PHARMACOGNOSY AND PHYTOCHEMISTRY-II

For

Second Year Degree Course in Pharmacy

Semester - IV

S.B. Gokhale

M. Pharm. AIC.

Former Co-ordinator
R. C. Patel College of Pharma Sciences and Research
Shirpur 425405.

Mrs. Aditi Kulkarni - Joshi

M. Pharm.

Assistant Professor, HOD, Pharmacognosy,
JSPM's Jayawantrao Sawant College of Pharmacy and Research,
Hadapsar, **Pune** 411 028.

NIRALI PRAKASHAN
ADVANCEMENT OF KNOWLEDGE

N1705

PHARMACOGNOSY AND PHYTOCHEMISTRY-II   ISBN 978-93-5164-596-2

First Edition   :   **February 2016**

©   :   **Authors**

Published By :   Polyplate

NIRALI PRAKASHAN
Abhyudaya Pragati, 1312, Shivaji Nagar,
Off J.M. Road, Pune – 411005
Tel - (020) 25512336/37/39, Fax - (020) 25511379
Email : niralipune@pragationline.com

☞ DISTRIBUTION CENTRES

PUNE

Nirali Prakashan   :   119, Budhwar Peth, Jogeshwari Mandir Lane, Pune 411002, Maharashtra
Tel : (020) 2445 2044, 66022708, Fax : (020) 2445 1538
Email : bookorder@pragationline.com, niralilocal@pragationline.com

Nirali Prakashan   :   S. No. 28/27, Dhyari, Near Pari Company, Pune 411041
Tel : (020) 24690204 Fax : (020) 24690316
Email : dhyari@pragationline.com, bookorder@pragationline.com

MUMBAI

Nirali Prakashan   :   385, S.V.P. Road, Rasdhara Co-op. Hsg. Society Ltd.,
Girgaum, Mumbai 400004, Maharashtra
Tel : (022) 2385 6339 / 2386 9976, Fax : (022) 2386 9976
Email : niralimumbai@pragationline.com

☞ DISTRIBUTION BRANCHES

JALGAON

Nirali Prakashan   :   34, V. V. Golani Market, Navi Peth, Jalgaon 425001,
Maharashtra, Tel : (0257) 222 0395, Mob : 94234 91860

KOLHAPUR

Nirali Prakashan   :   New Mahadvar Road, Kedar Plaza, 1st Floor Opp. IDBI Bank
Kolhapur 416 012, Maharashtra. Mob : 9850046155

NAGPUR

Pratibha Book Distributors   :   Above Maratha Mandir, Shop No. 3, First Floor,
Rani Jhanshi Square, Sitabuldi, Nagpur 440012, Maharashtra
Tel : (0712) 254 7129

DELHI

Nirali Prakashan   :   4593/21, Basement, Aggarwal Lane 15, Ansari Road, Daryaganj
Near Times of India Building, New Delhi 110002
Mob : 08505972553

BENGALURU

Pragati Book House   :   House No. 1, Sanjeevappa Lane, Avenue Road Cross,
Opp. Rice Church, Bengaluru – 560002.
Tel : (080) 64513344, 64513355,Mob : 9880582331, 9845021552
Email:bharatsavla@yahoo.com

CHENNAI

Pragati Books   :   9/1, Montieth Road, Behind Taas Mahal, Egmore,
Chennai 600008 Tamil Nadu, Tel : (044) 6518 3535,
Mob : 94440 01782 / 98450 21552 / 98805 82331,
Email : bharatsavla@yahoo.com

niralipune@pragationline.com | www.pragationline.com

Also find us on 🇫 www.facebook.com/niralibooks

PREFACE

As per revised syllabus of **'Bachelor of Pharmacy'** from academic year 2013-2014, with incorporation of **'Pharmacognosy and Phytochemistry-II'** for fourth semester, the course contents of the subject also have been updated by taking into consideration the developments in pharmacy profession.

Pharmacognosy and Phytochemistry-II is meant to illuminate relevance and significance of alkaloids and terpenoids pharmaceutical and industrial utility.

Authors have made an attempt and also have tried to make justice with the intention of framing the course contents.

Authors are thankful to Publisher Shri. Dineshbhai Furia, Shri. Jigneshbhai Furia and Staff members of Nirali Prakashan for their full co-operation in bringing out this book.

February 2016   **Authors**

SYLLABUS

SEMESTER – IV

1. Alkaloids   **(Periods)**

  A. General consideration: Definition, classification, occurrences, properties, nomenclature, and chemistry (including general biogenesis, qualitative / quantitative analysis) of alkaloids.   **(03)**

  B. Systematic pharmacognostic study including history & contribution to modern medicine: **(24)**

a.	**Pyridine-piperidine**	: Tobacco
b.	**Tropane**	: Belladonna, Datura, Coca
c.	**Quinoline and Isoquinoline**	: Cinchona, Ipecac, Opium.
d.	**Indole**	: Ergot, Rauwolfia, Catharanthus and Nux-vomica
e.	**Imidazole**	: Pilocarpus
f.	**Steroidal**	: Veratrum and Kurchi
g.	**Alkaloidal Amine**	: Ephedra and Colchicum
h.	**Glycoalkaloid**	: Solanum
I.	**Purines**	: Coffee and Tea

2. Terpenoids & Resins

  A. General consideration: Definition, classification, occurrences, properties, nomenclature and chemistry (including general biogenesis, qualitative / quantitative analysis) of terpenoids / resins.   **(03)**

  B. Systematic Pharmacognostic study (including history and contribution to modern medicine of followings):   **(15)**

a.	**Lower terpenoids**	: Clove, Cinnamon, Coriander, Lavender, Sandal wood, Artemisia
b.	**Diterpenoids**	: Taxus, Coleus
c.	**Triterpenoids**	: Ginseng
d.	**Tetraterpenoids**	: Annato and Saffron
e.	**Resins**	: Podophyllum, Guggul, Boswellia and Cannabis

❖❖❖

CONTENTS

Chapter 1

ALKALOIDS

Alkaloids are complex organic compounds containing one or more nitrogen atoms. They are primary, secondary, tertiary amines or as quaternary salts. The nitrogen is thus responsible for the basicity of alkaloids. The alkaloids are extremely difficult to define because they show variations either chemically, biochemically or physiologically, except for the fact that all are organic nitrogenous compounds.

HISTORY

The term 'alkaloid' was coined by **Meissner**, a German pharmacist, in 1819. The mankind has been using alkaloids for various purposes like poisons, medicines, poultices, teas, etc. The French chemist, **Derosne** in 1803, isolated narcotine. In the same year, morphine from opium was isolated by **Sertuerner**, a pharmacist of Paderborn near Hannover in 1803. **Pelletier** and **Calverton** from the Faculty of Pharmacy in Paris isolated emetine in 1817 and colchicine in 1819. This was followed by isolation of series of alkaloids from vegetable drugs, like strychnine (1817); brucine, piperine and caffeine (1819); quinine, colchicine and cinchonine (1820); coniine (1826), papaverine (1821) and thebaine (1835). By 1884, about 25 alkaloids were reported to be isolated from cinchona bark. From the beginning of 19th century till date, it has proved to be a perpetual work to discover new alkaloids from plants and animals. In the present century, the proper structures were assigned to various alkaloids with the help of chromatographic and other sophisticated physical methods of analysis.

Definition

The term alkaloid, is derived from the word 'alkali-like' and hence, they resemble some of the characters of naturally occurring complex amines. The term alkaloid also covers proto alkaloids and pseudo alkaloids. In view of all such variations, the only definition that brings all such compounds under one title is as follows: These are the organic products of natural or synthetic origin which are basic in nature and contain one or more nitrogen atoms, normally of heterocyclic nature, and possess specific physiological actions on human or animal body, when used in small quantities. The true alkaloids are toxic in nature, contain heterocyclic nitrogen which is derived from amino acids and always basic in nature. True alkaloids are normally present in plants as salts of organic acids. The 'proto alkaloids' or 'amino alkaloids' are simple amines in which the nitrogen is not in a heterocyclic ring. Sometimes, they are considered as biological amines. They are basic in nature and prepared in plants from amino acids. Some of the examples of these alkaloids are mescaline, N, N-dimethyl tryptamine, colchicine and ephedrine. The term 'pseudoalkaloids' includes mainly steroidal and terpenoid alkaloids and purines. They are not derived from amino acids. They do not show many of the typical characters of alkaloids, but give the standard qualitative tests for alkaloids. The examples of pseudoalkaloids are conessine and caffeine.

Occurrence and Distribution

Plants have been rich source of alkaloids but some are found in animals, fungi, bacteria and also synthesized in laboratories.

In the plant kingdom, alkaloids are distributed in certain families and genera. Among the Angiosperms families like Leguminosae, Piperaceae, Solanaceae, Rubiaceas, Ranunculaceae, Berberidaceae are considered to be the rich sources, while Labiatae and Rosaceae are free from alkaloids. Gymnosperms rarely contain alkaloid (e.g. Taxaceae). Among the monocotyledons, Amaryllidaceae and Liliaceae show some alkaloid yielding plants.

Alkaloids occur in various parts of plant

Seed	:	Nux-vomica, physostigma, areca.
Fruits	:	Conium
Leaves	:	Datura, belladonna, cocoa
Stems	:	Ephedra
Underground stem	:	Sanguinaria
Root and Rhizome	:	Ipecac
Bark	:	Kurchi, cinchona
Latex	:	Opium
Fangus	:	Ergot

Nomenclature of Alkaloids

There is no systematic nomenclature of alkaloids, the names are obtained in various ways, but chemical rules designate that names of all alkoids should end with 'ine'.

1) From the generic name – *Atropine* is obtained from *Atrop belladonna*, *Papaverine* from *Papaver somniferum*.

2) From the specific name of yielding plant – balladonnine (from *A. belladonna*)

3) From common name of yielding plant – Ergotamine from ergot, vincrystine and vinblastine from vinca.

4) From their physiologic action – emetine (from Greek word emetikos means to vomit), morphine from German word Morphus means God of dreams.

5) According to the name of discoverer – pelletierine was discovered by **P. J. Pelletier.**

6) Prefixes like epi, iso, neo, pseudo are used to name isomeric or to slight modification in structure.

7) The minor alkaloids are named by adding one of principal alkaloid e.g. cinchonidine derived from cinchonine.

PROPERTIES

1. Physical Properties

With few exceptions, all the alkaloids are colourless, crystalline solids with a sharp melting point or decomposition range. Some alkaloids are amorphous gums, while others like coniine, sparteine, nicotine etc. are liquid and volatile in nature. Some alkaloids are coloured in nature, e.g. betanidin is red, berberine is yellow and salts of sanguinarine are copper red in colour.

In general, the free bases of alkaloids are soluble in organic non-polar, immiscible solvents. The salts of most alkaloids are soluble in water. In contrast, free bases are insoluble in water and their salts are also very sparingly soluble in organic solvents. The alkaloids containing quaternary bases are only water soluble. Some of the pseudoalkaloids and protoalkaloids show higher solubility in water. For example, colchicine is soluble in alkaline water, acid or water and caffeine (free base) is freely soluble in water. Quinine hydrochloride is highly soluble in water i.e. 1 part of quinine hydrochloride is soluble in less than 1 part of water, while only 1 part of quinine sulphate is soluble in 1000 parts of water. Alkaloids are generally bitter in taste and optically active (except papaverine), usually levorotatory in nature (exception is coniine, which is dextrorotatory).

The solubility of alkaloids and their salts is useful in pharmaceutical industry for the extraction and formulation of final pharmaceutical preparations.

2. Chemical Properties

Most of the alkaloids are basic in reaction, due to the availability of lone pair of electrons on nitrogen. The basic character of the alkaloidal compound is enhanced if the adjacent functional groups are electron releasing. The alkaloid turns to be neutral or acidic when the adjacent functional groups are electron withdrawing like amide group which reduces the availability of the lone pair of electrons. But, alkaloids exhibiting basic character are very much sensitive to decomposition and cause a problem during their storage. Their salt formation with an inorganic acid prevents many a time their decomposition.

The alkaloids may contain one or more number of nitrogen and it may exist in the form as primary ($R - NH_2$), e.g. mescaline; secondary amine ($R_2 - NH$), e.g. ephedrine; tertiary amine (R_3N) e.g. atropine; and quaternary ammonium compounds $[R_4N^+X]$ e.g. tubocurarine chloride. In the last type, their properties vary from other alkaloids, owing to quaternary nature of nitrogen.

In the natural form, the alkaloids exist either in free state, as amine or as salt with acid or alkaloid N-oxides.

CHEMICAL TESTS FOR ALKALOIDS

The qualitative chemical tests used for detection of alkaloids are dependent on the characters of alkaloids to give precipitates as salts of organic acids or with compounds of heavy metals, like mercury, gold, platinum, etc.

The alkaloidal reagent tests are as follows :

1) **Mayer's reagent** (potassium mercuric iodide solution) gives cream coloured precipitate;

2) **Dragendorff's reagent** (potassium bismuth iodide solution) gives reddish brown precipitate;

3) **Wagner's reagent** (iodine-potassium iodide solution) yield reddish brown precipitate.

4) Alkaloids also give yellow coloured precipitates with picric acid called as **Hager's reagent** and picrolonic acid. Individual alkaloid gives colour or precipitate with certain specific reagent.

5) For purine alkaloids (Murexide colour reaction), take caffeine or any purine alkaloid in petridish to which add hydrochloric acid and potassium chlorate and heat to dryness. A purple colour will develop by exposing the residue to vapour of ammonia. Addition of alkali will fade the colour.

6) For opium alkaloids – The opium alkaloids are present as salts of meconic acid. Opium when dissolved in water and treated with ferric chloride, it develops reddish purple colour which persists after addition of hydrochloric acid.

The chemical tests with heavy metals are not solely limited to alkaloids. Proteins, coumarins and α- pyrone also give precipitates with these reagents. It may be also noted that some alkaloids do not give such tests, like caffeine which is highly water soluble. Hence, the tests with heavy metals are in some cases false positive reactions or false negative reactions. For this purpose, the specific tests for individual alkaloids are more important for qualitative evaluation of crude drugs. These tests are covered under individual drugs.

ISOLATION AND EXTRACTION OF ALKALOIDS

The alkaloids are present as a complex mixture, plants also contain different organic acids, pigments, glycosides etc. that may complicate the isolation process.

The steps involved in isolation of alkaloids are summarized as follows :

1) Qualitative analysis of plant extract to ascertain presence of alkaloids.

2) Separation of crude alkaloids from plant extract.

3) Isolation and purification of individual alkaloids from crude alkaloids.

The further purification of crude extract of alkaloids is done by following ways, which may, however, vary for individual alkaloid.

1. Direct Crystallisation from Solvent

It is a very simple method of isolation and may not be useful in case of complex mixtures.

2. Steam Distillation

This method is specially employed for volatile liquid alkaloids like coniine, sparteine and nicotine, but otherwise this process is not suitable for alkaloids with high molecular weights.

3. Chromatographic Techniques

This method has proved to be ideal for separation of a vast number of plant alkaloids. The different techniques of chromatography (thin layer, column, gas, liquid, ion exchange chromatography, HPTLC etc.) are used for separation of individual alkaloids from complex mixtures.

4. Gradient pH Technique

Though alkaloids are basic in nature, there are variations in the extent of basicity of various alkaloids of the same plant. Depending on this character, the crude alkaloidal mixture is dissolved in 2 % tartaric acid solution and extracted with benzene so that the first fraction contains neutral and/or very weakly basic alkaloids. pH of the aqueous solution is increased gradually by 0.5 increments upto pH 9 and extraction is carried out at each pH level with organic solvent. By this way, the alkaloids with different basicity are extracted. Strongly basic alkaloids are extracted at the end. The general scheme for extraction of alkaloids can be summarized as follows.

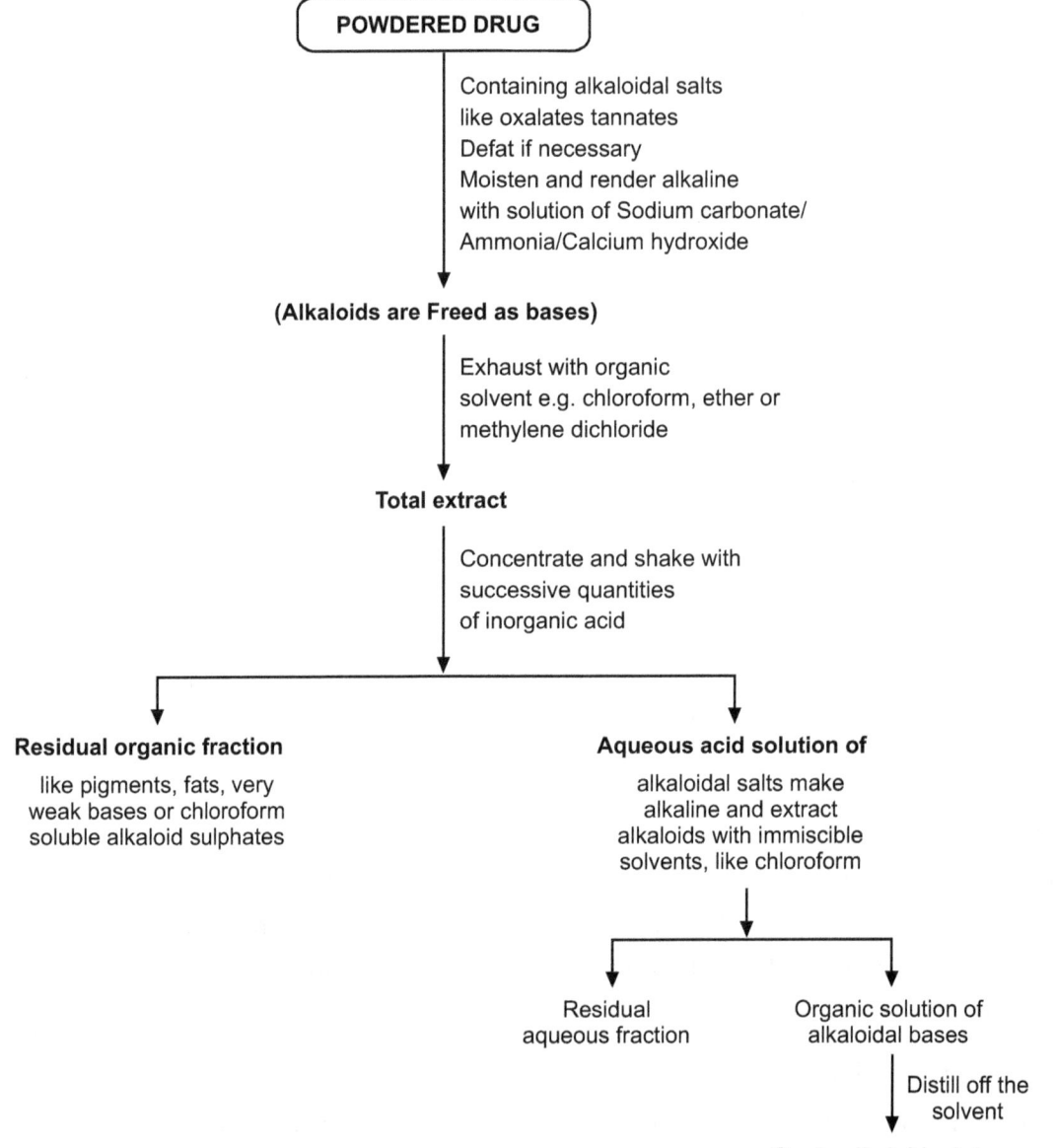

POWDERED DRUG

Containing alkaloidal salts
like oxalates tannates
Defat if necessary
Moisten and render alkaline
with solution of Sodium carbonate/
Ammonia/Calcium hydroxide

(Alkaloids are Freed as bases)

Exhaust with organic
solvent e.g. chloroform, ether or
methylene dichloride

Total extract

Concentrate and shake with
successive quantities
of inorganic acid

Residual organic fraction

like pigments, fats, very
weak bases or chloroform
soluble alkaloid sulphates

Aqueous acid solution of

alkaloidal salts make
alkaline and extract
alkaloids with immiscible
solvents, like chloroform

Residual
aqueous fraction

Organic solution of
alkaloidal bases

Distill off the
solvent

Crude alkaloid mixture

Purification by fractional crystallisation,
chromatographic separation, etc.

Structure identification by modern analytical
techniques such as UV, IR, MNR,
Mass spectrometry, etc.

CLASSIFICATION OF ALKALOIDS

The various methods proposed for classification of alkaloids are as follows:

1. Pharmacological Classification

Depending on the physiological response, the alkaloids are classified under various pharmacological categories, like central nervous system stimulants or depressants, sympathomimetics, analgesics, purgatives, etc. This method does not take into account chemical nature of crude drugs. Within the same drug, the individual alkaloid may exhibit different action e.g. morphine is narcotic analgesic, while codeine is mainly antitussive. In cinchona, quinine is antimalarial, while quinidine is cardiac depressant.

2. Taxonomic Classification

This method classifies the vast number of alkaloids based on their distribution in various plant families, like solanaceous or papillionaceous alkaloids. Preferably, they are grouped as per the name of the genus in which they occur, e.g. ephedra, cinchona, etc. From this classification, the chemotaxonomic classification has been further derived.

3. Biosynthetic Classification

This method gives significance to the precursor from which the alkaloids are biosynthesized in the plant. Hence, the variety of alkaloids with different taxonomic distribution and physiological activities can be brought under same group, if they are derived from same precursor. e.g. all indole alkaloids from tryptophan are grouped together. The alkaloidal drugs are categorised on the fact whether they are derived from amino acid precursor as ornithine, lysine, tyrosine, phenylalanine, tryptophan, etc.

4. Chemical Classification

This is the most accepted way of classification of alkaloids. The main criterion for chemical classification is the type of fundamental (normally heterocyclic) ring structure present in alkaloid. The alkaloidal drugs are broadly categorised into two divisions.

(a) Heterocyclic alkaloids (True alkaloids) are divided into twelve groups according to nature of their heterocyclic ring.

(b) Non-hetero-cyclic alkaloids or proto-alkaloids or biological amines or pseudoalkaloids.

The following Table 1.1 indicates types of alkaloids and their occurrence in various plants along with basic chemical ring.

Table 1.1 : Classification of Alkaloids

Basic structure	Type of alkaloid	Examples	Sources
TRUE ALKALOIDS			
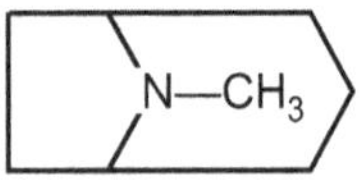 (N—CH₃ structure)	1. Tropane alkaloids	Atropine, cocaine, hyoscine, hyoscyamine	Datura, coca, belladonna, hyoscyamus, withania
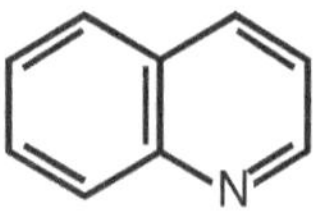 (quinoline structure)	2. Quinoline alkaloids	Quinine, quinidine, cinchonine, cinchonidine	Cinchona species
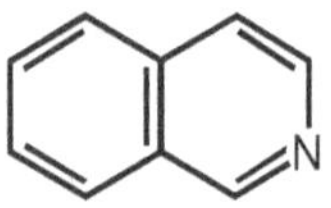 (isoquinoline structure)	3. Isoquinoline alkaloids	Papaverine, narcotine emetine, berberine	Opium, ipecacuanha, berberis
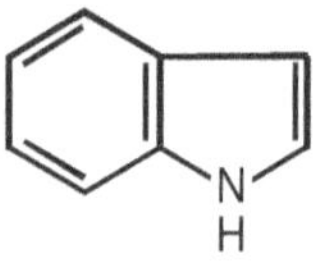 (indole structure)	4. Indole alkaloids	Strychnine, brucine, serpentine, ergometrine, reserpine	Nux-vomica, rauwolfia, ergot, vinca
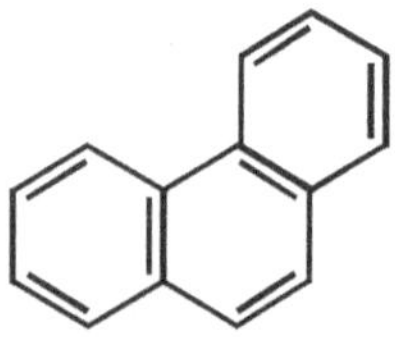 (phenanthrene structure)	5. Phenanthrene alkaloids	Morphine, codeine, thebaine	Opium
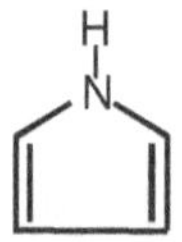 Pyrrole 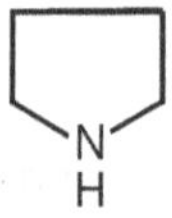 Pyrrolidine	6. Pyrrole and pyrrolidine alkaloids	Nicotine, hygrine, trigonelline	Tobacco, fenugreek, coca
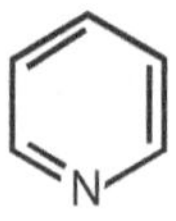 Pyridine 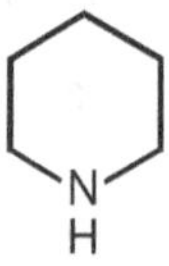 Piperidine	7. Pyridine and piperidine alkaloids	Coniine, lobeline, ricinine	Hemlock, lobelia, tobacco, castor
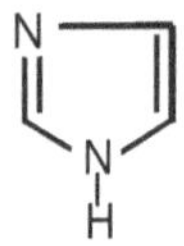 (imidazole structure)	8. Imidazole alkaloids	Pilocarpine	Pilocarpus

Contd...

PSEUDO ALKALOIDS			
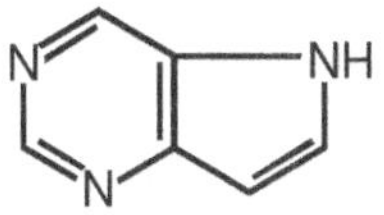	9. Purine alkaloids	Caffeine, theobromine	Tea, coffee
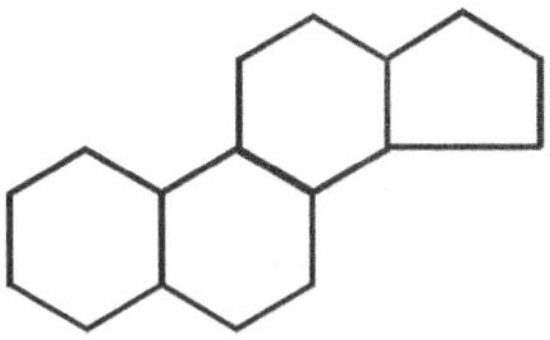 Cyclopentanoperhydro phenanthrene	10. Steroidal	Conessine, solanidine, solanine, veratramine, veratridine	Kurchi, veratrum, potato
AMINO OR PROTO ALKALOIDS			
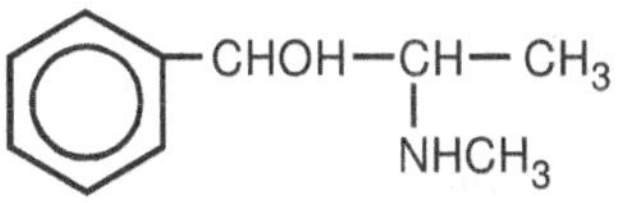	11. Alkaloidal amines	Ephedrine, pseudophedrine, colchicin	Ephedra, colchicum

ROLE OF ALKALOIDS IN PLANTS

The alkaloids are poisonous in nature, but when used in small quantities, exert useful physiological effects on animals and human beings and hence they have secured significant place in medicine. Their exact role in nature and functions in the plants, if any, are still a topic of ambiguity. Only one aspect is clearly understood that they are synthesized by a particular, stereospecific, many a time complicated, and energy consuming pathways and further they are metabolized to other alkaloidal or non alkaloidal substances. Some of the predicted roles of alkaloids in the plants are discussed below.

1. They are the reserve substances with an ability to supply nitrogen.

2. They might be the defensive mechanisms for plants growing in dry regions to protect from grazing animals, herbivores and insects.

3. It is also possible that they are end products of detoxification mechanism in plants, and by this way check formation of substances which may prove to be harmful to the plants.

4. They might have a possible role as growth regulatory factors in the plants.

5. They are present normally in conjugation with plant acids, like meconic acid, cinchotannic acid, etc. Therefore, alkaloids could be acting as carriers within plants for transportation of such acids.

(A) DRUGS CONTAINING PYRIDINE – PIPERIDINE ALKALOIDS
TOBACCO

Biological Source

This consists of dried leaves of *Nicotiana tabacum*, belonging to family Solanaceae.

Geographical Source

Tobacco is cultivated on a commercial scale to a very large extent in China, United States and India. China produces annually 22 lakh metric tonnes, while India produces about 5 lakh metric tonnes of tobacco in a year. The other tobacco producing countries are Brazil, Russia, Turkey and Italy. In India, it is produced mainly in Andhra Pradesh, Gujarat, Karnataka, Orissa and Bihar.

General Description

Tobacco as a whole is stout, ever green, viscid annual, 1 to 3 metres in height. It has thick erect stem and few branches. It bears about 20 leaves which are approximately 80 cm in length. Flowers are light-red, white or pink in colour, fruits and capsules, elliptic, ovoid 1.5 to 2.0 cm in size. Seeds are spherical and 0.5 mm in diameter, which are brown in colour. Various varieties are known to be cultivated in India. Few of them are Bidi tobacco, Cigar tobacco, chewing and hookah tobacco.

Cultivation and Collection

Depending upon the type of tobacco the requirements of soil and climate also vary. Warm climate, well drained fertile land is favourable for its cultivation. Seeds are used for cultivation. The seeds are sown on the seed beds in winter or early spring. When the seedlings are about 12 weeks old. They are transplanted. In the flowering season the flowering tops are cut so as to encourage the growth of foliage. Harvesting is done after 70 - 90 days of transplantation.

The leaves are then subjected to processing by air curing, fire curing or flue-curing. During this process only, the chemical changes occur and lead to development of flavour and aroma.

Organoleptic Characters

Colour   : Green or slightly brown.

Odour   : Characteristic to Nicotine.

Taste   : Bitter.

Size   : 60 - 80 cm in length and 35 - 45 cm in width.

Shape   : Ovate, elliptic or lanceolate.

Extra Features

The leaves are usually sessile, sometimes petiolate and with frilled wing.

Fig. 1.1 : Tobacco plant

Chemical Constituents

The tobacco contains pyridine-piperidine type of alkaloids, among which the most prominent is nicotine, which is about 0.5%. The other alkaloids are nornicotine and anabasine.

Chemical Test

Aqueous solution   +   Cyanogen bromide   → Orange colour.

Nicotine   **Nor-Nicotine**

Uses

Nicotine exerts stimulant effects on heart and nervous system. It is not used medicinally. It is powerful quick acting poison. Even 40 mg dose orally is fatal to humans. Rectified tobacco seed oil is used as edible oil in European countries. Nicotine is used in the manufacture of nicotinic acid and nicotinamide.

Contribution to Modern Medicine

Tobacco is not medicine basically it is never used therapeutically for any disorder.

Tobacco and nicotine are known insecticides for last three centuries. Nicotine controls a wide range of insects. It is mainly used against soft bodied insects like aphides. It acts as a contact poison. It is also effective against white flies, moths, termites, butterfly larvae, red-spider mites etc. Nicotine is sprayed on crops in the form of nicotine sulphate. It has certain advantages over synthetic insecticides that it is safer, easier to handle and much less toxic to warm blooded animals. Because of its volatility, it evaporates earlier and leaves no harmful residue on the marketable products.

(B) DRUGS CONTAINING TROPANE ALKALOIDS

Tropane is a dicyclic compound formed by condensation of pyrrolidine precursor with 3-acetate derived carbon atoms. It thus represents fusion of pyrrolidine and pipridien ring systems. 3-Hydroxy derivative of tropane is tropine, its esterfication with tropic acid yields (-) hyoscyamine. The hyoscyamine may be racemized to form ($\pm$) atropine.

Solanaceae family includes 72 genera, out of which only 8 genera contains solanaceous alkaloids. These genera are Datura, Atropa, Hyoscyamus, Scopolia, Duboisia, physoclaina, Mandrogora and Solandra.

Solanaceous Alkaloids:

The principal alkaloids of this group are (-) hyoscyamine, scopolamine (also known as hyoscine), atropine [($\pm$)-hyoscyamine], anhydride of atropine also known as apoatropine. All these alkaloids are tropiine derivatives and esters.

Hyoscyamine is tropine ester of tropic acid and is readily hydrolysed by boiling in dilute acids or alkalies to form these compounds.

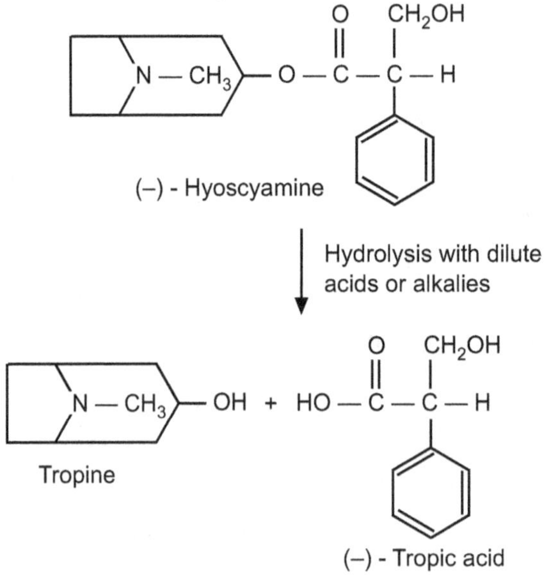

(–) - Hyoscyamine

Hydrolysis with dilute acids or alkalies

Tropine

(–) - Tropic acid

Hyoscine or scopolamine is abundantly found in *Datura metel.* It is an ester that upon hydrolysis, yield tropic acid and scopoline or oscine.

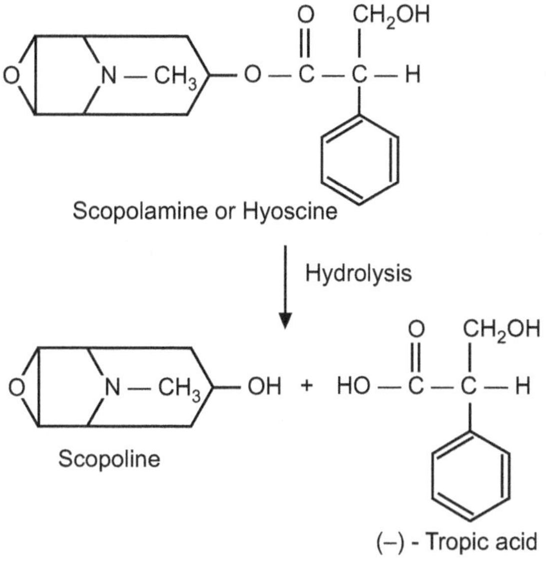

Scopolamine or Hyoscine

Hydrolysis

Scopoline   +   (–) - Tropic acid

Atropine is an alkaloid obtained from *Atropa belladonna, Datura, Hyoscyamus* linne or it may be produced synthetically.

Hyoscyamine sulphate occurs as white odourless, crystals or crystalline powder. It is anticholinergic, used to control gastric secretion and as antispasmodic agent in spastic coilitis, abdominal cramps. It is also used in parkinsonism.

Scopolamine hydrobromide or hyoscine hydrobromide occurs as colourless or white granular powder. It is an anticholinergic agent also used in prevention of nausea and vomitting associated with motion sickness. It is available in transdermal patch Transdermscope that is applied behind the ear.

Atropine sulphate occurs as colourless, needle like crystal or white crystalline powder. It is an anticholinergic agent, used in surgery to control bronchial, nasal and salivary secretion, prior to induction of anesthesia. It is also used as an antidote to cholineste inhibitors.

BIOGENESIS OF TROPANE ALKALOIDS

Tropane alkaloids are the esters of tropic acid. Formation of tropane ring system is generally similar in all members of solanaceae family. Ornithine acts as precursor for Tropine moiety. It is produced from L-arginine, in animals, by the action of an enzyme arginase but in plants ornithine is produced from L-glutamate.

The N-methyl group of tropane system is supplied by methionine and is incorporated at early stages of biogenesis putrescine and its N-methyl derivative is also involved to construct tropane skeleton. Putrescine is a diamine formed by decarboxylation of ornithine.

Tropane alkaloids are esters of tropic acid moiety, also termed as tropate. The tropic acid is derived from phenylalanine. Esterification of tropine and tropic acid leads to formation of tropane alkaloids.

1) Tropane formation :

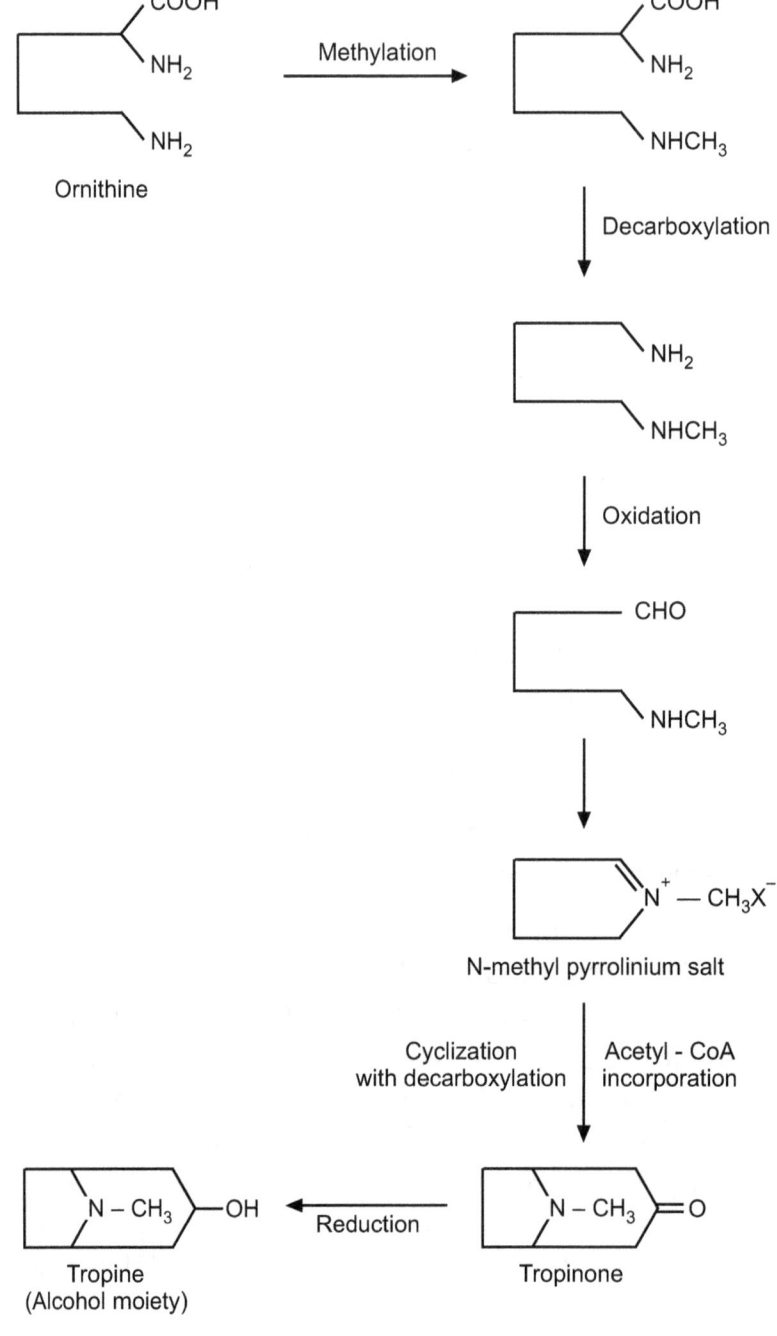

2) Tropic Acid formation :

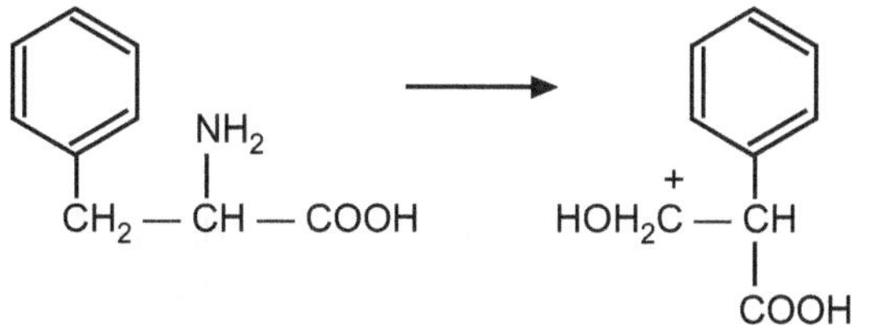

Phenyl alanine   Tropic acid

3) Esterification :

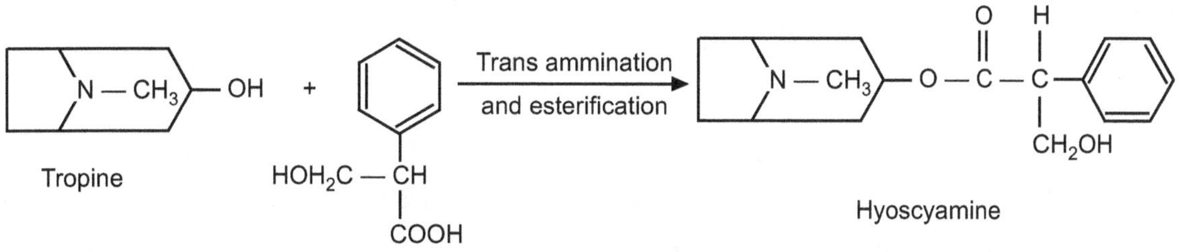

Tropine   HOH₂C — CH   Hyoscyamine

Tropic acid

BELLADONNA HERB

Synonyms

Belladonna Leaf; Belladonnae Folium; Deadly night shade leaf (European belladonna).

Biological Source

Belladonna herb consists of dried leaves or the leaves and other aerial parts of *Atropa belladonna* Linn. (European belladonna) or *Atropa acuminata* Royle ex-Lindley (Indian belladonna) or mixture of both the species collected when the plants are in flowering condition. It belongs to family Solanaceae. It contains not less than 0.3 % of the alkaloids of belladonna herb, calculated as *l*-hyoscyamine.

Geographical Source

It is indigenous to and cultivated in England and other European countries. In India, it is found in the Western Himalayas from Simla to Kashmir and adjoining areas of Himachal Pradesh. Its chief habitat is Jammu and in forests of Sindh, and Chinab valley.

History

Because of the hallucinogenic effect of this plant, it was used as witch craft in the middle ages. In ancient times, the juice of this plant was used as a cosmetic, because of its dilatory effect on the pupil of the eye. This drug was first introduced in the London Pharmacopoeia in 1809.

Cultivation and Collection

Cultivation of belladonna at an altitude of 1400 m above the sea level is found to be satisfactory, if proper irrigation facilities are provided. It is observed that the yield per hectare can be increased substantially by proper cultivation technology. The experimental trials of applications of several fungicides and insecticides right from the treatment of the seeds upto the foliar sprays were very encouraging. Its cultivation in Jammu and Kashmir is found to be successful.

Belladonna berries are crushed to get the seeds for cultivation. Proper processing like washing and sieving is performed. Only healthy seeds are used for cultivation. Seeds are sown by broadcasting method in well prepared beds with the application of fungicide like diathon.

Sowing is done in May and July. The seedlings are ready for transplantation by the end of September. Transplanting is done by keeping certain distance between two plants and the seedlings are irrigated carefully. Fertilizers like urea, potash and superphosphate are given as per the needs. Insecticidal sprays like sevin are also tried when the plant reaches maturity. The leaves, as well as, the flowering tops are cut and sundried or dried in shade. During drying, care is taken to retain the green colour. While grading and packing for market, woolly stems and foreign organic matter are rejected. The yield per hectare is found to be 200 to 600 kg. Its cultivation in Jammu and Kashmir was found to be successful.

Organoleptic Characters (Fig. 1.2)

Colour : Leaves - Green to brownish-green

Flowers - Purple to yellowish-brown

Fruits - Green to brown

Odour : Slight and characteristic

Taste : Bitter and acrid

Size : Leaves - 5 - 25 cm long and 2.5 - 12 cm wide

Flowers - Corolla 2.5 cm long and 1.5 cm wide

Fruits - About 10 cm in diameter.

Fig. 1.2 : Branch of *Atropa belladonna*

Shape : Leaves - Ovate, lanceolate to broadly ovate, with acuminate apex, decurrent lamina, entire margin, petiolate, brittle and transversely broken.

Flowers - Campanulate, 5, small reflexed lobes of corolla.

Fruits - Berries, sub-globular in shape with numerous flat seeds.

Extra Features

In general, the entire drug is seen as crumpled and twisted. The dropping flowers are associated with as many pairs of leaves. The flowers are with 5 stamens, superior bilocular ovary with numerous seeds.

Microscopic Characters (Fig. 1.3)

Epidermal cells with slightly sinuous anticlinal wall and striated cuticle, anisocytic stomata and occasionally uniseriate multicellular covering trichomes are present. There are glandular trichomes which are uniseriate and with unicellular heads. The palisade ratio is 5 to 7.

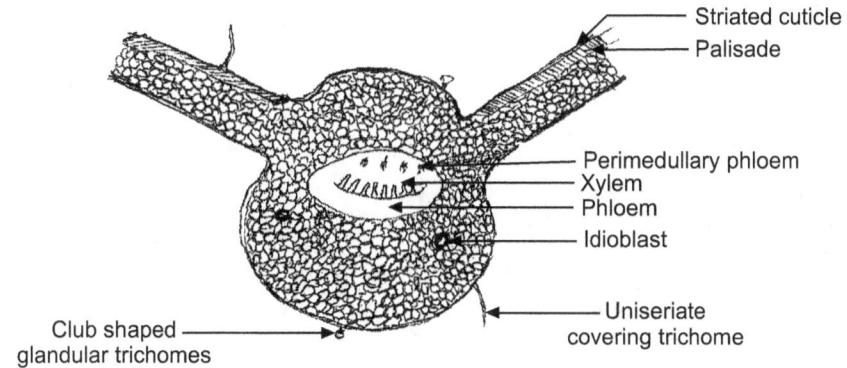

Fig. 1.3 : T. S. of Belladonna Leaf

Chemical Constituents

The total alkaloidal content of drug is 0.4 - 1 % and varies in different parts of plant, roots (0.6 %), stems (0.05 %), leaves (0.4 %), unripe and ripe berries (0.19 - 0.21 %) and seeds (0.33 %).

The main alkaloids are *l*-hyoscyamine and its racemic form atropine. Atropine exists only in traces in fresh plant material but is formal by racemization during extraction process. The drug also contains apotropine, belladonine, scopoletin (*l* - methyl aesculetin), hyoscine, cuscohygrine. The later two are the volatile bases. Homotropine is a synthetic compound and is preferred in the medical profesion as the synthetic process of atropine and hyoscyamine is very costly.

Atropine (Tropine (±) - Tropate)   **Hyoscyamine (Tropine (–) - Tropate)**

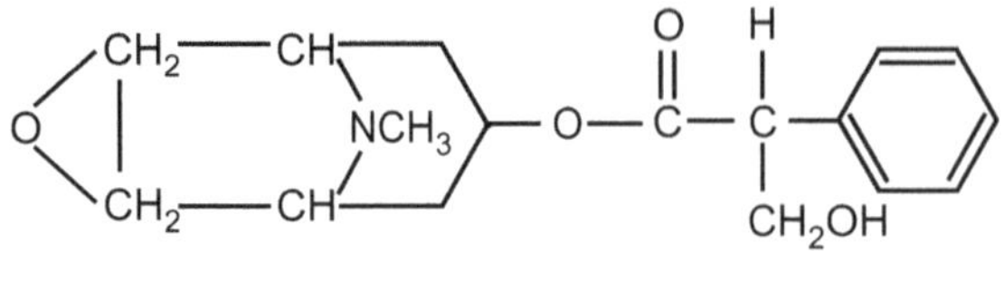

Hyoscine (Scopalamine) 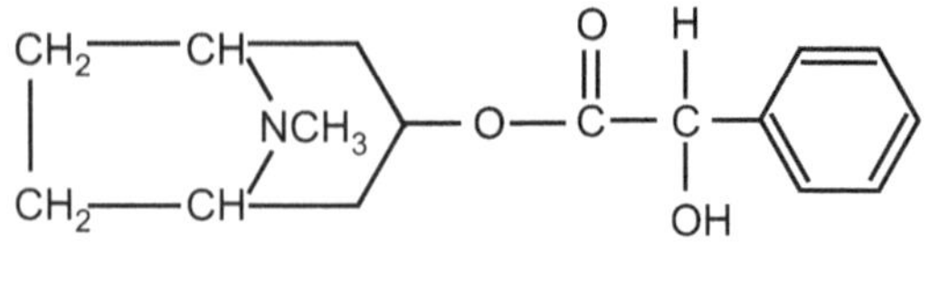   **Homotropine**

Standards

1. Total ash   - 14 %
2. Acid-insoluble ash   - 3 %
3. Foreign organic matter   - not more than 3 %

It gives Vitali - Morin reaction   - positive

Uses

It is the parasympatholytic drug with anticholinergic properties. It is used to reduce the secretions such as sweat, saliva and gastric juice and also to reduce spasm in cases of intestinal gripping due to strong purgatives. It is also used as adjunctive therapy in the treatment of peptic ulcer, digestive disorders like ulcerative colitis and diarrhea. It is also used as an antidote in opium and chloral hydrate poisoning.

Dose

0.6 to 1 ml in the form of belladonna tincture - 4 times a day.

Adulterants and Substitutes

The drug is adulterated with the leaves of *Phytolacca americana, Solanum nigrum,* and *Ailanthus glandulosa.* Each of them is distinguished by their histological character. Idioblast is present in *Phytolacca* leaves, lamina is denser, needle shaped crystals are present and anomocytic stomata are distinct. Palisade ratio is from 2 - 4 in *S. nigrum* leaves. Clustered crystals of calcium oxalate near the veins are present in *Ailanthus* leaves. The leaves also show the presence of unicellular lignified trichomes.

DATURA

Synonyms

Datura herb, Angel's trumpet.

Biological Source

Datura consists of the dried leaves and flowering tops of *Datura metel* and *D. metel* var. *fastuosa* Safford. It belongs to family Solanaceae.

It should contain not less than 0.20 % of total alkaloids of Datura, calculated as *l*-hyoscyamine.

Geographical Source

It is found in India, England and other tropical and subtropical regions.

Cultivation and Collection

The drug is cultivated by sowing the seeds. The germination is normally very slow. If the seeds are soaked in water and kept overnight, the rate of germination increases. About 7 - 8 kg of seeds per hectare are required for sowing purpose. The seeds require about 15 - 20 days for germination. Weeding and thinning are necessary and performed when are 10 - 15 cm tall. The distance kept in between 2 plants is about 75 - 100 cm. The plants should be supplied with organic fertilizers and proper irrigation. The drug is collected after 4 months of its cultivation. The leaves and branches are removed, drug is dried in the sun and marketed by packing in gunny bags.

Organoleptic Characters (Fig. 1.4)

The drug has a characteristic but unpleasant odour and a bitter taste. The drug contains entire, broken wrinkled, crushed leaves along with stem fragments and floral parts. The entire leaf has length of 9 - 18 cm and width of 8 - 13 cm. Normally, the margin is of entire, but in some cases sinuated with rounded or acute 2 - 4 broad lobes. The leaf is covered with minute hairs, lower surface is slightly pale in colour and the leaf has a thin texture. The leaf is unequal at the base with acute apex and glabrous lamina.

Fig. 1.4 : *Datura metel* herb

Flowers are reddish-purple on outer side and whitish on inner side. Corolla is thin, acuminate, triangular to circular in shape. Flowers are funnel shaped with pedicel which is never erect. The stems, as well as, branches of drug are purple coloured. Brown coloured seeds are triangular and are found in the thorny capsule.

Microscopic Characters (Fig. 1.5)

Through the transverse section, it shows its dorsiventral character. The epidermal cells of both sides show anisocytic or cruciferous stomata. The cells are covered with thin cuticle and glandular and non-glandular simple trichomes. About 40 % of the lamina is occupied by single layer of palisade cells. Approximately 6 - 8 layers of spongy parenchymatous cells are present. The midrib shows vascular tissue with protoxylem and metaxylem. Trichomes are more on the midrib region. Stomatal index is 12.7 - 19.5 for upper surface and 21.2 - 24 for lower surface.

Palisade ratio is 3.5 - 6.5. The spongy parenchyma contains calcium oxalate crystals.

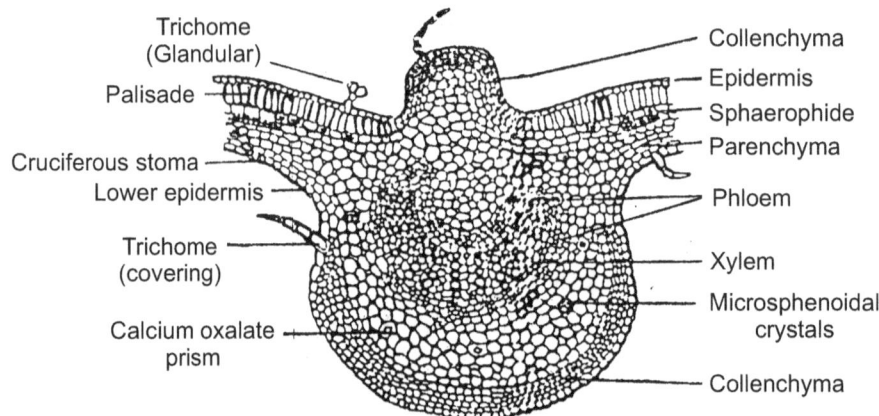

Fig. 1.5 : Transverse section of Datura leaf

Chemical Constituents

Datura herb contains upto 0.5 % of total alkaloids, among which hyoscine (scopolamine) is the main alkaloid, while *l*-hyoscyamine (scopoline) and atropine are present in very less quantities (see belladonna herb).

Hyoscine ($C_{17}H_{21}O_4N$) is an ester of tropic acid and scopine. It is the principal alkaloid of *Datura*, *Scopolia* and *Duboisia* species. The occurrence of hyoscine is restricted only to Solanaceae family.

Standards

1. Stems, flowers, fruits   : not more than 20 %
2. Foreign organic matter   : not more than 2 %
3. Acid-insoluble ash   : not more than 4 %

Chemical Test (Vitali-Morin reaction)

1. The tropane alkaloid is treated with fuming nitric acid, followed by evaporation to dryness and addition of methanolic potassium hydroxide solution to an acetone solution of nitrated residue. Violet coloration takes place due to tropan derivative.

2. On addition of silver nitrate solution to solution of hyoscine hydrobromide, yellowish white precipitate is formed, which is insoluble in nitric acid, but soluble in dilute ammonia.

Uses

Datura herb and its main alkaloid hyoscine are parasympatholytic with anticholinergic and central nervous system depressant effects. The drug is used in cerebral excitement.

Along with morphine, it is used as preoperative medication. It is also used in treatment of asthma and cough.

Hyoscine hydrobromide is used in motion sickness, gastric or duodenal ulcers.

STRAMONIUM

Synonym

Jimson weed, Jamastown weed, Thornapple.

Biological Source

Stramonium consists of dried leaves and flowering or fruiting taps with branches of *Datura stramonium or Datura stramonium* var. *tatula* linne, family Solanaceae. It yields not less than 0.25 % of alkaloids.

Geographical Source

It is indigenous to Caspian sea, Europe, North America and cultivated in central Europe and South America.

Cultivation and Collection

The plant is an annual herb that attains the height of about 2 meters. The leaves and tops are collected when plant bears flowers. Then it is carefully dried and preserved.

History

Stramonium was grown in England in about 16th century from seeds near Jamestawn, herb was used as "pot herb" hence its common name is Jamestawn weed, which was subsequently modified as jimson weed. The fruits of the plant are thorny, hence it is also known as thornapple plant.

Organoleptic Characters

Datura stramonium var. *tatula* is known as purple stramonium as both stems and flowers are purplish, while *Datura stramonium* shows white coloured funnel shape flowers. The drug has characteristic but unpleasant odour and bitter taste. The dried leaves are grayish-green in colour, thin, brittle, twisted and broken. Whole leaves are 8 – 25 cm long, 7 – 15 cm wide, shortly petiolate ovate in shape with acuminate apex and vary in colour from light olive brown (D. stramonium) to purple (*D. stramonium* var. *tatula*).

Microscopic Characters

A transverse section shows bifacial structure. Both surfaces have smooth cuticle, stomata and trichomes. Mesophyll contains cluster and microsphenoid crystals of calcium oxalate. Both anisocytic and anomosytic stomata are present. Three to five celled uniserriate covering trichomes are present. Glandular trichomes have one to two celled stalk with multicellular head. The midrib is bicolateral type and sclerenchyma is absent.

Chemical Constituents

The total alkaloidal content is 0.2 – 0.45%, where chief alkaloids are hyoscyamine and hyoscine, but little amount of atropine is formed by racemization of hyoscyamine stramonium seeds containing about 0.2% of alkaloid and 15 – 30% fixed oil.

Allied Species

Datura metel and *Datura innoxia* are major allied drugs. The *Datura* available in commerce comprise mainly of these two species. These leaves are twisted but brown in colour with entire margin. *D.metel* contains about 0.5% of alkaloids. During development *D. metel* show variation in hyoscine and atropine content. *D. innoxia* shows 30 different types of alkaloids. The alkaloidal content is about 0.2%. Both these species are common in India.

Quantitative Analysis

A. Estimation of total topane alkaloids using UV-visible spectroscopy :

Vitali-Morin Method :

1. Prepare Atropine working standard solution from range of 200-1000 µg/ml.
2. To it add 0.2 ml of fuming nitric acid and evaporate to dryness. To this residue add 2 ml acetone and 0.1 ml of 3% methanolic KOH.
3. Make up the volume to 10 ml with acetone.
4. Measure the absorbance using green filter or at 430 nm and plot calibration curve.
5. Follow the same procedure for crude alkaloid. Chloroform extract of plant is used as sample.
6. Calculate total tropane alkaloid in the sample from calibration curve.

B. Assay for belladonna leaf as per USP :

1. Extract the alkaloids with ether and purify by re-extracting into 0.5 N sulphuric acid (as free base).
2. Evaporate chloroform extract to dryness. Add this residue to excess of sulphuric acid to form sulphate salt.
3. The quantity of unreacted acid is determined by titration with alkali.
4. The quantity of alkaloid is calculated from molar quantity of acid which has reacted with alkaloids to form salt.

COCA LEAVES

Synonym

Coca

Biological Source

These are the dried leaves of *Erythroxylon coca, Erythroxylon truxillense, Erythroxylon novogranetensc* and varities belonging to family Erythroxylaceae.

Geographical Source

It is native to South American countries like Peru and Bolivia. Commercially, it is cultivated in Java, Peru, Bolivia, Columbia, Sri Lanka and India.

History

Since ancient times, the coca leaves have been used by South Americans as a masticatory and were reserved for only native chiefs and Incas. It was considered as 'divine plant'. The first report about coca leaves was prepared by **Monardes** in 1569. The plant was brought to Europe in 1688. Cocaine was isolated in 1860 and its local anaesthetic effects were discovered in 1884 by **Koeller** from Vienna. It was introduced into medicine some time in the later half of nineteenth century.

Cultivation, Collection and Preparation

The principle constituent cocaine has local anaesthetic effects and also has hallucinogenic actions, leading to addiction. Therefore plantation is strictly governed by Narcotic Drugs and Psychotropic Substances Act 1985 in India and by relevant acts in other countries.

Coca plant is mainly cultivated in Java, Peru and Bolivia. The open fields at an altitude of 500 - 2000 metres are suitable for cultivation of this drug. Propagation is done by sowing the seeds in nursery beds and then transplanted to open field. The drug is collected over a period of 3 years, at an interval of one year. The leaves are collected in dry weather and dried in the shed or by artificial means.

Varieties of Coca

1. **Huanco or Bolivian coca :** It consists of leaves of *E.coca* obtained from Bolivia and Peru leaves are petiolate, elliptical, 2-5 - 7.5 cm long, 1 - 4 cm wide with entire margin. The lower surface shows two characterstic curved lines. Odour is characteristic, taste at first bitter and slightly aromatic.

2. ***E.coca* var. *ipadu* :** It is known as Amazonian coca. Leaves are broadly elliptical, rounded at base with characteristic parallel lines on lower surface.

3. ***C. Columbian coca* :** It consists of leaves of *Erythroxylon novogranatense* var. *novogranetense*. It is cultivated throughout Columbia.

4. **Truxillo or Peruvia coca :** It is obtained from *Erythroxylon novogranetense* var. *truxillense*. The leaves are smaller, narraower, thinner and lighter green than those of var. *coca*.

Organoleptic Characters [Fig. 1.6 (a) and (b)]

These are described under varieties of coca above.

 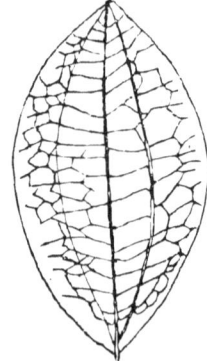 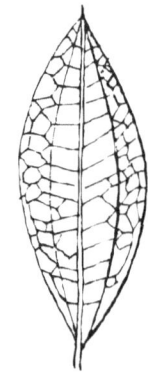

Fig. 1.6 (a): *Erythroxylum coca* herb   Fig. 1.6 (b) E.Coca and (c) *E. truxillense leaves*

Microscopic Characters (Fig. 1.7)

Microscopically, both the varieties have similar characters. They are isobilateral leaves and show presence of parenchyma under both epidermal layers. Midrib is typical and is partly encircled by considerable amount of collenchyma. The lower epidermis shows presence of papillae and numerous paracytic stomata. The drug

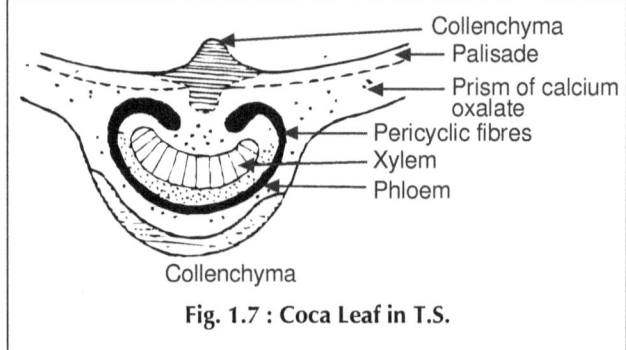

Fig. 1.7 : Coca Leaf in T.S.

does not show trichomes, but some of the cells of epidermis contain mucilage. Numerous lignified idioblasts are present near the veins. Starch grains, stone cells and rarely calcium oxalate crystals are present in epidermal cells.

Chemical Constituents

The drug contains 0.7 - 1.5 % of total alkaloids. The majority of alkaloids are tropane esters. Both Peruvian and Bolivian coca contain less alkaloids, but higher proportion of cocaine among them. Java coca has higher percentage (upto 2 %) of alkaloids, but low amount of cocaine. The composition of the alkaloid mixture varies qualitatively and quantitatively according to variety or plant.

The coca plant yields the tropane derived alkaloids such as cocaine (methyl benzoyl ecgonine), cinnamyl cocaine (methyl cinnamoylecgonine), α-truxilline (methyl - α - truxilloylecgonine), tropocaine, benzoyltropine, dihydroxytropane and benzoylecgonine.

In commerce, the price of leaves is determined on the basis of ecgonine content, because it is converted synthetically into commercial cocaine. In this process, ecgonine is obtained from crude alkaloids which are first isolated by treatment with lime and organic solvents or dilute sulphuric acid. All free bases may be converted to their hydrochlorides. Further, they are hydrolysed by boiling with dilute hydrochloric acid. Due to this, the different bases liberate ecgonine in following way.

1.

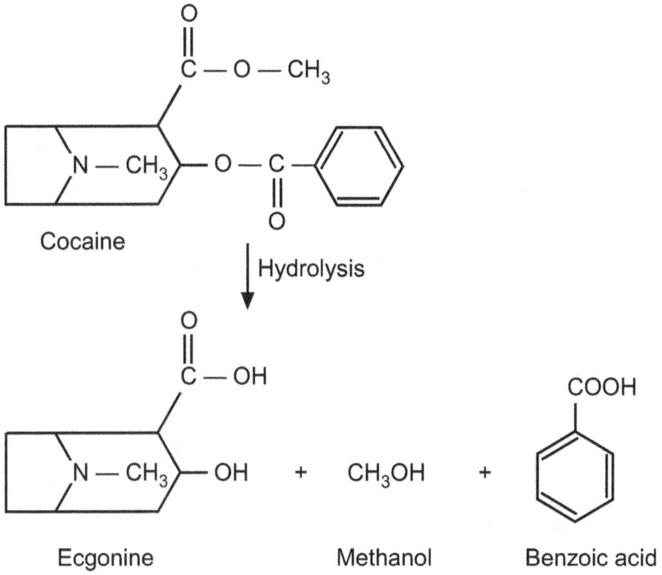

Cocaine

Hydrolysis

Ecgonine + Methanol + Benzoic acid

2.

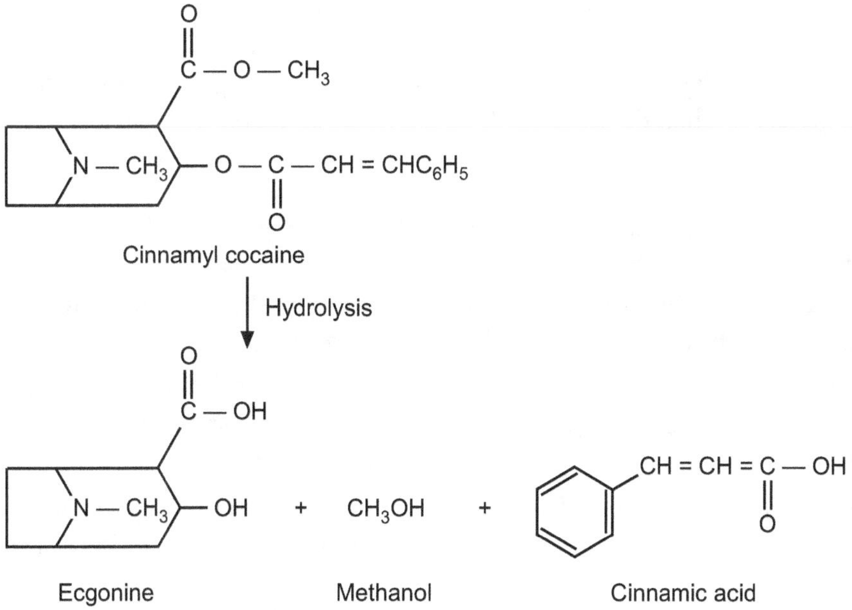

Cinnamyl cocaine

Hydrolysis

Ecgonine + Methanol + Cinnamic acid

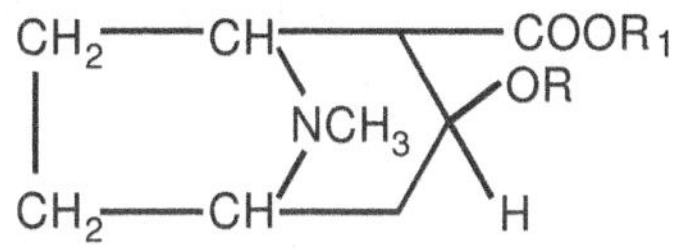

General strucutre of coca alkaloid

Ecgonine Derivatives

R	R'	Name of Alkaloid
H	H	Ecgonine
CH$_3$	C$_6$H$_5$CO (benzoyl)	Cocaine
H	CH$_3$	Methyl ecgonine
H	C$_6$H$_5$CH = CHCO (cinnamoyl)	Cinnamoyl ecgonine
H	C$_6$H$_5$CO	Benzoyl ecgonine

Hygroline   Hygrine

Ecgonine liberated from all the alkaloids is obtained as its hydrochloride. It is further converted to benzoylecgonine by treating with benzoic anhydride. The benzoylated base is next treated with methyl iodide and sodium methoxide in methyl alcohol by which methylation occurs and brings out cocaine i.e. methyl benzoyl ecgonine. This synthetic cocaine is isolated as cocaine hydrochloride.

Chemical Test

Cocaine powder is treated with sulphuric acid, heated, followed by addition and mixing of water. It gives the characteristic smell of methyl benzoate.

Uses

Cocaine hydrochloride is an ingredient of Brompton's cocktail which is widely used to control severe pain in terminal cancer.

Cocaine is a local anaesthetic. It is the first known local anaesthetic from which various other synthetic substitutes with similar activity have been prepared.

In general, coca leaves are used as stimulant, restorative and also in convulsions. Cocaine reduces the sedative and respiratory depressant effects of morphine and allied drugs, due to CNS stimulant properties.

Owing to hallucinogenic and addictive effects of cocaine, it has become the drug of abuse and hence, its uses are limited to ophthalmic surgery and surgery of ear, nose and throat.

(C) DRUGS CONTAINING QUINOLINE ALKALOIDS

Alkaloids containing quinoline as their basic nucleus includes quinine, quinidine, cinchonine, cinchonidine etc. These are obtained from cinchona plant quinine and quinidine are stereoisomers while cinchonine is isomeric with cinchonidine.

BIOGENESIS OF QUINOLINE ALKALOIDS

Quinine is biosynthesized from monoterpenoid – trypthophan pathway. The cleavage of benzopyrrole ring of tryptophan and rearrangement leads to formation of quinoline nucleus. Detailed mechanism of biosynthesis of quinoline is not yet known, but strictosidine and corynantheal are important intermediates.

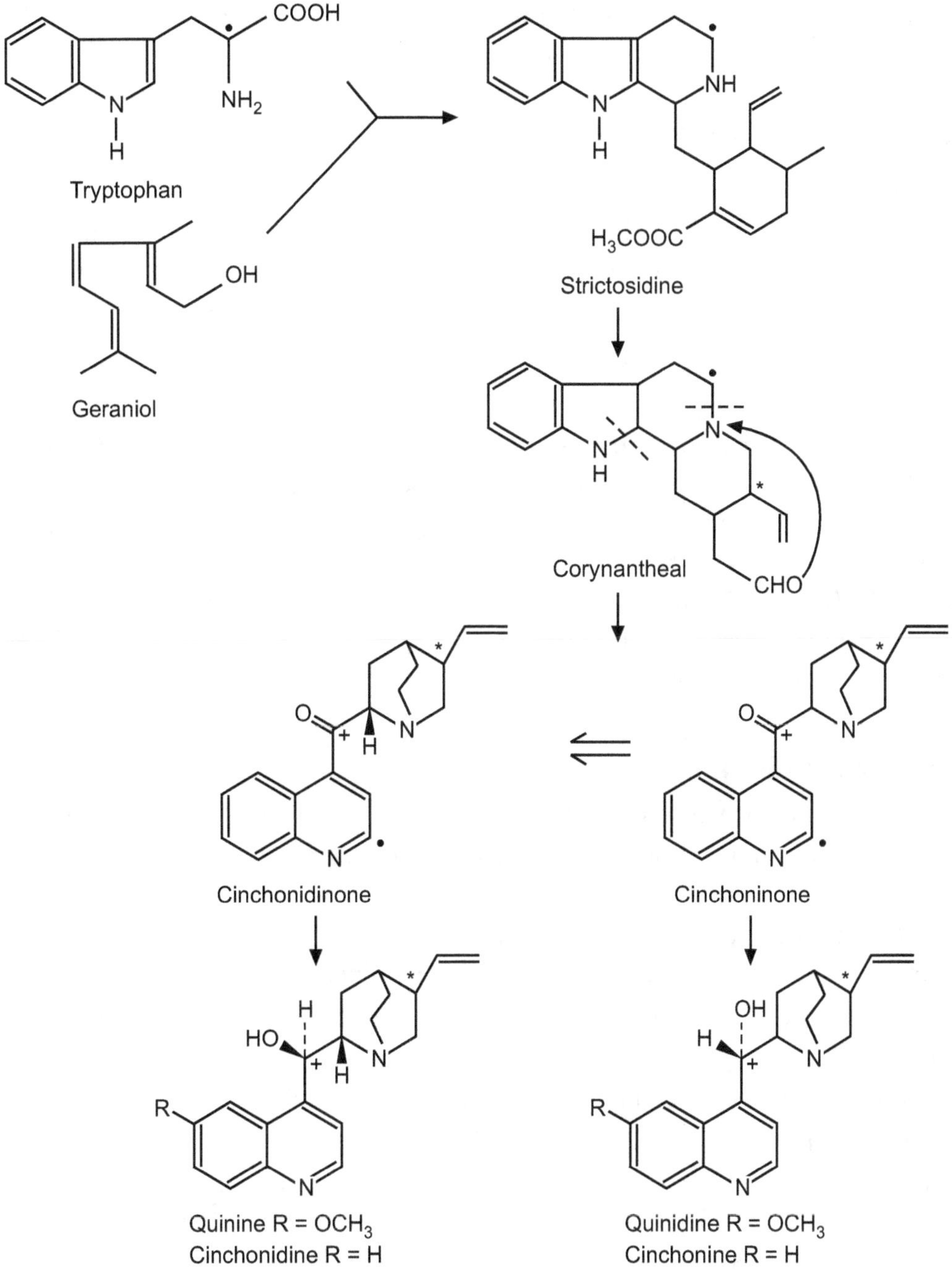

Tryptophan

Geraniol

Strictosidine

Corynantheal

Cinchonidinone

Cinchoninone

Quinine R = OCH_3
Cinchonidine R = H

Quinidine R = OCH_3
Cinchonine R = H

CINCHONA

Synonyms

Jesuit's bark, Peruvian bark.

Biological Source

It is the dried bark of the cultivated trees of *Cinchona calisaya* Wedd., *C. ledgeriana* Moens, *C. officinalis* Linn, *C. succirubra* Pav. ex-klotzsch, or of hybrids of either of the last two species with either of the first two. Cinchona belongs to family Rubiaceae. It contains not less than 6 % of total alkaloids of cinchona.

Geographical Source

India, Bolivia, Columbia, Ecuador, Peru, Tanzania, Guatemala, Indonesia and Sri Lanka are the countries where cinchona is found. In India, it is cultivated in Annamalai hills (Coimbatore district) and Nilgiri hills (Nilgiri district) in Tamil Nadu and in Darjeeling area of West Bengal.

History

Cinchona is native to Eastern slopes of the Andes at high altitudes (1500 to 2500 metres). It is known that the bark was first used as an antipyretic in 1630 by Jesuits, although it was discovered in 1513 in Peru. Owing to the efforts of Viceroy of Peru, Count Chinchon it was introduced as a drug in Europe around 1655. It was officially reported as an infusion in London Pharmacopoeia in 1677. In the honour of viceroy, the genus was described by Linnaeus as Cinchona in 1742. After the isolation of quinine and cinchonine in 1820 by Pelletier and Canventon, the alkaloids or their mixtures came into use as a medicine.

Cultivation and Collection

Most of the cinchona species thrive best in tropical climate at an altitude of 1000 to 3000 metres. The soil, temperature, rainfall and other requirements of cinchona plant are as under :

1. Altitude : 1000 to 3000 metres above sea level. It also grows satisfactorily below 1000 metres, but it has been found to contain low quinine.

2. Temperature : The optimum temperature for the favourable growth of cinchona is 60° to 75° F.

3. Rainfall : In between 250 to 380 cm; well distributed throughout the year.

4. Soil : Light, well drained forest soil rich in organic matter is found to be suitable for cinchona cultivation. The acidic soil with a pH of 4.2 to 5.6 and a little nitrogen content is found conductive to the maximum growth of cinchona. High humidity, sloping situation, shelter from wind are also necessary for cinchona plantation.

Cultivation of the cinchona trees can either be done by sowing the seeds or budding and layering. In Tamil Nadu, the budding and layering methods of vegetative propagation are followed, while in West Bengal only budding is followed. The seeds of cinchona are very small and light and about 3500 seeds weigh only one gram. The seeds are supplemented with sand to keep them in position while sowing. It takes about 3 to 6 weeks for their germination in the nursery beds. The seeds are sown as early as possible after their collection as they loose the variability on storage. The seedlings which bear about two pairs of leaves are transplanted in the nursery beds. Since cinchona consists of stem as well as root bark, the age of the plants selected for harvesting the bark varies from 4 to 20 years. Maximum alkaloidal content is found in 10 to 12 years old plants. The technique of coppicing is followed for collection of bark. The vertical incisions are made on the branches, as well as, trunk of the trees with copper knieves and these incisions are connected by horizontal circles. The bark is then removed and dried. Mostly, drying of bark is done by natural method or if done artificially, it is dried below 175°F. Bark looses about 70 % of its weight on drying. The dried barks are then packed in gunny bags and marketed.

Organoleptic Characters (Fig. 1.8)

Cinchona bark has a slight and characteristic odour, but somewhat astringent and intensely bitter taste. In general, the bark is available in the form of quills and curved pieces.

Fig. 1.8 : Flowering bunch of Cinchona and Piece of Cinchona Bark

Stem bark: It is upto 30 cm in length and about 2 to 6 mm in thickness. The outer surface shows dull brown grey or grey colour and many a time, shows presence of mosses and lichens owing to its growth in heavy rainfall areas. The bark is rough and has transverse fissures. These fissures are different in different species. It is furrowed or wrinkled longitudinally. The outer bark in some varieties shows exfoliation. The inner surface is pale yellowish-brown to deep reddish-brown and the colour depends on the species. The fracture is short in external layers and fibrous in the inner portion.

Root bark: It occurs in length of 2 - 7 cm. The bark is curved, twisted or irregularly channelled. The outer and inner surfaces are similar in colour. The outer surface is scaly and shows depressions. The inner surface is striated.

The different commercial varieties have some special characters. *C. succirubra* is also called as red bark, while *C. ledgeriana* is referred to as yellow bark. *C. robusta* is the hybrid between *C. succirubra* and *C. officinalis*.

Table 1.2: The typical characters of 4 main species of cinchona

Characters	*C. calisaya*	*C. ledgeriana*	*C. officinalis*	*C. succirubra*
Size	Diameter is from 12 - 25 mm and thickness from 2 - 5 mm	Diameter is 12-25 mm and thickness varies from 2 - 5 mm	Diameter is upto 12 mm and thickness is upto 1.5 mm	Diameter is from 20 - 40 mm and thickness from 2 - 5 mm
Other features	Broad longitudinal fissure with transverse cracks.	Broad longitudinal fissures and cracks more in number, but less deep. Some pieces show longitudinal wrinkles and reddish warts.	It shows a number of transverse cracks	Well marked longitudinal wrinkles, but less number of transverse cracks. Only some pieces show reddish warts.
Powder	Cinnamon brown	Cinnamon brown	Yellow	Reddish brown

Microscopic Characters (Fig. 1.9)

Cinchona exhibits the typical histological characters of the bark. The cork cells are thin-walled, followed by phelloderm. The cortex consists of several secretory channels and phloem fibres. Medullary rays with radially arranged cells are present. Idioblast of calcium oxalate is the specific characteristic of cinchona bark. Starch grains are present in the parenchymatous tissues. Stone cells are rarely present in the structure. A few of the cork cells are lignified. Medullary rays are 2 to 3 cells wide.

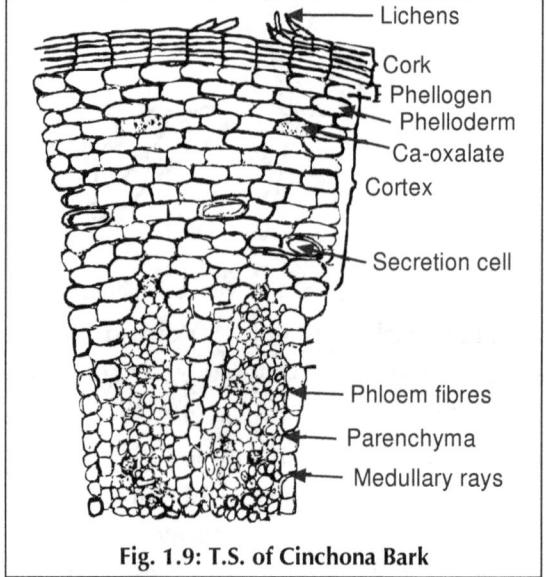

Fig. 1.9: T.S. of Cinchona Bark

Chemical Constituents

Cinchona bark contains about 25 alkaloids, which belong to quinoline group. The important alkaloids are quinine, quinidine, cinchonine and cinchonidine. The alkaloids of lesser importance are quinicine, cinchonicine hydroquinine, hydrocinchonidine and homocinchonidine.

Quinine and Quinidine are stereoisomers of each other. Quinidine is also obtained commercially from cuprea bark i.e. *Ramijia pendunculata* Fluckiger belonging to family Rubiaceae, or by isomerization of quinine.

Quinine and Quinidine form many salts, but medicinally their sulphates are more significant. Cinchonine and cinchonidine are also isomers of each other.

Apart from alkaloids, cinchona also contains quinic acid and cinchotannic acid (2 – 4%). In the plant, the alkaloids are present as salts of these acids. Cinchotannic acid decomposes into insoluble cinchona red, due to its phlobatannin nature it is present to the extent of 10%. Cinchona bark also contains a glycoside called quinovin, tannins and bitter essential oil.

Table 1.3 : Cinchona alkaloids present in different species

Sr. No.	Name of Species	Total Alkaloid (in %)	% of quinine present
1.	C. succirubra	5 – 7	upto 30
2.	C. ledgeriana	10 – 14	upto 75
3.	C. calisaya	6 – 8	upto 50

The hybrids of *Cinchona ledgeriana* and *Cinchona calisaya* produce higher yield of alkaloids than any other parent species.

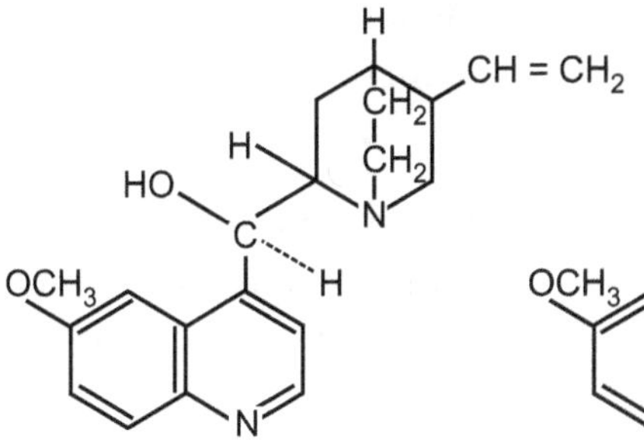

Quinine 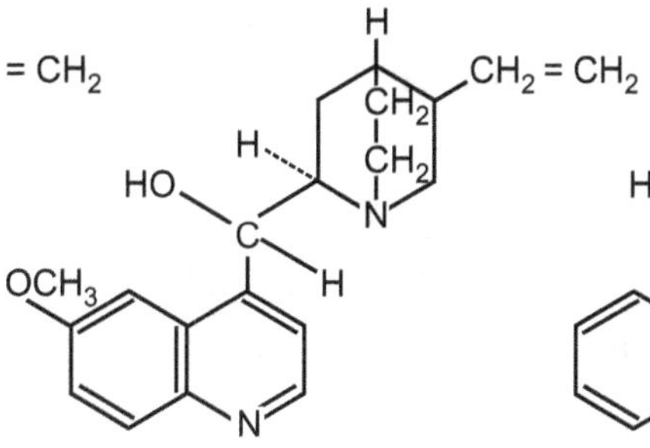   Quinidine 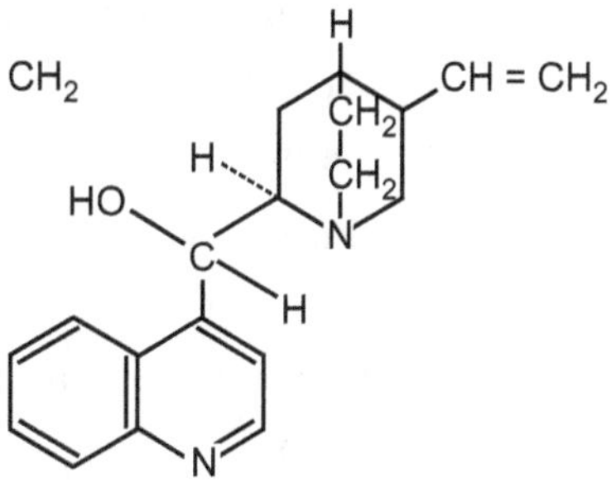   Cinchonine

Cinchonidine   Cupreine   Hydroquinine

The alkaloid quinine occurs as bitter white crystals and it darkens when exposed to light and has fluorescent properties. It shows a strong blue fluorescence in ultra-violet light. This fluorescence is enhanced in presence of dilute sulphuric acid. Quinine forms salts with different acids. Quinine sulphate $(C_{20}H_{24}N_2O_2)_2$. H_2SO_4. $2H_2O$ is important from pharmaceutical point of view. It has very less solubility in water (1 in 810 parts of water), due to which, it is suitable for oral use.

Quinidine $(C_{20}H_{24}N_2O_2)$ is similar to quinine in its physical and chemical properties and has higher water solubility. The free base is soluble in water, ethyl alcohol, methyl alcohol and chloroform.

Chemical Tests

1. **Thalleoquin test :** The powdered drug gives emerald green colour with bromine water and dilute ammonia solution. The coloured product formed is known as thalleoquin. Quinidine and cupreine, a 'Remijia alkaloid, also give positive response to this test, but cinchonine and cinchonidine do not respond to this test.

2. **Fluorescence test :** Quinine gives a distinct and strong blue fluorescence with oxygenated acids like acetic acid, and sulphuric acid. The hydrochloride and hydroiodide salts do not respond to this test.

3. **Erythroquinine or Rosquin test :** A solution of quinine in dilute acetic acid instantly turns red when treated with bromine water, 10% w/v potassium ferrocyanide and strong ammonia.

4. **Herpathite test :** To boiling mixture of quinine and glacial acetic acid, add ethanol, few drops of conc. sulphuric acid and solution of iodine in ethanol, iodosulphate crystals of quinine are formed. This product is known as herpathite, having olive green colour.

5. Quinidine solution gives a white precipitate with silver nitrate solution, which is soluble in nitric acid.

Schematic Method of Isolation of Cinchona Alkaloids :

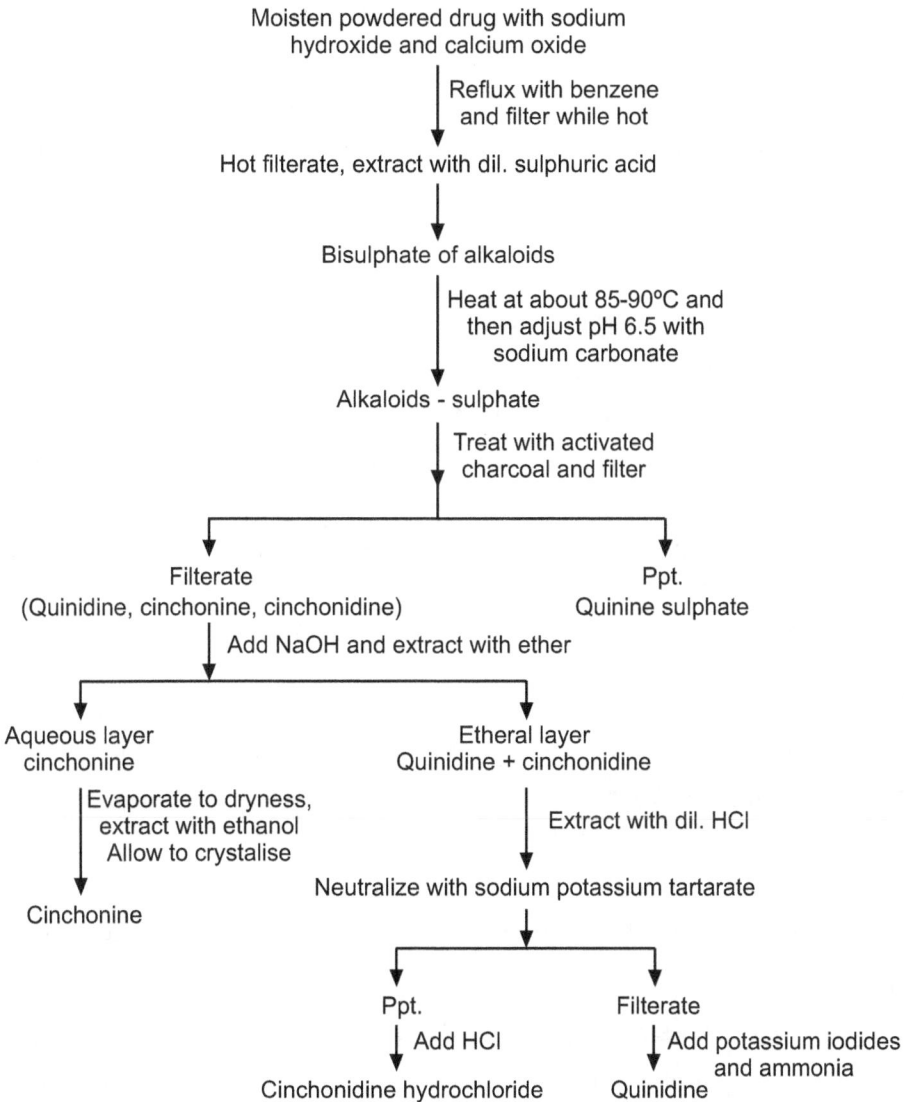

Standards

(1) Total ash   -   not more than 4 %

(2) Foreign organic matter   -   nor more than 2 %

The UV spectrophotometric method of estimation is carried out for quinine.

Uses

Cinchona bark is antimalarial in nature. The cinchona preparations like cinchona extract, compound cinchona tincture etc. are also employed as bitter stomachics and antipyretics. Quinine and its salts are used in the treatment of malaria. Quinine is a protoplasmic poison, especially for protozoa like *Plasmodium vivax, P. falciparum, P. malarie and P. fatal,* and hence, used as powerful antimalarial drug.

Recently the pharmacokinetic studies on quinine have shown that it can be better used in other forms. Infusion of quinine rather than intravenous injection eliminates the risk of sudden death. Secondly, quinine in microencapsulated form has been reported to give better bioavailability.

Quinine has also been found to be highly active *in vitro* against *Trypanosoma cruzi* epimastigotes.

Quinidine is primarily a cardiac depressant and used to prevent certain arrhythmias and tachycardia. Quinidine is valuable in prevention of atrial fibrillation. Quinidine is also available as quinidine gluconate and quinidine polygalacturonate salt.

The antimalarial action is due to intercalation of quinoline moiety into DNA of *Plasmodium* parasite, thereby reducing effectiveness of DNA to act as template.

It is important in chloroquine-resistant falciparum malaria in combination with pyrimethamine.

Dose

    1. Cinchona powder   -   0.3 - 1 g

    2. Quinine sulphate   -   1 g daily for 2 days and then 600 mg daily for 5 days

    3. Quinidine sulphate   -   0.2 - 0.4 g every two to four hours to a total dose of 3 g daily in atrial fibrillation.

Overdose of cinchona products results in temporary loss of hearing and blurred vision. Ringing in ears is symptomatic toxicity. Cinchona toxicity is known as cinchonism.

Substitutes

Cuprea bark (*Remijia pedunculata*), a coppery red coloured drug, contains quinine, quinidine and other alkaloids which resemble to those from cinchona bark. The bark contains numerous stone cells. Along with cinchona alkaloids, it also contains cupreine. False cuprea bark (*R. purdiena*) contains an alkaloid called cusconidine, traces of cinchonine, cinchonamine, but no quinine.

Quantitative Estimation of Cinchona Alkaloids

Non-aqueous titration : Weigh accurately about 0.2 g of quinine sulphate/quinidine sulphate and dissolve in a mixture of chloroform (50 ml) and acetic anhydride (20 ml). Determine equivalence point potentiometerically using 0.1 M perchloric acid. Each ml of 0.1 M perchloric acid = 0.02490 gm of quinine or quinidine.

(D) DRUGS CONTAINING ISOQUINOLINE ALKALOIDS

The important drugs in this class are ipecac, opium, sanguinaria, curare etc. Opium alkaloids include both isoquinoline (like papaverine) and phenanthrene type (like morphine, codeine thebaine). These phenanthrene alkaloids are biosynthetically derived from benzyl-isoquinoline intermediates, hence opium is included in this group.

IPECACUANHA

Synonym

Ipecac.

Biological Source

It consists of the dried roots, or the rhizomes and roots of *Cephaelis ipecacuanha* (Brot.) A. Rich. or of *Cephaelis acuminata* Karsten, both belonging to family Rubiaceae. It should contain not less than 2 % of the ether soluble alkaloids, in which at least 50 % should be emetine.

Geographical Source

Cephaelis ipecacuanha is called Rio or Brazilian ipecac, which is obtained from Brazil, India, Myanmar, and Malaysia. *C. acuminata* is called Panama or Cartagena ipecac, which is procured from Columbia, Panama, Nicaragua and India.

History

Ipecacuanha means the small wayside plant with vomiting effects. Even before it was introduced in Europe as a medicine, ipecac was known in Brazil and used as an antidysenteric drug. Helvetius, a Dutch physician, launched use of this drug in Europe in 1688 under the name Brazilian root. In 1817, Pelletier and Magnedi first isolated emetine in crude form and later in 1894, Paul and Cownley separated emetine in pure form. Pyman succeeded in isolating two more alkaloids, viz. emetamine and o–methyl psychotrine in 1917.

Cultivation, Collection and Preparation

The commercial cultivation of Rio ipecac (also called Brazilian or Matto Grosso ipecac) in India is discussed here as large areas from West Bengal are under the cultivation of Rio ipecac. The drug from W. Bengal is also called as Johore ipecac. Better results have been obtained by cultivating ipecac at the lower foot hills of Eastern Himalayas. But the cultivation needs special attention and precautions.

The propagation is done by sowing the seeds in mid January to mid February. The germination is improved by treatment of seeds with lime water or hydrogen peroxide. It favourably grows in the temperature range of 23 - 38°C, with a rainfall of 300 cm. The humid atmosphere helps in the growth of plant. The nitrogenous fertilizers have significant effect in increasing the quantity of emetine. The percentage of all alkaloids is maximum in third year and hence, harvesting of roots is done after three years of vegetative growth.

Organoleptic Characters (Fig. 1.10)

1. Brazilian ipecacuanha

(a) Roots

Colour : Dark brick red to dark brown

Odour : Faint

Taste : Bitter

Size : Upto 150 mm in length and 6 mm in thickness

Shape : Roots are found in tortuous pieces.

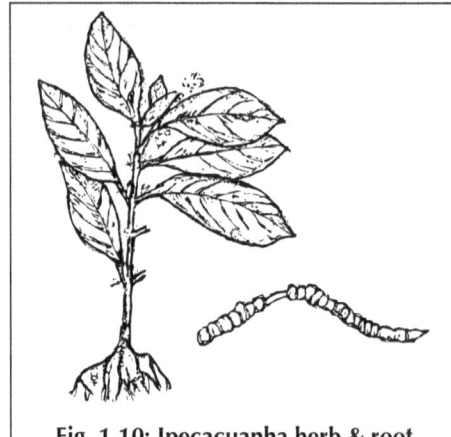

Fig. 1.10: Ipecacuanha herb & root

Extra Features : They are closely annulated externally, ridges rounded and completely encircling roots. Fracture is short in the bark and splintery in the wood. Pith is absent.

(b) Rhizomes

Colour : Brick red to dark brown.

Size : About 2 mm in diameter and short, attached to the roots

Shape : Cylindrical.

Extra Features : They are wrinkled longitudinally and show the presence of prominent pith.

2. Panama ipecacuanha

Colour : Greyish-brown to reddish-brown

Odour and taste : Same as in Brazilian variety

Size : Characterized by large size upto 9 mm in thickness.

Shape : Cylindrical

Extra Features : They are characterised by the absence of annulations and the presence of transverse ridges at an interval of 1 to 3 mm. They partially encircle the roots.

Microscopic Characters (Fig. 1.11)

Roots : Transverse section of root shows the presence of cork layer with brown contents, which is followed by phelloderm composed of thin walled parenchyma. It is full of starch grains and acicular crystals of calcium oxalate. Xylem consists of tracheids and small vessels. Secondary medullary rays with starch grains are also present. Size of the starch grains is up to 15 microns. Sclerenchyma is absent.

Rhizomes : Pericycle is with thick walled sclereids, sclerenchymatous fibres, protoxylem and spiral vessels. Pith at centre shows pitted parenchyma.

Columbian variety differs only in one aspect i.e. the starch grains are larger in size and upto 22 microns.

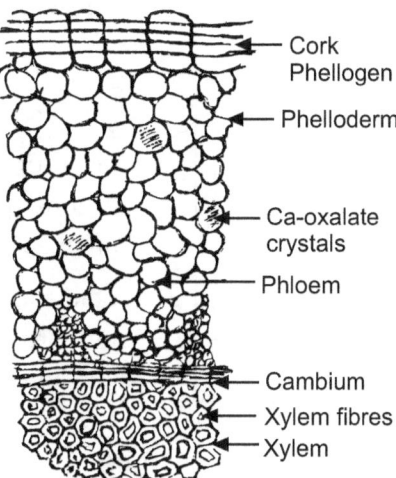

Fig. 1.11: T. S. of Ipecacuanha Root

Chemical Constituents

Ipecac contains isoquinoline alkaloids which belong to phenolic and non-phenolic groups. The total alkaloids in Rio-ipecac are upto 2%, and in Panama ipecac, about 2.2%. The main alkaloids are emetine, cephaeline, psychotrine, o-methyl psychotrine and emetamine.

Cephaeline is converted into emetine by methylation of phenolic C (6) hydroxyl group. Medicinally, emetine is most important. It was discovered by Pelletier and Magendie in 1817. Non-phenolic alkaloidal group includes emetine and o-methyl psychotrine, while phenolic alkaloidal group includes cephaeline and psychotrine. Ipecac also contains ipecacuanhic acid, glycoside ipecacuanhin, about 40% starch and calcium oxalate.

Emetine hydrochloride is a hydrated hydrochloride salt of emetine. It is white, odourless, crystalline powder that becomes yellowish when exposed to light.

Chemical Tests

(1) To about 2.5 g powdered drug, add 20 ml hydrochloric acid and 5 ml water. Shake it well and filter. To the filtrate, add 0.5 g potassium chlorate. The presence of yellow colour gradually changing to red, after standing, is due to emetine.

(2) The addition of sulphuric acid and sodium molybdate (Frohde's reagent) to small quantity of emetine gives bright green colour.

Standards

(1) Total ash   - not more than 5 %
(2) Acid-insoluble ash   - not more than 2 %
(3) Foreign organic matter - not more than 1 %

Table 1.4 : Comparison between Rio Ipecac and Panama Ipecac

Rio or Brazilian Ipecac	Panama or Cartagena Ipecac
1) It is obtained from *Cephaelis ipecacuanha*.	1) It is obtained from *Cephaelis accuminata*.
2) The drug is indigenous to Brazil, also cultivated in Malaysia and in India.	2) The drug is indigenous to northern portions of Columbia that extends into Panama, Nicaragua and Cartagena.
3) Total alkaloid content is about 2%, about one-third cephaeline and two-thirds emetine.	3) Total alkaloid content is 2.2%, about one-third emetine and two-third cephaeline.

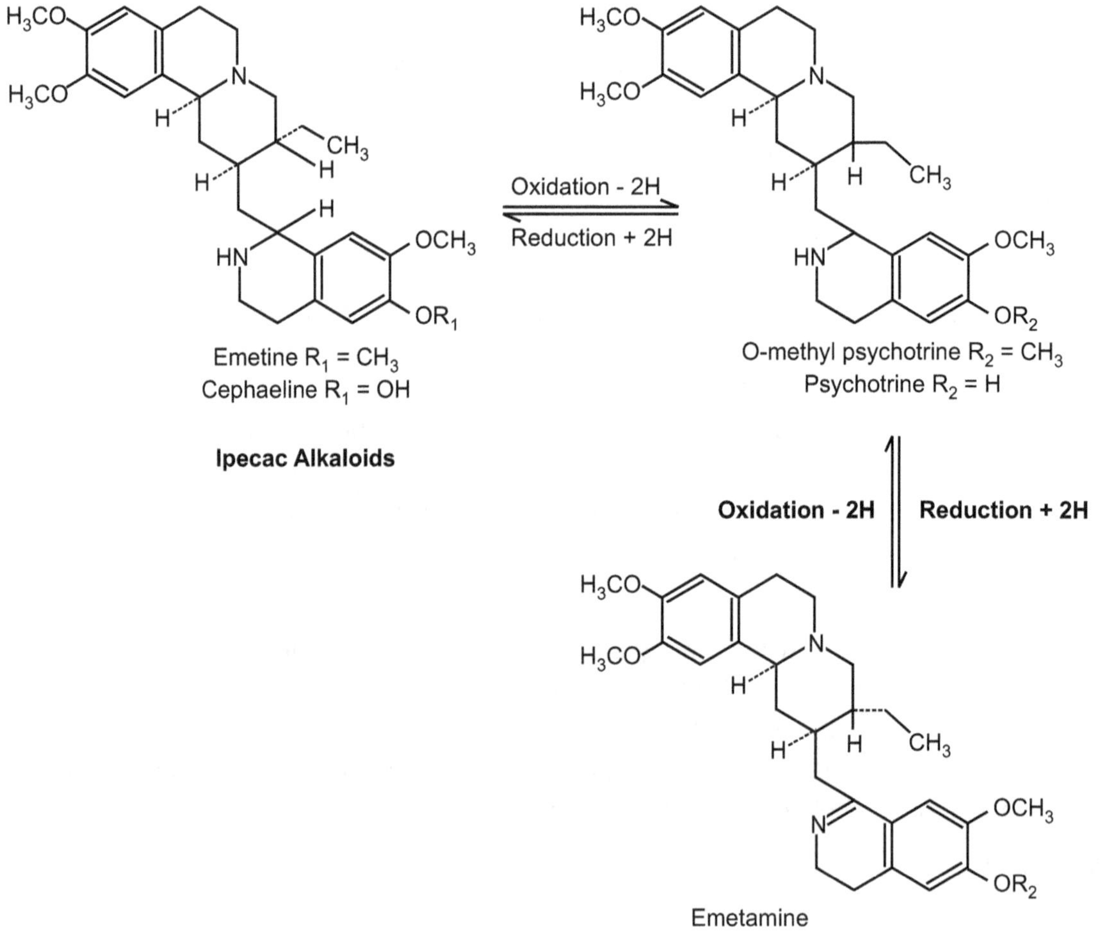

Emetine $R_1 = CH_3$
Cephaeline $R_1 = OH$

Ipecac Alkaloids

Oxidation - 2H
Reduction + 2H

O-methyl psychotrine $R_2 = CH_3$
Psychotrine $R_2 = H$

Oxidation - 2H   Reduction + 2H

Emetamine

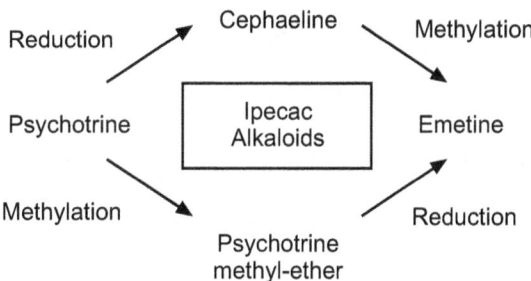

Inter-relationship between ipecac alkaloids

Uses

Ipecacuanha is expectorant in small doses and emetic in higher doses. Cephaeline has more emetic and less expectorant action as compared to emetine.

Emetine hydrochloride is used as antiprotozoal, as it is highly toxic to amoeba i.e. *Entamoeba histolytica* even in very low concentrations like 1 in 6 millions. Hence, it is used by administering parenterally, in treatment of amoebic dysentery. It acts by inhibiting polypeptide chain elongation, thereby blocking protein synthesis.

Ipecacuanha is used for isolation of emetine and cephaeline. It is also reported that emetine has anti-tumour properties.

Dose

Emetine hydrochloride : 1 mg per kg body weight, subcutaneously or intramuscularly, but should not exceed 60 mg and maximum for 5 days.

Allied Plants

Various genera belonging to family Rubiaceae contain emetine. Some of them are *Alangium, Hillia, Manettia Psychotria, Borreria, Remijia* and *Ferdinandusa*.

BIOGENESIS OF PHENANTHRENE AND ISOQUINOLINE ALKALOIDS

Isoquinoline alkaloids are derived from condensation reaction of phenylethylamine derivative with a phenylacetaldehyde derivatives. Both these moieties are derived from tyrosine or phenylalanine.

Morphine is also formed from two molecules of tyrosine. Enzymatically controlled methylation gives rise to formation of (–)-reticuline. This reticuline then facilitate formation of dienone known as salutaridine. This is the first intermediate from phenanthrene class of alkaloids. After salutaridine formation, stepwise demethylation leads to first, formation of thebaine (therapeutically less important), then codeine (mild analgesic and antitussive) and lastly morphine (a potent analgesic and narcotic).

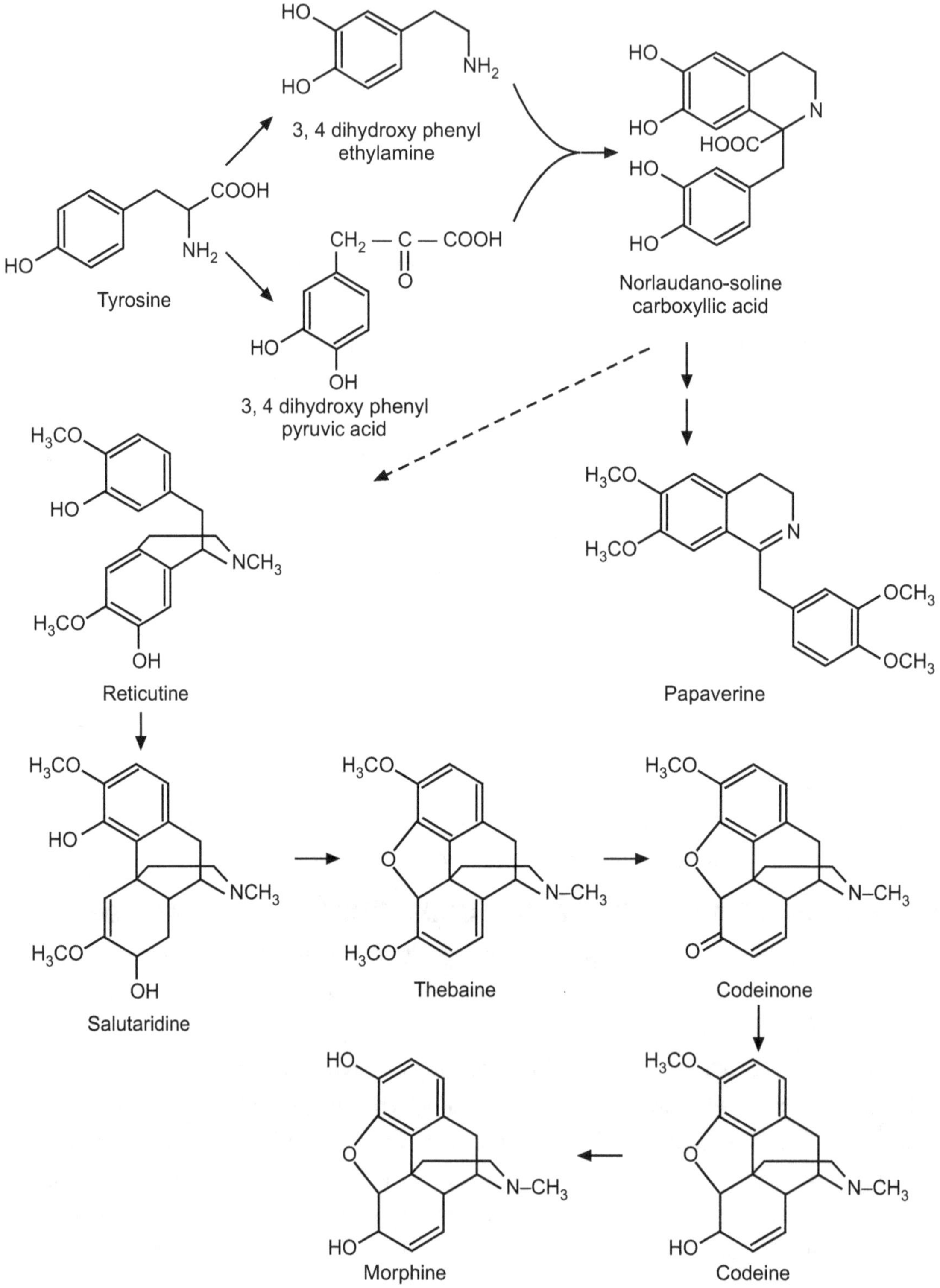
HO
HO
NH2
3, 4 dihydroxy phenyl ethylamine
COOH
NH2
HO
Tyrosine
CH2 — C — COOH
O
HO
OH
3, 4 dihydroxy phenyl pyruvic acid
HO
HO
N
HOOC
HO
HO
Norlaudano-soline carboxyllic acid
H3CO
HO
NCH3
H3CO
OH
Reticutine
H3CO
H3CO
N
OCH3
OCH3
Papaverine
H3CO
HO
NCH3
H3CO
OH
Salutaridine
H3CO
O
N–CH3
H3CO
Thebaine
H3CO
O
N–CH3
O
Codeinone
HO
O
N–CH3
HO
Morphine
H3CO
O
N–CH3
HO
Codeine

OPIUM

Synonym

Raw opium

Biological Source

It is the dried latex obtained by incision from the unripe capsules of *Papaver somniferum* Linn., dried or partly dried by heat or spontaneous evaporation, and worked into somewhat irregularly shaped masses (natural opium) or moulded into masses of more uniform size and shape (manipulated opium). Poppy plant belongs to family Papaveraceae. It contains not less than 10 per cent of morphine, and not less than 2.0 per cent of codeine, both calculated as anhydrous morphine.

Geographical Source

India, Pakistan, Afghanistan, Turkey, Russia, China, and Iran.

History

Opium has been known to mankind since centuries due to its narcotic properties. It was first cultivated in Mediterranean regions and probably brought by Alexander in 327 B.C. to India. It is known that Dioscorides and Theophrastus were aware of the medicinal properties of opium. The earliest written record about opium is revealed from *Historia plantarum* (some where in 300 B.C.) and *De Materia Medica* (78 A.D.). Narcotine was the first alkaloid reported both from opium and among alkaloidal series, to be isolated in 1803 by Derosne. In 1806, Serturner isolated the alkaloid Morphine from opium. Magendi and Bally first introduced it in medical practice in 1818. Gulland and Robinson elucidated the structure of morphine in 1923. In 1833, Robiquet isolated codeine from opium, and in 1881, Grimaux reported that codeine is o-methyl derivative of morphine. Merck company isolated papaverine in 1848.

Cultivation, Collection and Preparation

Being a potent narcotic drug, the cultivation and other aspects of opium are governed by respective governments in different countries, including India. Opium cultivation is controlled internationally by International Narcotic Control Board of United Nations. In India, all the activities about opium and its derivatives are controlled under Narcotic Drugs and Psychotropic Substances Act, 1985.

The genus *Papaver* has 50 different species, of which six species are found in India, viz. *P. somniferum* (Opium poppy), *P. nudicaule* (Iceland poppy), *P. rhoeas* (corn poppy), *P. orientale, P. argemone,* and *P. dubium.*

Poppy is an erect plant attaining 60 - 120 cm height. It is rarely branched. The leaves are linear, oblong or ovate oblong and have a dentate or serrate margin. It bears bluish white, purple or violet coloured large flowers. Accordingly, the varieties *P. somniferum* var. *glabrum*, *P. somniferum* var. *album*, *P. somniferum var. nigrum* are described. The second variety is cultivated in India. Indian opium is considered as the only legal source of opium to many countries including United States of America and Britain.

In India, about 54 thousand hectares of land is under opium poppy cultivation. It is under government control, and cultivation of poppy is restricted to Madhya Pradesh, Rajasthan and Uttar Pradesh.

The weather conditions affect, upto a large extent, the yield of opium. Although, temperate climate is the natural requirement of opium poppy, it can be grown with success under subtropical climate in winter season, as there is a favourable effect on yield by cold weather. But, extreme cold conditions, including frost, adversely affect the plant and ultimately yield of opium. In short, the best climatic conditions for opium poppy are cool weather without freezing temperature and cloudiness, and sufficient sunshine.

Opium poppy is grown from November to March. Propagation is done by sowing the seeds, for which 3 - 4 kg of seeds per hectare are necessary. The seeds admixed with about 3 - 4 parts of sand are sown. Opium poppy requires highly fertile, well drained loamy soil with fine sand. The soil should contain organic matter, nitrogen and should have a pH around 7. The distance between two plants maintained is usually 25 cm and the plant reaches maximum height of one metre.

Latex

Fig. 1.12: Opium poppy capsule

Periodically, the thinning of plants is done to get uniform growth and better development. The plants are kept totally free from weeds with the use of suitable weedicides. The plant should be protected from various insect pests like cut worms, leaf minor and poppy borer. The use of manures and fertilizers markedly improve the quality and yield of opium poppy. Especially, nitrogen and phosphorus have remarkable effects on growth of plant.

After sowing, within 3 - 4 months, the plant bears flowers, which are converted to capsules within few days and attain maturity after 15 - 20 days. During the maturity period, the capsule exudes maximum latex which shows a colour change from dark green to light green. Such capsules (Fig. 1.12) are incised vertically in the afternoon with the help of specific needle like apparatus called 'nushtur'. It penetrates maximum upto 2 mm into the capsule. Because of incisions, latex exudes out and thickens due to cold weather in night which is eventually scrapped and collected next morning by an iron scoop called

Charpala. The incising process is repeated for about 4 times on the same capsule with 2 days interval. The incisions must remain superficial, so as to maintain the external exudation of latex. The latex is collected in plastic containers. Then, capsules are collected and dried in open areas and further the seeds are separated by beating. The average yield of opium is about 25-26 kg per hectare and for seeds, it is from 4-5 quintals per hectare. Opium is exported traditionally from India. The exports for 95-96 and 96-97 were ₹ 2365.5 lacs and 4102 lacs respectively.

The opium collected by this way is either exported or some of the part is further processed at Government opium factory at Ghazipur. Additional processing of raw opium takes place at government centres. About 35 kg of latex is kept in Sun for drying purpose and after every 30 minutes, each pan is stirred with wooden paddles. 8 – 20 days of stirring is required to reduce the moisture from 30% to 10%. When sufficiently dry, it is formed into 5 kg cakes. Externally it is olive-brown to olive gray in colour. It is shipped in polyethylene bags. Indian opium yields about 10% anhydrous morphine.

Organoleptic Characters

Odour :   Strong characteristic

Taste :   bitter

1. Indian opium: Dark brown in colour. It is found in the form of cubical pieces weighing about 900 g for marketing purposes. It is enclosed in tissue paper and is brittle and plastic in nature. Internally, it is homogenous.

2. Persian opium: Dark brown in colour, found in the form of brick shaped masses, weighing 450 g. It is hygroscopic in nature, granular or nearly smooth with brittle fracture.

3. Natural Turkish or European opium: Brown or dark brown in colour. It is found in conical or rounded and somewhat flattened masses, weighing 250 to 1000 g. On keeping, it becomes hard and brittle. It is covered with poppy leaves.

4. Manipulated Turkish opium: It is chocolate brown or dark brown internally and covered with broken poppy leaves externally. The masses of this type are oval and flattened on upper and lower surface weighing about 2000 g. It is somewhat plastic or even brittle.

5. Manipulated European opium: It is dark brown in colour internally and covered with broken leaves. It is found in the form of elongated masses with rounded ends weighing 150 to 500 g. It is firm, plastic and with brittle fracture.

Chemical Constituents

The latex contains mainly the alkaloids derived from amino acids phenylalanine and tyrosine. Chemically, they are placed under benzylisoquinoline and phenanthrene types.

Narcotine (also called noscapine), narceine and papaverine are benzylisoquinoline type of alkaloids, while morphine, codeine and thebaine are phenanthrene type.

Morphine :   4 - 21 %,   Noscapine : 4 - 8%

Codeine   :   0.8 - 2.5%,   Papaverine : 0.5 - 2.5%,

Thebaine :   0.5 - 2%

A generalised process is outlined to cover the industrial method for extraction of alkaloids of opium.

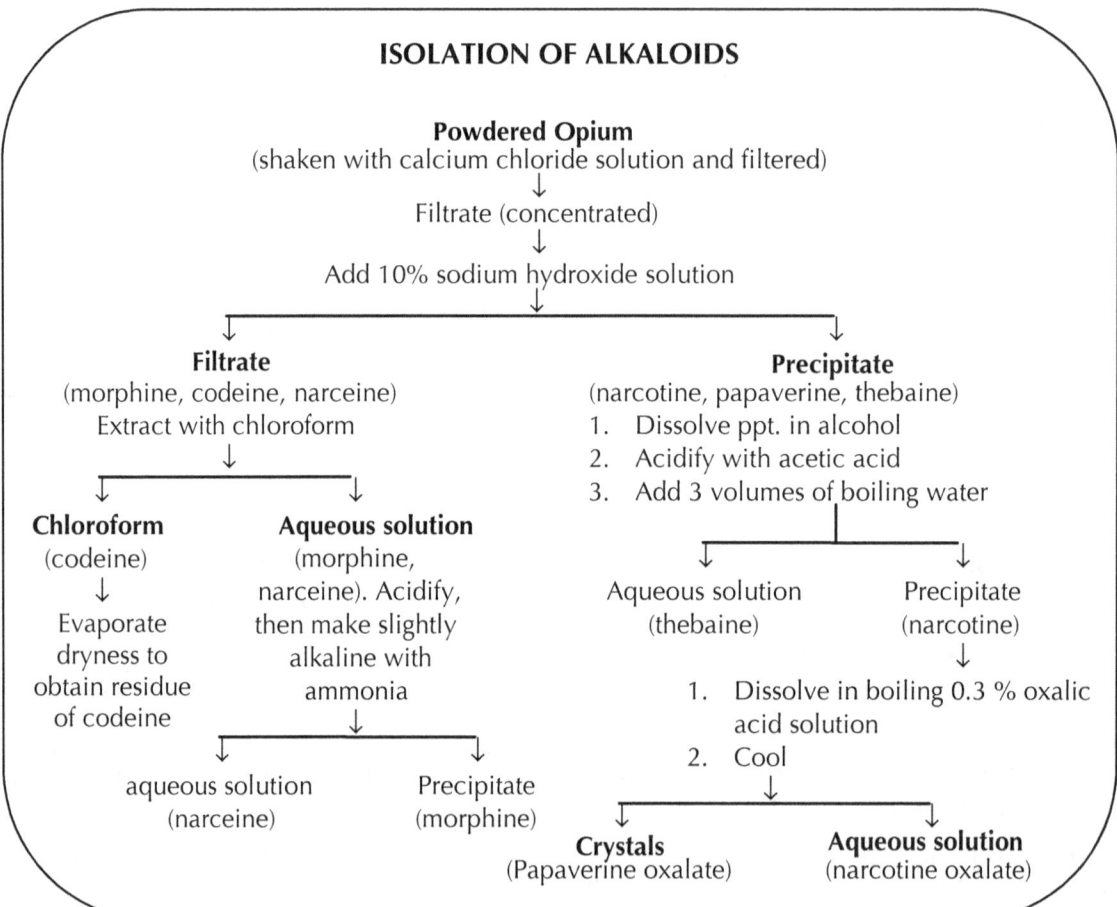

Opium also contains 3 – 5% meconic acid, which is present either in free form or in combination with morphine and other alkaloids. It is known as chemotaxonomic marker of Papaveraceae family. It also contains one more dibasic acid known as chelidonic acid.

Fruits of poppy contain numerous off-white coloured and minute seeds. These seeds contain 30-35 % drying fixed oil, which is used commercially in oil paint industry, which is colourless, tasteless and transparent.

OPIUM ALKALOIDS

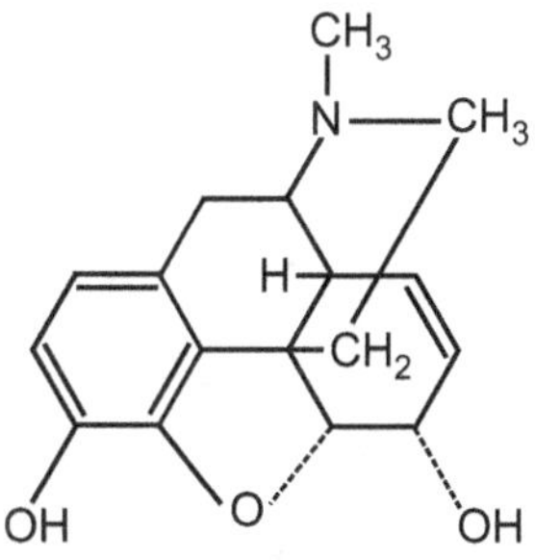

Morphine 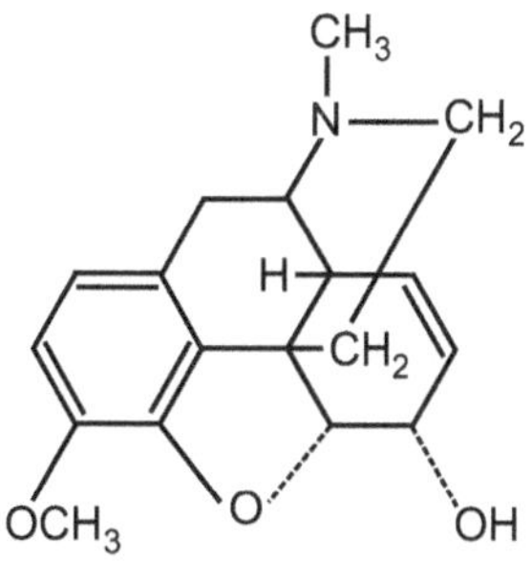   Codeine

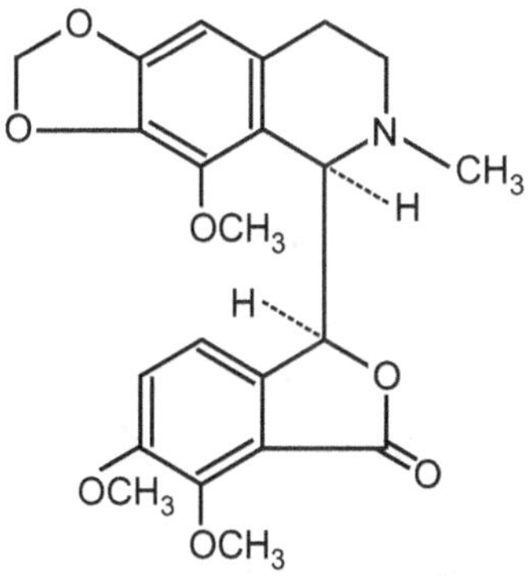

Narcotine 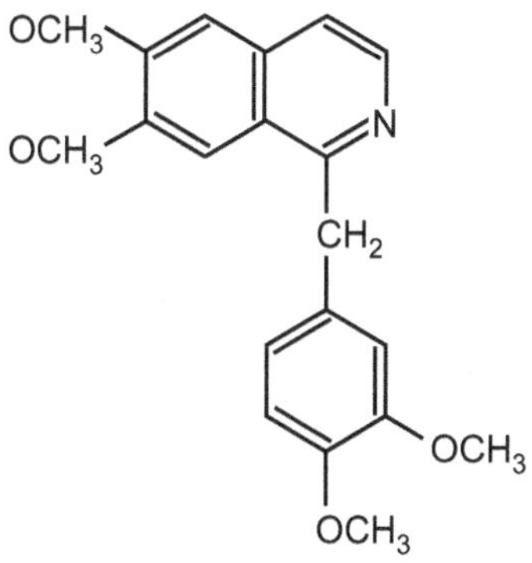   Papaverine 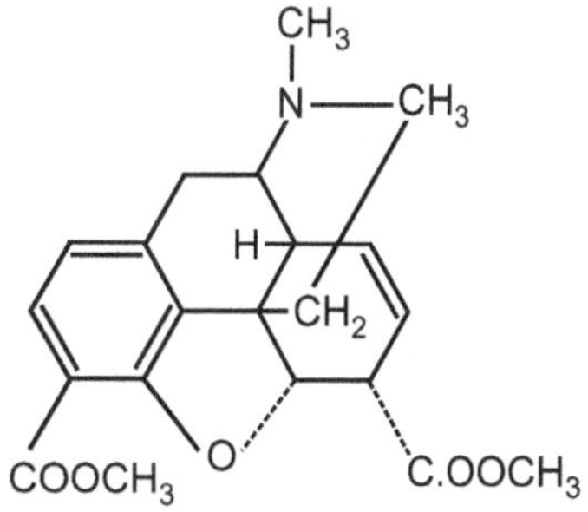   Heroin

Morphine is monoacidic, laevorotatory phenolic alkaloid and also contains an alcoholic hydroxyl group at C (6) position. Due to presence of phenolic hydroxyl group, it is soluble in alkali hydroxides, except ammonium hydroxide. Morphine is very less soluble in different solvents like ether (1 in 600), chloroform (1 in 1200), alcohol (1 in 200) and water (1 in 3000). Diacetyl derivative of morphine is heroin.

Codeine (methyl morphine) is a strong monoacidic base and laevorotatory. It is soluble in water and organic solvents. Codeine and its salts occur as fine needles or as white crystalline powders.

Papaverine is a weak monoacidic base and inactive optically. It is slightly soluble in organic solvents, but insoluble in water. It occurs as white crystals or crystalline powder. It is odourless, but has slightly bitter taste.

The other important benzylisoquinoline alkaloid narcotine is also a weak monoacidic base and is laevorotatory, while its salts are dextrorotatory. Narcotine is soluble in acetone, benzene, chloroform, but insoluble in water, alcohol and ether.

The opium alkaloids are present as salts of meconic acid.

Protopine and hydrocotarnine are the minor alkaloids of opium. Opium also contains sugar, wax, mucilage and salts of calcium, potassium and magnesium. Opium does not contain tannins, starch and calcium oxalate.

Standards

Total ash   :   4 – 8%

Acid insoluble ash   :   0.55 %

Raw opium (BP/EP)   :   It should contain -

Not less than 10% morphine

Not less than 2% codeine

Not less than 3% thebaine

Prepared opium (BP/EP) dried upto 70°C and should contain -

9.8 – 10.2 % morphine

minimum 1% codeine

upto 3% thebaine

Chemical Tests

(1) The general test to detect opium is by testing presence of meconic acid. Opium is dissolved in water and to the filtrate, ferric chloride solution is added by which deep reddish purple colour is obtained, which persists even on addition of hydrochloric acid.

(2) Morphine when sprinkled on nitric acid gives orange red colour. Codeine does not respond to this test.

(3) The treatment of morphine solution with potassium ferricyanide and ferric chloride solutions gives bluish green colour. Codeine does not respond to this test.

(4) Papaverine solution in hydrochloric acid gives a lemon yellow colour with potassium ferricyanide solution.

Meconic acid   **Chelidonic acid**

Uses

Opium belongs to the category of hypnotic sedative and analgesic in which the action is mainly due to morphine. Morphine is a potent analgesic. Due to its central narcotic effects, it causes addiction. Hence, it is given only in severe pains and in those cases, when patient does not show response to other analgesics. Morphine has a biphasic action on central nervous system. It sedates the cerebrum and has a mixture of stimulation and sedation on the medulla. In the medulla, it sedates the respiratory centre, emetic centre and the cough reflex. It also stimulates chemoreceptor trigger zone in the medulla, which leads to nausea and vomitting and is considered as a side effect. Morphine also produces respiratory depression and constipation.

Codeine relieves local irritation in the bronchial tract and as an antitussive used in various cough medicines. It has mild analgesic effects, which are potent than aspirin, but only one tenth activity of that of morphine. Papaverine has relaxant effects on smooth muscles of the intestinal and bronchial tract and the blood vessels. Noscapine has a specific depressant action on cough reflex and is used in the preparation of cough linctuses.

Opium alkaloids are semisynthesized like other medicinal agents. Diacetyl morphine (heroin) has more narcotic, analgesic property than morphine. By losing one molecule of water, morphine gives apomorphine which is emetic and used subcutaneously to treat poisoning cases. Hydromorphone is formed by replacing one of the hydroxyl groups and also removal of adjacent double bond. It is also a potent narcotic analgesic, but habit forming tendencies are less.

The synthetic morphine like compounds are called 'opioids', which are non-habit forming, but possess the medicinal activity of morphine.

Dose

    (1) Morphine Sulphate   : 10 mg, 6 times a day parenterally.

    (2) Codeine sulphate/phosphate : 10 - 20 mg every 4 - 6 hours, orally.

    (3) Narcotine (noscapine)   : 15 mg, 4 times a day, orally.

    (4) Papaverine hydrochloride : 150 mg orally and 30 mg parenterally.

Commercial Varieties of Opium

(1) Indian opium: It is dark brown in colour and found in the form of cubical pieces weighing 900 g. It is brittle and plastic in nature. The powdered form is available as 5 - 10 kg packs. It contains 10 % anhydrous morphine.

(2) Persian opium: It is dark brown in colour and available as brick shaped masses of 450 g. It is hygroscopic, granular or smooth.

(3) Turkish opium: It is commonly called as druggists opium or soft opium. It is brown or dark brown in colour and available as conical rounded or flattened masses.

(4) Chinese opium: It comes in market in the form of flat globular cakes and contains 4 - 11 % morphine.

Different Forms of Opium

(1) Powdered opium :   It contains 10 % anhydrous morphine with lactose, caramel and powdered cocoa husks.

(2) Opium concentratum : It contains different alkaloid hydrochlorides of opium in following proportions:

        Anhydrous morphine - 47.5 - 52.5 %

        Codeine   - 2.5 - 5 %

        Narcotine   - 16 - 22 %

        Papaverine   - 2.5 - 7 %

(3) Camphorated opium tincture: It contains alcoholic solution of opium, benzoic acid, camphor, anise oil and the formulation is prepared in alcohol. It is used in treatment of diarrhoea as antiperistaltic.

Storage

Opium is preserved in a well closed container to prevent loss of morphine.

Adulteration

Since the production of opium is under government control, it is not found to be adulterated. The adulterated forms show presence of opium capsules in powdered form, gum and sugary fruits.

Allied Plants

The various other species of poppy, which do not contain morphine are *Papaver argemone, P. dubium, P. orientate, P. bracteatum, P. strigosum, P. intermedia, P. paeoniflorum,* hybrid of *P. somniferum* and *P. orientate, P. pseudo orientate,* and plants from genera *Argemone* and *Eschscholzia* (both belonging to family Papaveraceae).

Among all these species, *P. bracteatum* has scored more importance, as it does not contain morphine, which causes addiction. The amount of total alkaloids and consequent percentage of thebaine is also very high. Because of such morphine free contents, this species is more significant as a potential new source of opiates.

(E) DRUGS CONTAINING INDOLE ALKALOIDS

Most of the indole alkaloids are biosynthesized in the plants from amino acid tryptophan. It is considered as one of the most important group of alkaloids, as they yield the drugs with very useful therapeutic effects. The indole alkaloids normally contain two nitrogens, out of which one is present as indolic nitrogen and the other one is present in the position created by removal of two carbons from the p-position of the indole ring. The important drugs and their alkaloids of indole group are rauwolfia (reserpine), vinca (vincristine and vinblastine) nux-vomica (strychnine and brucine), ergot (ergotamine and ergonovine), physostigma (physostigmine).

BIOGENESIS OF INDOLE ALKALOIDS

Tryptophan and its decarboxylation product tryptamine give rise to large class of indole alkaloids. These alkaloidal bases contain two nitrogen atoms. Within indole class, there are several alkaloid groups present, so depending upon type of condensation occuring in between tryptamine and an aldehyde or ketoacid, different bases are formed.

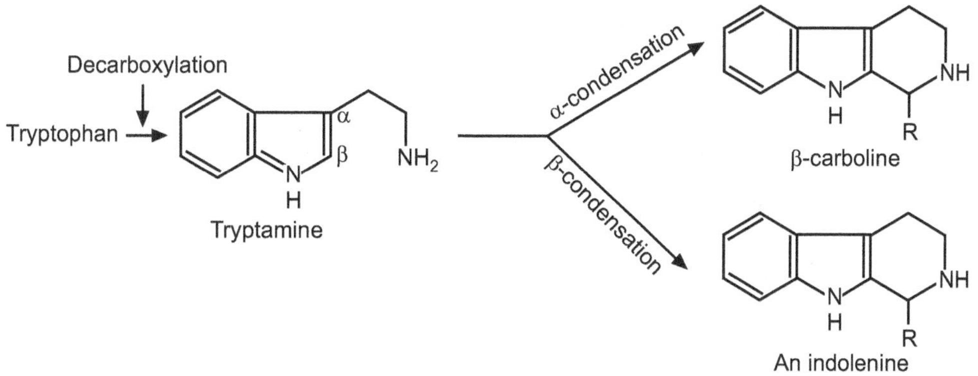

Tryptophan → Tryptamine

β-carboline

An indolenine

A Mannich reaction is involved, the α-carbon atom gives rise to β-carboline moiety while β-carbon atom gives rise to an indolenine moiety.

Different alkaloids of indole class involve tryptamine and mevalonic acid participation. A key intermediate in biosynthesis of monoterpene indole alkaloids is strictosidine. It is formed from enzymatic condensation of tryptamine and secologanin. The enzyme strictosidine synthase is involved in this condensation reaction.

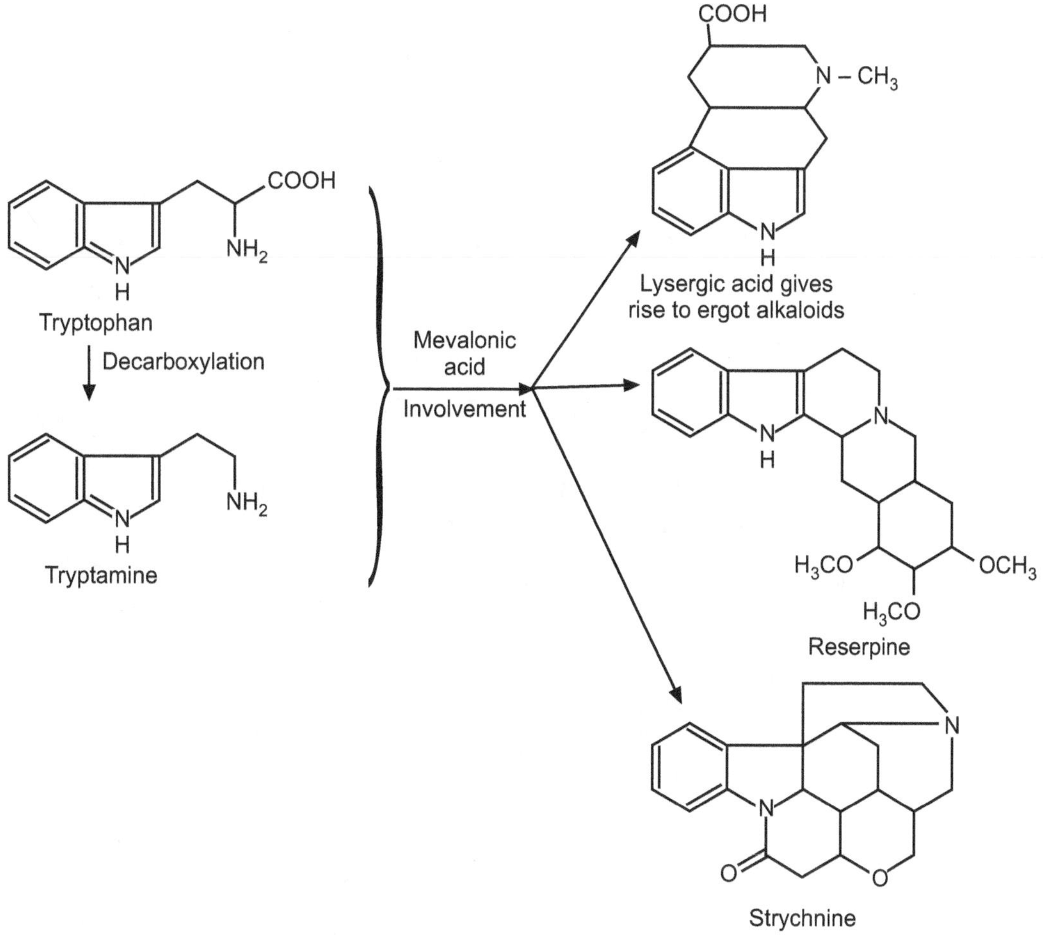

Tryptophan
Decarboxylation
Tryptamine

Mevalonic acid Involvement

Lysergic acid gives rise to ergot alkaloids

Reserpine

Strychnine

BIOGENESIS OF ERGOT ALKALOIDS

The ergoline nucleus is derived from tryptophan and mevalonate.

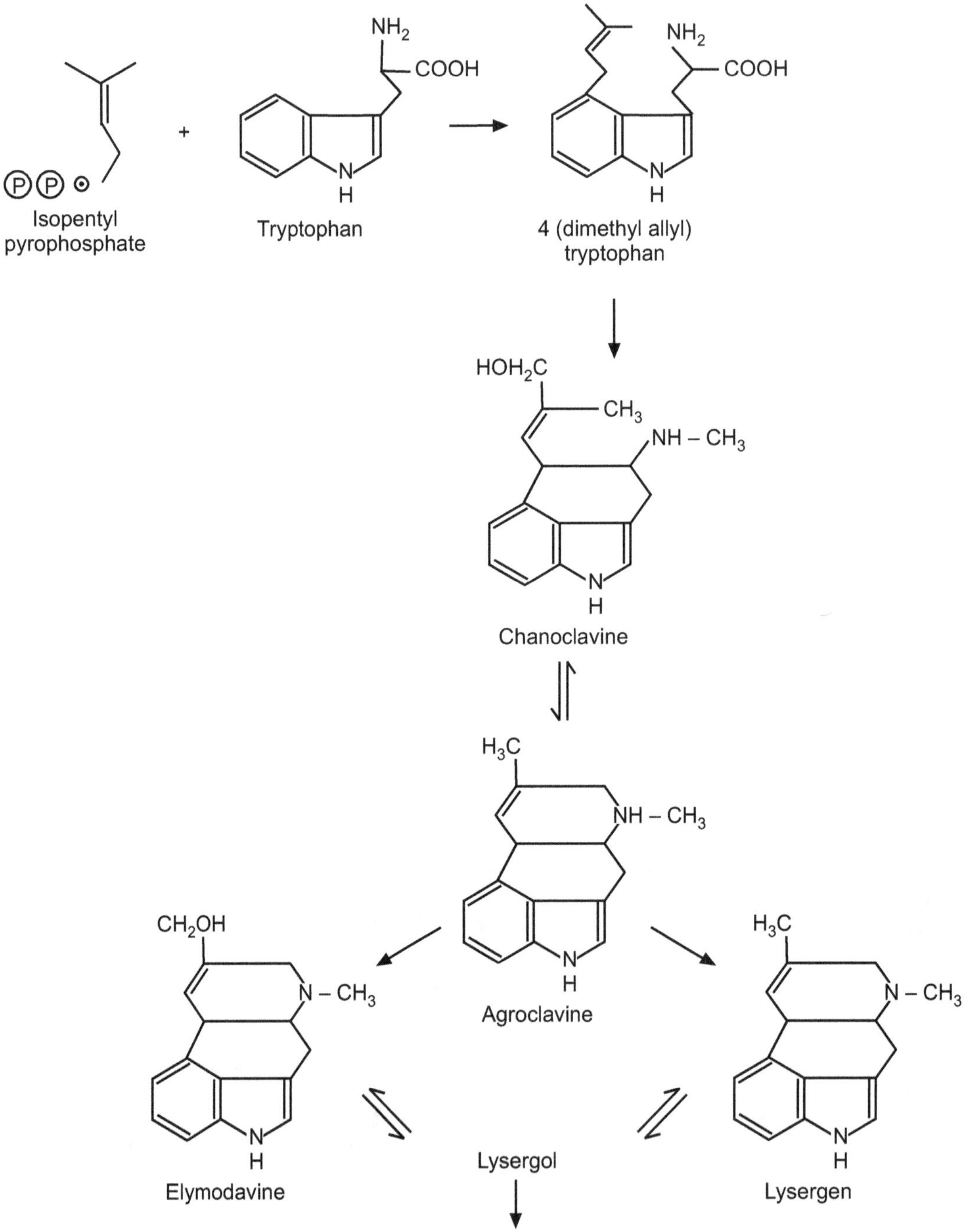
NH2
COOH
+
Isopentyl pyrophosphate
Tryptophan
4 (dimethyl allyl) tryptophan
HOH2C
CH3
NH – CH3
Chanoclavine
H3C
NH – CH3
Agroclavine
CH2OH
N – CH3
Elymodavine
Lysergol
H3C
N – CH3
Lysergen

contd...

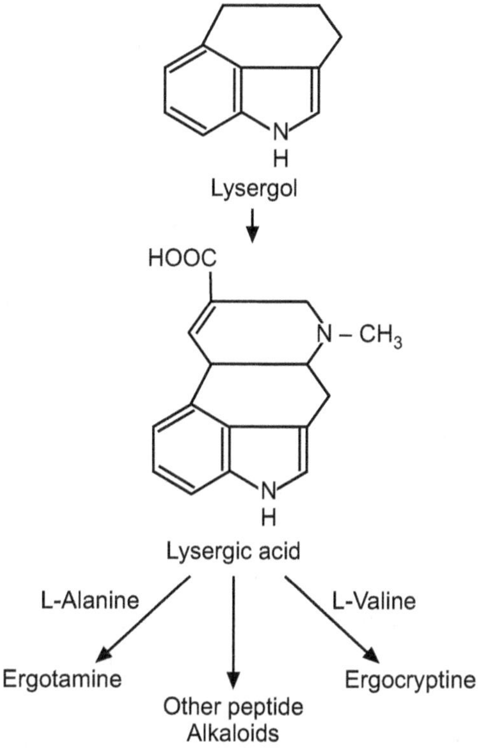

Lysergol

HOOC

$N - CH_3$

Lysergic acid

L-Alanine   L-Valine

Ergotamine   Ergocryptine

Other peptide
Alkaloids

ERGOT

Synonyms

Ergot of Rye, Ergota.

Biological Source

Ergot is the dried sclerotium of a fungus, *Claviceps purpurea* Tulasne (Clavicipitaceae or Hypocraceae) developed in ovary of rye plant, *Secale cereale* Linne (Graminae). It contains not less than 0.19 % of the total alkaloids of ergot, calculated as ergotoxine, of which not less than 15 % consists of water soluble alkaloids of ergot, calculated as ergometrine.

Geographical Source

Switzerland, Yugoslavia, Hungary and Czechoslovakia.

History

The name of this drug is originated from a French word 'Argot,' which means fur and indicates the shape and attachment of the sclerotia to the infected rye spikes, like the fur which is attached to the body of the birds. Even in old days, ergot fungus was known to be a pathogen, infecting the rye fields in European countries and Russia. It is known that the toxic effects both in human and in cattles were observed owing to contamination of ergot with rye grains. Two distinct types of toxic effects were observed. One was characterised by the appearance of gangrene in the extremities. The gangrene was caused by restricted blood flow due to vasoconstrictor action of ergot alkaloid. It was common in some parts of France. The second type which was common in Germany, rised by couvulsions. Before causative agent was known, gangrenous ergotism was referred as "St. Antony's fire". Further, it was discovered that ergot has specific uses in obstetrics and came into wide use from nineteenth century onwards. In 1836, it was introduced in London Pharmacopoeia. The life history of fungus was studied and the name *Claviceps purpurea* was first coined by Tulasne in 1853.

Collection and Preparation of Ergot

Presently, ergot is produced by natural way i.e. cultivation of rye plants and subsequently infecting with this fungus, as well as, by artificial way i.e. saprophytic production.

For the natural way of production, rye plant is host and ergot is a parasite. It is known that more than 600 plants from different families of wild and cultivated grasses act as hosts for ergot fungus as a parasite or pathogen. The various other known species of this fungus are *C. microcephala, C. nigricans* and *C. paspali,* which can produce ergot. Among all the hosts, rye is the better host for the large scale production of ergot by way of quality and quantity.

Among the various stages of development of this fungus, sclerotial stage or a dormant stage contains the maximum amount of drug. For a systematic study, it is necessary to know the other developmental stages of fungus or more precisely the life history of ergot (Fig. 1.13).

Life Cycle of Ergot

Ergot is a parasitic. The ovary of the rye plant at its base, gets infected by ascospores of the fungus in spring or summer season. The spread of ascospores to ovaries is influenced by wind and insects. After infecting, the ascospore germinate in the favourable conditions, like moisture and damp climate. The germination of ascospores leads to formation of hyphal strands which go on invading the wall of ovary. Thus the hyphae form a soft, white mass of tissue over the surface of the ovary which is called as mycelium. Some hyphal strands produce asexual spores called as conidio-spores which remain suspended in sugary, viscous liquid. The liquid is known as Honey-dew, secreted by mycelium. Due to the sugary fluid i.e. honey-dew, the insects and ants are attracted which further help in the spread of the fungus to other host plants. This developmental stage is the sexual stage and called as **Sphacelial stage**.

The hyphae further invade into the deeper parts of ovary and slowly replace the entire tissue of ovary by a compact hard and dark purple tissue called pseudoparenchyma. It is called as **Sclerotium stage** and is considered as resting or dormant stage of the fungus and contains maximum amount of ergot alkaloids. If this sclerotium is left uncollected, it eventually falls on the ground and in the favourable season, i.e. spring gives out 'stromata' which are in the elongated form. Each stromatum has a globular head and a stalk. The head portion contains a large number of perithecia and every perithecium is like a flask shaped structure which contains a number of sacs, each sac containing the ascospores which are thread like in appearance. Ascospores are the sexual spores capable of inducing fresh life cycle of fungus by infecting the ovary of rye plant.

Fig. 1.13 : Life Cycle of Ergot

Selection of a correct strain of fungus (*Claviceps purpurea*), appropriate containers for preparing large scale ergot inoculum and an ideal nutrient medium are important requirements for commercial production of ergot. The various chemical races of fungus can produce only specific ergot alkaloids like ergotamine, ergometrine and ergotoxin in appreciable quantities from their sclerotia. The ascospores of this species with the specific chemical race are germinated on nutritive medium and by this way large bulk of conidiospores are formed. The suspension of this strain of fungus is sprayed on rye plants in large cultivated areas.

Saprophytic Production of Ergot Alkaloid :

Apart from field cultivation, other method which is much practised is saprophytic production of ergot. This process was initiated by Prof. Abe of Takeda Pharmaceutical Industries in Japan. Saprophytic production is convenient in many ways as it eliminates the variation in yield due to weather conditions and production can be achieved throughout the year. For this method, various strains of ergot are used depending on the type of ergot alkaloid to be obtained. *Claviceps paspali* gives clavines and simple lysergic acid derivatives.

It is much easier to manufacture clavines and simple lysergic acid derivatives and then convert them to different peptide alkaloids, i.e. ergot alkaloids. For nutrition of cultures of fungus, specific nutrients are used and fermentation is carried out in temperature range of 20° - 30°C and in a pH range of 4.6 - 6.3. The fermentation process for these submerged cultures in shaking flasks or fermenters takes from 7 - 21 days. The isolation, separation and purification of simple lysergic acid derivatives or synthesized alkaloids is done by usual ways applied for other alkaloids. The lysergic acid derivatives are converted to lysergic acid and further partly synthesized into ergometrine and other peptide alkaloids. Large scale production of lysergic acid derivatives in submerged culture was achieved in 1960 by A. Tanolo and co-workers.

The artificially virulented strain of *C. Palspali* was used to produce simple lysergic acid derivatives. The alkaloids obtained were utilized for semisynthesis of ergonovine and ergotamine.

The saprophytic production is much practised now-a-days, because mycelial dry weight gives even more than 20 % of alkaloids, while natural sclerotia contain less than 1 % of alkaloids. The process of fermentation is properly regulated or controlled for optimum bioproduction of useful metabolites.

Organoleptic Characters (Fig. 1.14)

Colour	:	Externally, it is dark violet to black. Internally, it is whitish or pinkish white.
Odour	:	Disagreeable and faint.
Taste	:	Unpleasant.
Size	:	The sclerotia are 1 - 3 cm in length and 1 - 5 mm in width.
Shape	:	Sclerotia are fusiform, triangular and usually tapering on both the ends.
Fracture	:	It is brittle with short fracture.

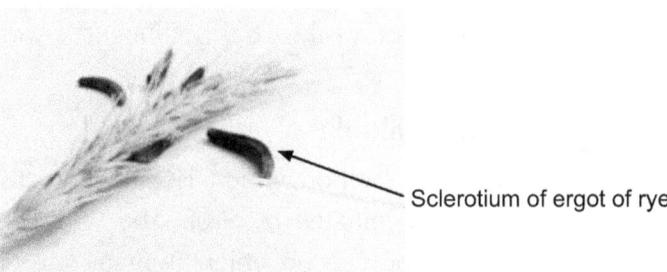

Sclerotium of ergot of rye

Fig. 1.14 : Sclerotia of Ergot

Extra Features

Longitudinal furrows and transverse cracks are present on each surface. Sclerotia are highly susceptible for fungal growth.

Microscopic Characters (Fig. 1.15)

The outermost layer of the sclerotium is made up of few thin, flattened, polygonal cells of purple to dark brown colour, while inner part is made up of dense pseudo parenchymatous cells composed of chitin. The mycelial cells (central region) are round or oval, thick and with high refractive walls. They also contain cells with fixed oil. Sclerotium does not contain starch, calcium oxalate or any of the lignified tissue.

Chemical Constituents

Ergot contains large number of potent indole alkaloids (0.1 - 0.25 %), known as ergolines. It is categorized as clavin type (which are derivatives of 6-8 dimethyl ergoline) and lysergic acid derivatives (peptide alkaloids). The peptide alkaloids are pharmacologically significant. Each active alkaloid occurs with an inactive isomer. The leavo (–) form is active while dextro (+) form is inactive or inert in action. The six pairs of alkaloids are broadly grouped into water soluble and water insoluble categories. The water soluble

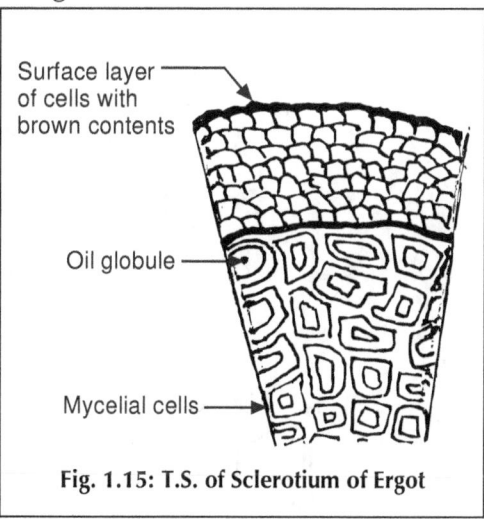

Fig. 1.15: T.S. of Sclerotium of Ergot

alkaloids are present in ergometrine ergonovine group, while the water insoluble group is divided into Ergotamine and ergotoxine group. The ergotamine and ergotoxine group of alkaloids are polypeptide in nature in which lysergic acid and isolysergic acid are linked to other amino acids.

Table 1.5: Ergot alkaloids

(–) Laevorotatory alkaloids	(+) Dextrorotatory alkaloids
Ergometrine	Ergometrinine
Ergotamine	Ergotaminine
Ergosine	Ergosinine
Ergocristine	Ergocristinine
Ergocryptine	Ergocryptinine
Ergocornine	Ergocorninine

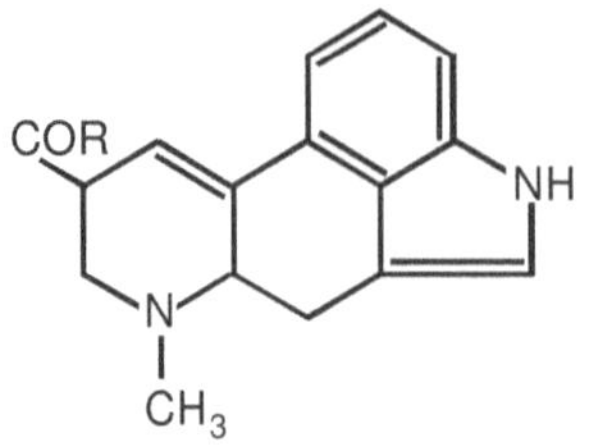

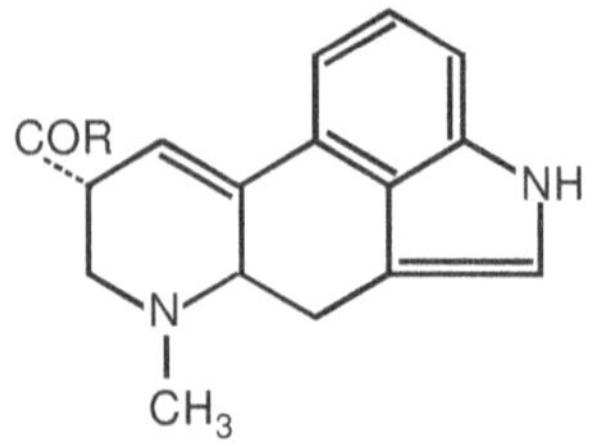

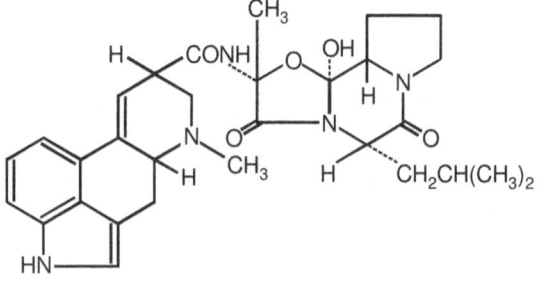

R = – OH	Lysergic acid	Isolysergic acid
R = –NH$_2$	Lysergic acid amide	Isolysergic acid amide
	(Ergine)	**(Erginine)**

R = – NH—C—CH$_3$ (with H above C and CH$_2$OH below C) Ergometrine   Ergometrinine

R = – N (C$_2$H$_5$)$_2$ Lysergic acid diethylamide (LSD)

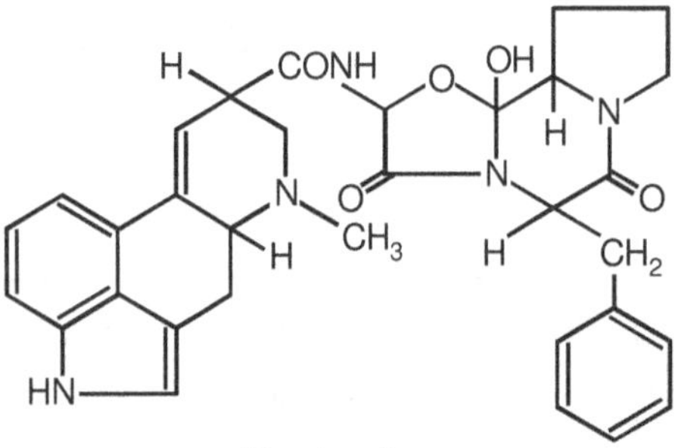

Ergotamine

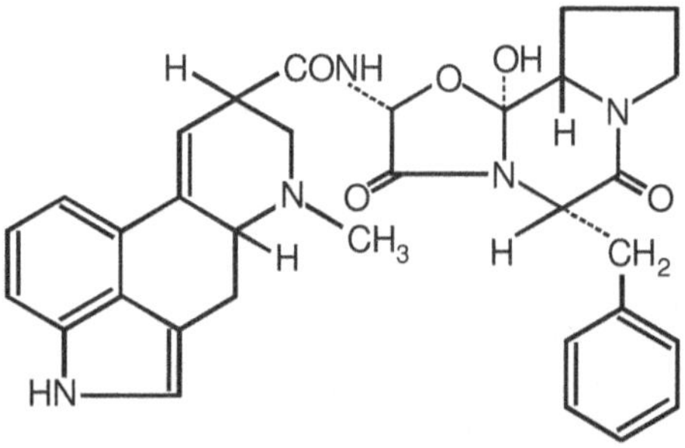

Ergocristine

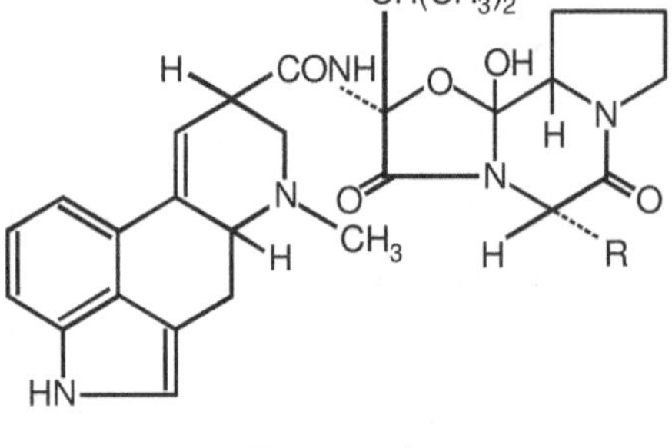

Ergocryptine

Ergosine

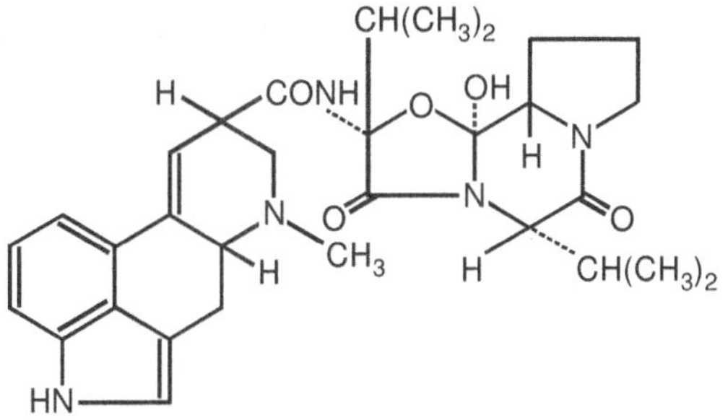

Ergocornine

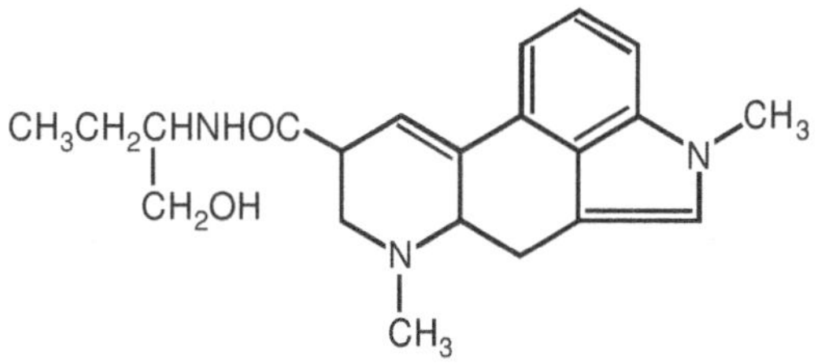

α-Ergocryptine $R = CH_2CH(CH_3)_2$
β-Ergocryptine $R = CH(CH_3)CH_2CH_3$

Methysergide

(Derivative of Lysergic acid used
as migraine prophylactic)

Semi-synthetic derivatives:

1. Methyl ergonovine (discussed in uses of ergot).

2. **Dihydroergotamine mesylate :** It is a semisynthetic salt prepared from hydrogenation of ergotamine. It is also used in migraine, but is more effective and better tolerated by the patients than ergotamine tartarate, the parent drug.

3. **Methysergide maleate :** It is salt of methyl ergonovine. It is serotonin antagonist used in prophylaxis of vascular headache.

Besides the alkaloids, ergot also contains pigments, ergosterol and fungisterol, histamine, tyramine, amino acids, acetyl choline, chitin, upto 30 % fixed oil and 8 % moisture cellulose and lignin is absent.

Chemical Tests

1. Ergot powder gives a blue colour with p-dimethylaminobenzaldehyde (Van-Urk's reagent).

2. Ergot is treated with solvent ether and sulphuric acid and the filtrate obtained shows red violet colour in its aqueous layer, when treated with saturated solution of sodium bicarbonate.

3. Ergometrine gives a blue fluorescence in water.

4. Ergotamine responds to a specific test. Little quantity of ergotamine is dissolved in glacial acetic acid and ethyl acetate. A small portion of this is treated with sulphuric acid and shaken well by which blue colour with red tinge appears. By addition of ferric chloride, blue colour deepens, while red tinge becomes faint.

Uses

Ergot and its alkaloids have many different uses. Now-a-days, ergot is not used as a whole, but the isolated alkaloids are used in therapeutics. Ergot and ergometrine maleate (in the United States, ergometrine is called as ergonovine) are used as oxytocic and sometimes used to enhance the labour pains in delivery cases and also to prevent the post partum haemorrhage.

Methyl ergonovine maleate is a semisynthetic homologue of ergonovine prepared from lysergic acid and amino butanol. It is more active than ergonovine.

Ergotamine tartarate is used as a specific analgesic in treatment of migraine. It is given along with caffeine. Ergotoxine methanesulphonates (mesylates) are used in geriatric patients. Lysergic acid diethylamide (LSD) is a semisynthetic derivative, and possesses psychotomimetic action and used in psychiatry, but owing to its abuse, its use is controlled under Narcotic Drugs and Psychotropic Substances Act, 1985.

Ergonovine and methyl ergonovine have the capacity to directly stimulate contractions of uterine and vascular smooth muscles by interacting with tryptaminergic, dopaminergic and alpha-adrenergic receptors. Small doses produce uterine contractions with increased force and frequency and with normal resting muscle tone. Intermediate doses cause more forceful and prolonged contractions with an elevated resting muscle tone, while large doses cause sustained contractions and tetany. Small doses of these drugs are used after delivery to control bleeding and maintain uterine firmness.

Ergotoxine is a mixture of ergocristine, ergocryptine and ergocrine. Hydrogenated derivatives of this mixture was prepared. The methanesulphonates of this mixture is known as ergoloid mesylate. It is used in elderly patients. It produces vasorelaxation and lower systemic blood pressure.

Dose

1. Ergometrine maleate and methyl ergometrine maleate, oral 200-400 µg, 2-4 times a day, i.m./i.v. → 200 µg every 6-8 hours.

2. Ergotamine tartarate → 1-2 mg sublingual; 250-500 µg intramuscular/subcutaneous.

3. Ergotoxine methanesulphonates → 0.5 mg sublingual, 4 - 6 times a day.

Substitutes

1. **Ergot of wheat :** The sclerotia are shorter and thicker than that of rye. It is medicinally used in France.

2. **Ergot of Oats :** The sclerotia are black in colour, 10-12 mm long and 3-4 mm diameter. It is medicinally used in Algeria.

3. **Ergot of Diss :** It is produced on *Ampelodesma tenax*, sclerotia are upto 9 cm long and spirally twisted.

Prepared Ergot

The powdered and immediately defatted ergot is called as prepared ergot. It is required to contain 0.19 % of total ergot alkaloids, calculated as ergotoxine of which 15 % should be ergometrine. Its dose is 0.15 - 0.5 g by oral route.

Storage

Ergot should be dried thoroughly and kept in entire form in cool place. It should be stored in well closed containers as ergot alkaloids are very sensitive to moisture. The broken sclerotia are very susceptible to the fungal growth and hence broken pieces should not be stored. Ergot alkaloids are sensitive to light and temperature. Hence, the drug is stored at low temperature in cool place away from light. If powdered ergot is required to be stored, it should be defatted first and then stored or, otherwise, decomposition of active constituents takes place.

Quantitative Analysis

(I) Estimation of total alkaloids of ergot

1. Defat ergot powder with ether.
2. Reflux defatted powder with acetone containing 10% ammonia solution for one hour.
3. Filter and concentrate the extract and add 0.2 ml of 20% tartaric acid.
4. Extract this acetone - ether mixture with 1% tartaric acid.
5. Separate acid layer and concentrate at 40°C.
6. Transfer this solution in 50 ml volumetric flask and make up the volume with 1% tartaric acid solution.
7. Take 4 ml of above solution and add 8 ml Van-Urk's reagent.
8. Allow to stand for about 3 - 5 min.
9. Read the absorbance at 550 nm.
10. To prepare calibration curve, carry out procedure using standard ergotoxine sulphate.
11. Estimate total alkaloids from calibration curve.

(II) Colorimetric method (USP 1995)

For estimation of ergometrine standard solution : 40 µg/ml of standard ergometrine in water.

Sample solutions : 40 mg/ml of sample of ergometrine in water.

Procedure : Take 5 ml from stock solution and add 10 ml paradimethyl amino benzaldehyde. Allow to stand for 20 min. and measure absorbance at 555 nm against blank.

BIOSYNTHESIS OF RESERPINE, AJMALINE AND SERPENTINE

Rauwolfia alkaloids reserpine, ajmaline and serpentine are derived from a monoterpenoid precursor known as "Corynanthe". The amino acid tryptophan is decarboxylated to form tryptamine, while non-tryptophan portion is derived from different monoterpenoid moiety. The tryptamine reacts with secologanin to form strictosidine. This strictosidine then reacts with monoterpenoid moiety, to form Rauwolfia alkaloids.

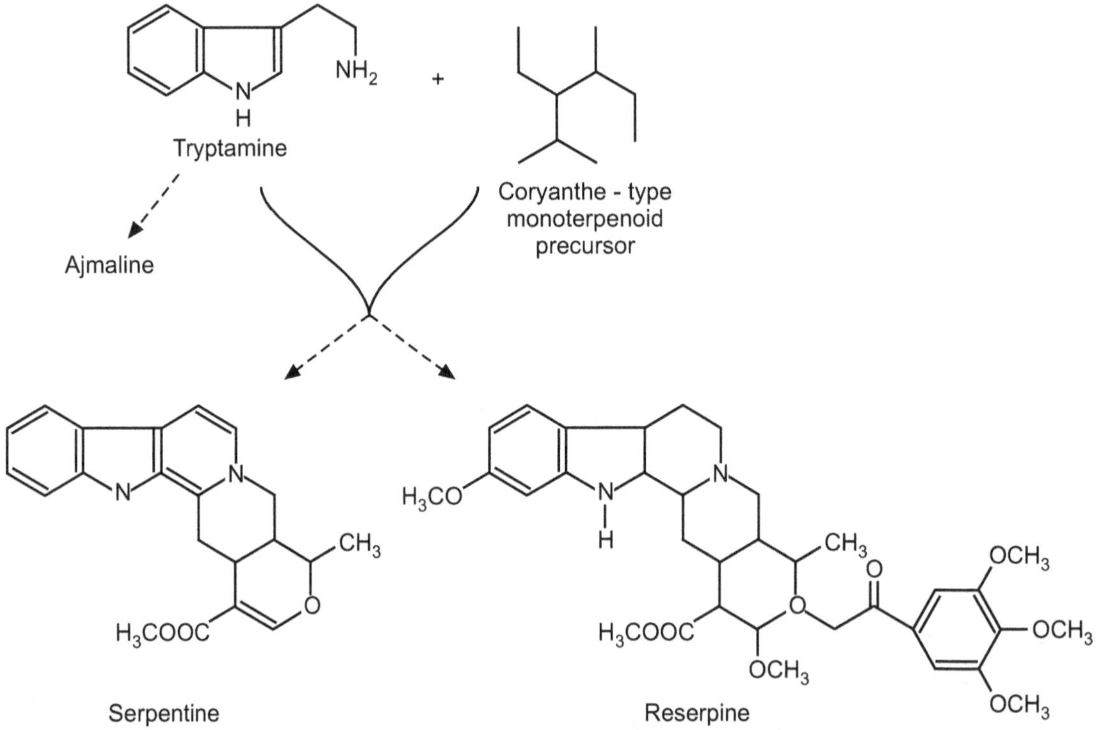

Tryptamine

Coryanthe - type monoterpenoid precursor

Ajmaline

Serpentine

Reserpine

RAUWOLFIA

Synonyms

Rauwolfia root, Serpentina root, Chhotachand, Sarpagandha

Biological Source

Rauwolfia consists of dried roots of the plant known as *Rauwolfia serpentina* Benth, belonging to family Apocynaceae. Sarpagandha contains not less than 0.15 % of reserpine calculated on dried basis.

Geographical Source

Several species of *Rauwolfia* are found distributed in the tropical regions of Asia, America and Africa. Commercially, it is produced in India, Sri Lanka, Myanmar, Thailand

and America. In India, it is cultivated in Uttar Pradesh, Bihar, Orissa, Tamil Nadu, West Bengal, Karnataka, Maharashtra, and Gujarat.

History

This drug is known to Indian System of Medicine since last many centuries. Because of snake like shape of the drug, it has been known as 'Sarpagandha'. It has found its place as an important drug in treatment of insanity and snake bite since traditional times. But the drug came into limelight only after the isolation of reserpine, its most significant alkaloid, in 1952 by Mueller. Since then a large interest has been generated regarding the activity of this drug.

Cultivation and Collection

Under wide range of climatic conditions, rauwolfia grows luxuriantly. However, it flourishes in hot humid condition and grows satisfactorily in shade. In wild state, it grows in variety of soils. But for cultivation, clay loamy soil with large amount of humus and good drainage are supposed to be ideal. The pH of the soil should be acidic and around 4. The temperature range for cultivation is 10° to 38°C. Rainfall should be in the range of 250 - 500 cm. Soils containing large amount of sand make the plants more susceptible to diseases.

In can be propagated by various methods, such as by seeds, roots, cutting, root stumps, etc. The propagation from seeds is usually the method of choice. The healthy seeds are sown into the nursery beds in the month of May or at the break of monsoon. The seedlings are then transplanted in the month of August at a distance of 16 to 30 cm. The plants are provided with various chemical fertilizers like ammonium sulphate, urea and manures like the bone-meal. The plants are kept free from weeds. When the plants are about 3 to 4 years old, they are uprooted. The roots are cut properly, washed so as to remove the earthy matter and dried in air.

Organoleptic Characters (Fig. 1.17)

Colour : Root bark is greyish yellow to brown and wood is pale yellow.

Odour : Odourless

Taste : Bitter

Size : About 10 to 18 cm long and from 1 to 3 cm in diameter.

Shape : Roots are sub-cylindrical, slightly tapering and tortuous.

Fracture is short and irregular. The transversely cut surface is white, dense with finely radiating xylem.

Extra Features

Roots are rough with longitudinal marking and slightly wrinkled surface. Rootlets are usually absent, but few small circular root scars with tetrastichous arrangements are seen.

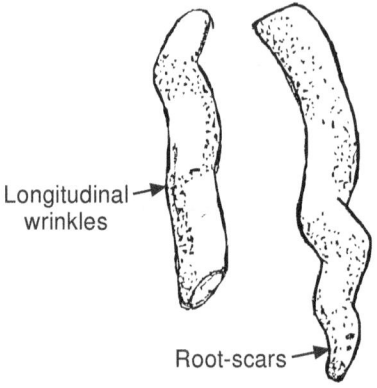

Longitudinal wrinkles

Root-scars

Fig. 1.16: Pieces of Rauwolfia Roots

Microscopic Characters (Fig. 1.18)

Cork
Phelloderm

Phloem
Medullary rays

Primary xylem

Fig. 1.17: *Rauwolfia serpentina* (entire herb)   **Fig. 1.18: T.S. of Rauwolfia Root**

The cork is made up of stratified cells followed by phelloderm of few rows of parenchyma. Phloem is narrow, parenchymatous with small scattered sieve tissue. Parenchyma contains starch grains and few latex cells, with brown resinous matter. Secondary phloem contains calcium oxalate crystals. Xylem is about 4/5th of the diameter of the root and consists of vessels, tracheids, wood parenchyma and wood fibres. Xylem vessels are elongated upto 350 μ in length and 50 μ in width and contain simple or bordered pits. Stone cells and phloem fibres are absent.

Chemical Constituents

About 30 indole alkaloids have been reported in drug and total alkaloidal content of rauwolfia roots ranges from 0.7 - 3 %, depending upon the source. Alkaloids are concentrated mostly in the bark of the roots. The alkaloids of rauwolfia are broadly classified into the following types, (a) indole alkaloids, (b) indoline alkaloids, (c) indolenine alkaloids, (d) oxyindole alkaloids and (e) pseudo indoxyl alkaloids. The important alkaloid of rauwolfia is reserpine. Apart from the alkaloids, it also contains oleo-resin, phytosterol, fatty acids, alcohol and sugars. The other alkaloids present in the drug are ajmaline, ajmalicine, rauwolfinine, rescinnamine, reserpinine, yohimbine, serpentine and serpentinine. The major alkaloids reserpine and rescinnamine are esters derived from methyl reserpate and trimethoxybenzoic acid in reserpine and trimethoxycinnamic acid in case of rescinnamine. Syrosingopine is methyl carbethoxy syringoyl reserpate.

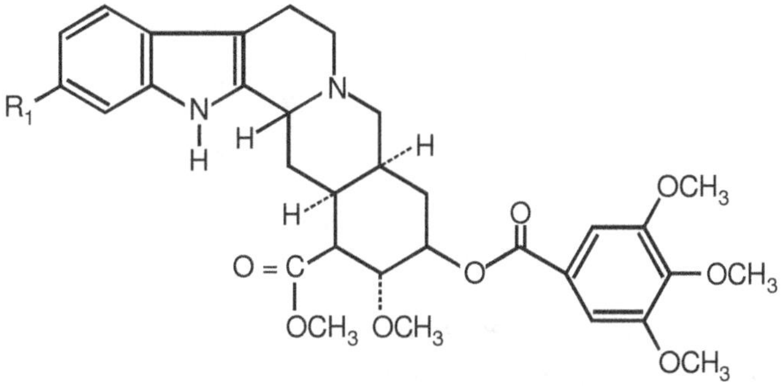

Deserpidine R$_1$ = H

Reserpine R$_1$ = OCH$_3$

Hydrolysis of Reserpine :

Reserpine $\xrightarrow{\text{Hydrolysis}}$ 3,4,5-trimethoxy benzoic acid + Methanol + Reserpic acid

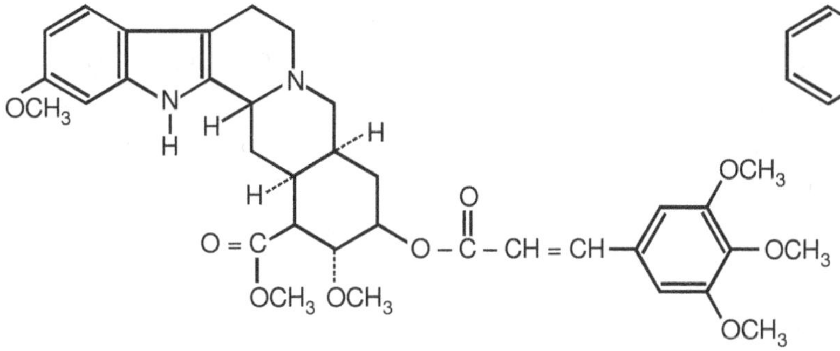

Rescinnamine

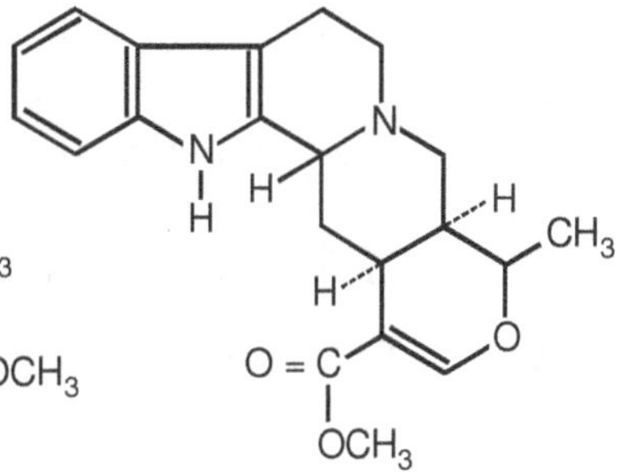

Ajmalicine

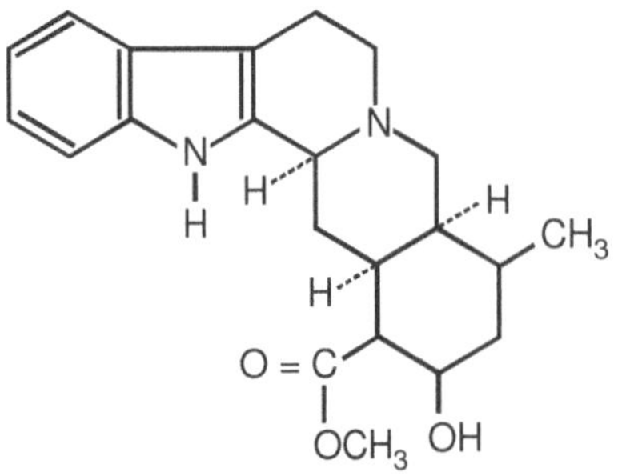

Yohimbine

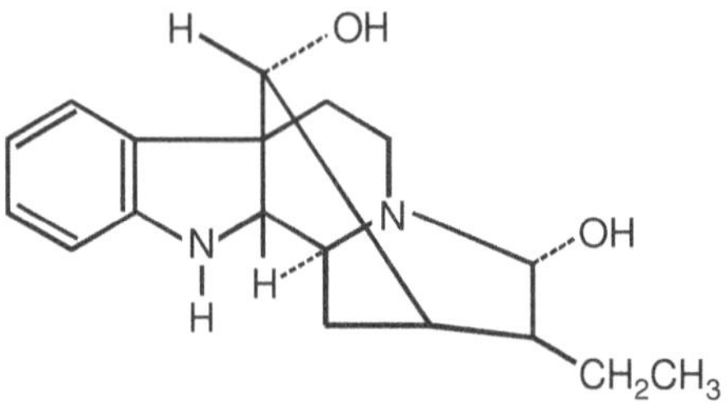

Ajmaline

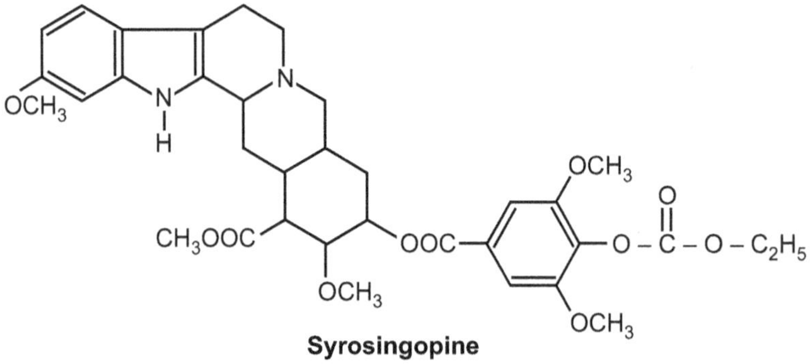

Syrosingopine

Chemical Tests

1. A red coloration along the medullary rays is observed when the freshly fractured surface is treated with concentrated nitric acid.

2. Reserpine shows violet red colour when treated with solution of vanillin in acetic acid.

3. Powdered rauwolfia when treated with sulphuric acid and p-di-methyl amino benzaldehyde, develops violet to red colour.

Uses

Rauwolfia is antihypertensive in activity. Among the various alkaloids of rauwolfia, reserpine, rescinnamine and ajmalicine are clinically important. Reserpine lowers the blood pressure by depleting stores of catecholamines at nerve endings. It prevents re-uptake of nor-epinephrine at storage sites, allowing enzymatic destruction of neuronal transmitter. It is used to treat mild essential hypertension and may be an effective adjunct to the treatment of more severe hypertension.

Because of the tranquillising effects, the drug is used in mild anxiety conditions and reserpine in some of the neuropsychiatric disorders.

Rescinnamine is also used as antihypertensive, but it causes mental depression in higher doses.

Deserpidine is used as antihypertensive and tranquilliser. It shows very less side effects.

Ajmalicine, though less in quantity, has the uses in treatment of circulatory diseases, in relief of obstruction of normal cerebral blood flow.

Syrosingopine shows peripheral effects similar to reserpine. It has less sedative actions and it is used for the treatment of mild or moderate hypertension.

Dose

Rauwolfia	: 100 to 150 mg twice daily (oral)
Reserpine	: Initial dose 250 μg once a day (oral)
	Maintenance dose 100 - 250 μg once a day
Rescinnamine	: Initial dose 500 μg twice a day (oral)
	Maintenance dose 250 μg daily (oral)

Allied Drugs and Substitutes

African Rauwolfia :

It consists of dried roots of *R. vomitoria*. The plant is widely distributed in Africa.

Macroscopy

Size and shape	: Cylindrical or flattened, 0.15 – 1.5 cm diameter and about 30 cm long.
Outer surface	: Longitudinally furrowed
Colour	: Greyish brown
Fracture	: Short and splintery.
Odour and taste	: Odourless and bitter.

Microscopy

Sclerides are arranged in five discontinuous bands (distinction from *R. serpentina* where sclerenchyma is absent). It also shows large vessels upto diameter 180 mm (*R. serpentina* shows vessels upto 57 μm).

Chemical Constituents

It contains reserpine, rescinnamine, serpentine and reserpoxidine. Other alkaloids present in small amounts are ajmaline, alstonine and yohimbine etc. but *R. vomitoria* serves as commercial source for isolation of reserpine.

Other allied drugs are as follows :

The other known species of rauwolfia from Africa are *R. caffra*, *R. cumminsfi*, *R. mombasiana*, *R. oreogiton*, *R. obscura*, *R. rosea* and *R. volkensii*. All of them contain reserpine.

The other rauwolfia species with reserpine content are *R. tetraphylla* and *R. nitida*. *Catharanthus roses* contain ajmalicine.

Pausinystalia yohimba, known as yohimbe bark, contains yohimbine, which is structurally related to reserpine.

The root bark of *Alstonia venenata* and *A. constricta* also contain reserpine. The various species of *Aspidosperma* genus contain indole alkaloids which resemble to those from rauwolfia.

The various other species with which rauwolfia is found to be substituted are *Rauwolfia tetraphylla, R. densiflora* and *R. vomitoria* (African rauwolfia). *R. densiflora* contains sclerenchyma, while *R. tetraphylla* has uniform cork, abundant sclereids and fibres, but devoid of rescinnamine.

Extraction of Reserpine :

1. Extract coarsely powdered drug i.e. Rauwolfia root powder with 90% alcohol in soxhlet apparatus.
2. Concentrate the extract and then evaporate to dryness.
3. Extract the residue with mixture of ether-chloroform-alcohol in proportion of 20 : 8 : 2.5.
4. Filter and add dilute ammonia to the filterate.
5. Wash the precipitate with water and then dissolve in sulphuric acid.
6. Add ammonia to liberate alkaloid.
7. Extract with three volumes of chloroform.
8. Evaporate the chloroform to obtain total rauwolfia alkaloids. Seperate the reserpine by column chromatography.

Chromatographic Profile :

Stationary phase – Silica gel.

Solvent system – 1) Toluene : Ethyl acetate : Diethyl amine (70 : 20 : 10)

       2) n-butanol : Glacial acetic acid : Water (4 : 1 : 1)

Detection

1) Dragendroff's reagent : Orange-brown colour root.
2) UV – 365 nm

Standardization

The BPC 1988 and USP/NF 1995 determine reserpine and rescinnamine by colour reaction between acid solution of alkaloid and sodium nitrite.

BIOGENESIS OF VINCA ALKALOIDS

It involves incorporation of mevalonic acid into vinca alkaloids.

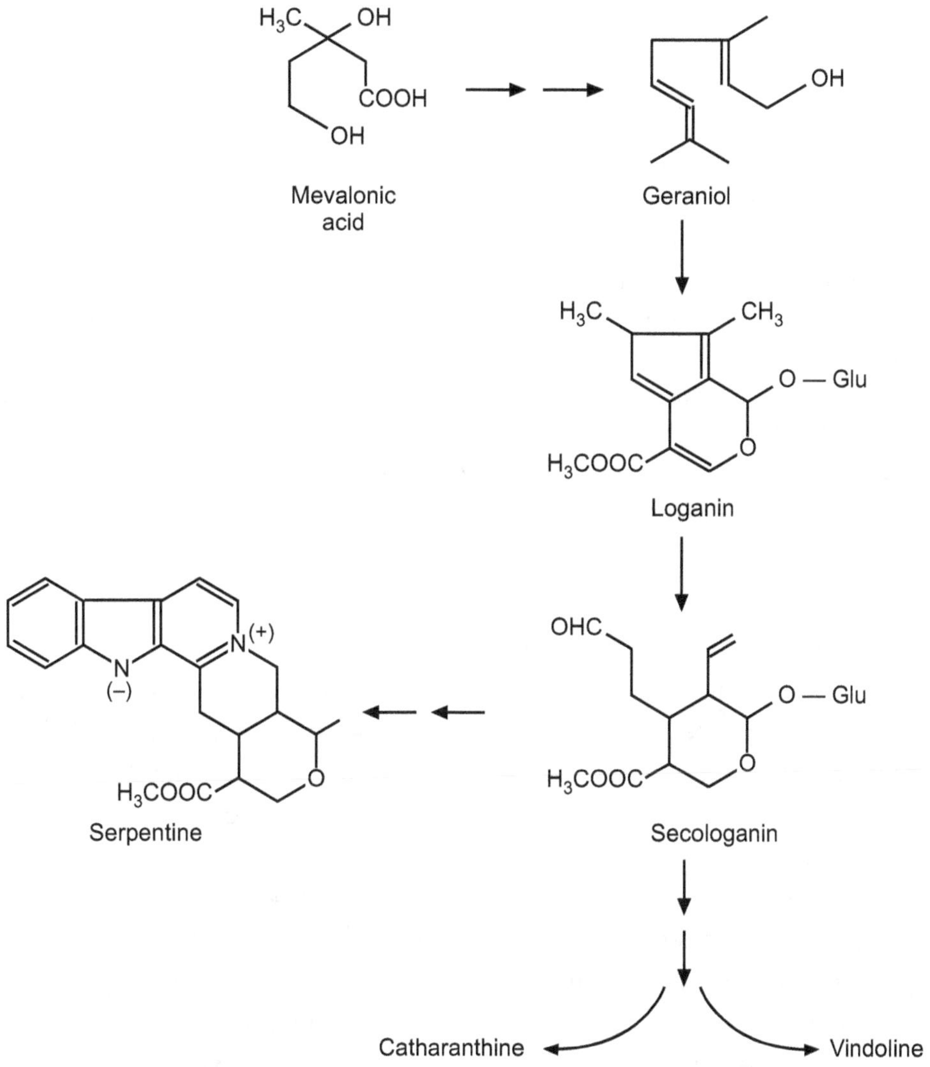

Mevalonic acid

Geraniol

Loganin

Serpentine

Secologanin

Catharanthine   Vindoline

Both are monomeric units of vinca alkaloid that form a dimer of vincristine and vinblastine.

VINCA

Synonyms

Catharanthus, periwinkle.

Biological Source

It is the dried whole plant of *Catharanthus roseus*, belonging to family Apocynaceae. It is also known as *Vinca rosea*.

Geographical Source

It is probably indigenous to Madagascar. It is cultivated in South Africa, India, U.S.A., Europe, Australia and Caribbean islands as an ornamental plant, as well as, for its medicinal properties.

History

Probably the use of vinca has been known since B.C. 50 in European countries as antidysentric, antihaemorrhagic, diuretic and wound healing. This plant was used in the form of 'tea' for treatment of diabetes in Jamaica and in Brazil for toothache. This plant was first scientifically investigated by Canadian workers Noble, Beer and Cutts. During these studies, it was found that it does not have any oral hypoglycemic principle, but contains alkaloid possessing antileukemic principle and the alkaloid was named as vincaleucoblastine. Because of such activity, the plant was thoroughly investigated at M/s Eli Lilly by Svoboda and his colleagues and they reported four dimeric indole alkaloids, viz. vinca-leucoblastine, leurosine, leurosidine and leurocristine. All these compounds exhibited anticancer activities. Some changes were later reported for the names of these compounds such as vincaleucoblastine to vinblastine and leurosine, leurosidine and leurocristine to vinleurosine, vinrosidine and vincristine respectively.

Cultivation, Collection and Preparation for the Market in India

Vinca grows all over India up to 500 metres. It is grown well in tropical and subtropical area in South Indian and North Eastern States of India. It favourably grows in light sandy soils, rich in humus. The rainfall of about 100 cm is most suitable for it. For the propagation, the fresh seeds are used and sown in nurseries or some times direct sowing is also done. They are mixed with 10 times quantity of sand and sown in monsoon in rows of 45 cm apart. In February or March, they are sown in nursery and transplanted in open fields. The plants do not need much water supply and are drought resistant. Though, the plant does not require any special supply of fertilizers, a mixture of nitrogen, phosphorus, potassium manure gives favourable results. Weeding is done periodically. The stems are cut about 7 - 8 cm above the ground level after one year of growth and the leaves, stems and seeds are separated and air dried. For collection of roots, the field is profusely irrigated and roots are dug out by ploughing, which are further washed, dried in shades and packed in bales.

As the plant contains very less percentage of alkaloids, it is not used as a galenical, but for extraction of the alkaloids. The extraction and separation procedure for alkaloids is based on their separation into soluble and insoluble tartarates in other solvents. Due to this vinblastine, vincristine and other weak bases are separated and then fractionated with the help of column chromatography, using alumina as adsorbent.

Cell Culture :

The production of alkaloids by tissue culture technique yields upto 1.5% of total alkaloids. The cultures produced catharanthine and tebersonine and not vindoline, so for production of climetic alkaloid, one precursor is not produced by cell culture. Hence the research is still necessary to find out means for production of such important alkaloid.

Organoleptic Characters (Fig. 1.19)

The leaves are green, roots are pale grey, flowers are violet, pink, white or carmine-red in colour. The odour is characteristic and taste is bitter. Vinca is an erect, pubescent herb, with branched tap-root. Leaves are simple, petiolate, ovate or oblong, unicostate, reticulate, entire, brittle with acute apex and glossy appearance. Flowers are bractate, pedicellate, complete, hermaphrodite, normally 2 - 3 cm in cymose axillary clusters. Fruits are follicles with several black seeds.

Fig. 1.19: **Catharanthus roseus**
with flowers

Microscopic Characters (Fig. 1.20)

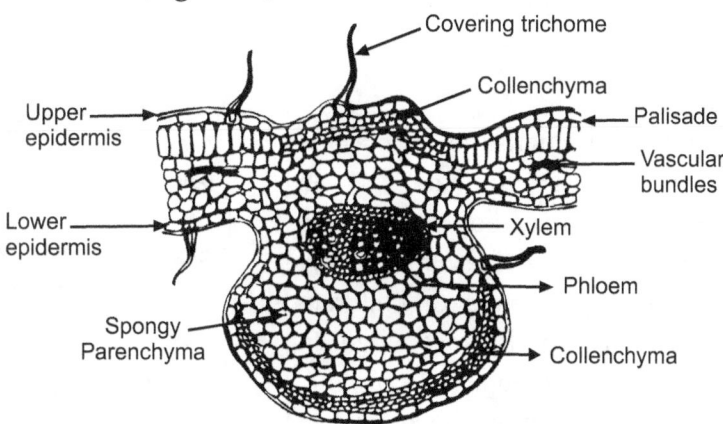

Fig. 1.20 : T.S. of Vinca Leaf

Upper surface shows presence of single layer of rectangular celled epidermis with unicellular covering trichomes. Palisade is made up of single layer beneath upper epidermis and contains compact elongated cells. Spongy parenchyma is 5 - 8 layered with intercellular spaces. Midrib shows presence of collenchyma below the upper epidermis and above the lower epidermis. Xylem and phloem are present in the centre. Cruciferous stomata are present more frequently on lower epidermis. Calcium oxalate crystals are absent.

Chemical Constituents

A large number of indole alkaloids are present in vinca. Out of them, about 20 dimeric indole-dihydroindole alkaloids possess oncolytic activity, and among them, vincristine and vinblastine are most significant. Vinblastine contains indole alkaloid part called catharanthine and dihydroindole alkaloid part called vindoline. The other alkaloids present in vinca are ajmalicine, lochnerine, serpentine and tetrahydroalstonine. It requires about 500 kg crude drug to extract out 1 g of vincristine, because of its extreme low content, viz. 0.0002 %. This makes these alkaloids very costlier and hence, the efforts for their synthesis are under attempts. From their structure, the five-ring dihydroindole system is present in few other natural drugs. Therefore, the attempts towards the synthesis of four-ring indole system are going on presently. Such two systems can be further coupled.

Semisynthetic Derivatives of Vinca Alkaloids :

1) **Vinorelbine :** It is orally active anhydro derivative of 8' nor vinblastine having broader anticancer activity and lower nurotoxicity. It is used in non-small cell lung cancer, breast cancer, testicular cancers and ovarian cancers. It is available in market with trade name Novelbine.

2) **Vindesine :** It is used in acute lymphoid leukemia in children, as it possess less nurotoxic effects. It is also used in lung carcinomas, breast cancer and in colorectal cancer.

Uses

Vinca is used to extract vincristine, vinblastine and ajmalicine. Vincristine sulphate is an antineoplastic agent which may act by arresting mitosis at the metaphase. It is given intravenously in the treatment of acute leukemia of children; some childhood leukemias are also responded. In adults, hodgkin's diseases, reticulum cell sarcoma, lymphosarcoma and myosarcoma have shown short remission.

Vinblastine sulphate is an antineoplastic agent, which may act by arresting mitosis at metaphase or by interfering with amino acid metabolism. It suppresses immune response and is mainly used in the treatment of hodgkin's disease and other lymphomas and choriocarcinoma. Vinca also exhibits hypotensive and antidiabetic actions.

Vinblastine   R = CH_3
Vincristine   R = CHO

Mechanism of Action :

Vinca alkaloids are cell-cycle specific agents. They block mitosis in metaphase (M-phase). They block the ability of tubulin to polymerize to form microtubules. The resulting dysfunctional spindle apparatus, frozen in metaphase, preventing chromosomal segregation and cell prolliferation.

Dose

1. Vincristine sulphate (USP) : 10 to 30 µg/kg of body weight intravenously, but maximum upto 2 mg.

2. Vinblastine sulphate (USP) : 100 µg/kg body weight intravenously.

NUX VOMICA

Synonyms

Crow-fig, Semen strychni, Nux vomica seed.

Biological Source

Nux Vomica consists of dried ripe seeds of *Strychnos nux vomica* Linn, family Loganiaceae. It should contain not less than 1.2 % of total alkaloids calculated as strychnine.

Geographical Source

It is indigenous to East India and is largely collected from forests in Sri Lanka, Northern Australia and India. It is found abundantly in South India i.e. in Tamil Nadu, Kerala and on Malabar Coast. It is also available in the forests of Bihar, Orissa, Konkan, Mysore and Gorakhpur.

History

Because of its poisonous nature, this drug was used in sixteenth century to kill the animals. It is derived from a Greek word *Strychnos*, meaning poisonous and nux vomica indicates a nut with vomiting effects. Strychnine and brucine, the alkaloids present in this drug, are some of the few alkaloids which were first isolated. It was introduced in medical practice from 1640 onwards.

Collection

In India, the entire drug is collected from wild grown plants by the local tribal community. The nux vomica tree is found throughout the tropical area, 1300 m above the sea level. The plants are about 10 - 12 metres in height with a crooked trunk and several branches. The leaves are orange, oppositely arranged, with oval shape, entire margin and acute apex. The flowers are greenish-white and the bark is greyish to yellow. Fruits of the plants are orange yellow, berries of normal size. Each fruit contains about 4 - 5 seeds and heavy bitter pulp. The ripened fruits are collected and seeds are freed of the pulp. They are washed with water thoroughly. Unripened seeds are separated by the floating test in water. The seeds are dried on mat and packed in gunny bags for marketing. The collection of the fruit and seeds is carried out from November to February. In India, about 15,000 tones of seeds are collected annually. Seeds, pure and crude alkaloids of Nux-vomica are regularly exported from India. Exports of the alkaloids for 1988 - 89 and 1989 - 90 were ₹ 407.7 lacs and ₹ 429.5 lacs respectively.

Organoleptic Characters (Fig. 1.21 and 1.22)

(a) Nux vomica plant

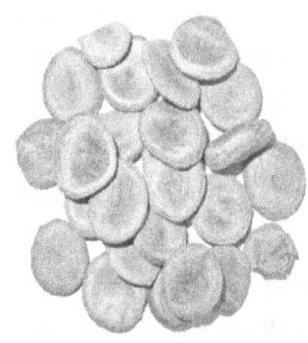
(b) Nux vomica seeds

Fig. 1.21

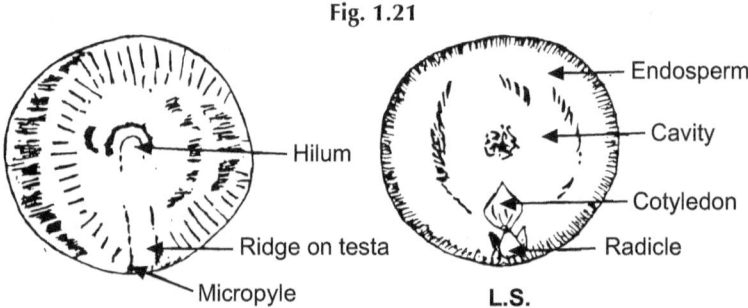

Fig. 1.22: Internal structure of Nux vomica Seed

Colour   : Greenish-brown

Odour   : None

Taste   : Intensely bitter

Size   : Seeds are 10 to 30 mm in diameter and 4 to 6 mm in thickness.

Shape   : The seeds are disc shaped, somewhat flat or irregularly bent and concavo-convex. Margin of the seeds is rounded.

Extra Features

Surface of the seeds is silky due to the radially arranged, densely covered, closely appressed unicellular lignified covering trichomes.

Microscopic Characters (Fig. 1.23 and 1.24)

The epidermis consists of strongly thickened, pitted and lignified trichomes. Epidermis is followed by a layer of collapsed cells. Endosperm is characterised by thick walled polyhedral unlignified cells with plasmodesma, aleurone grains and oil globules. Calcium oxalate crystals and starch grains are absent in drug.

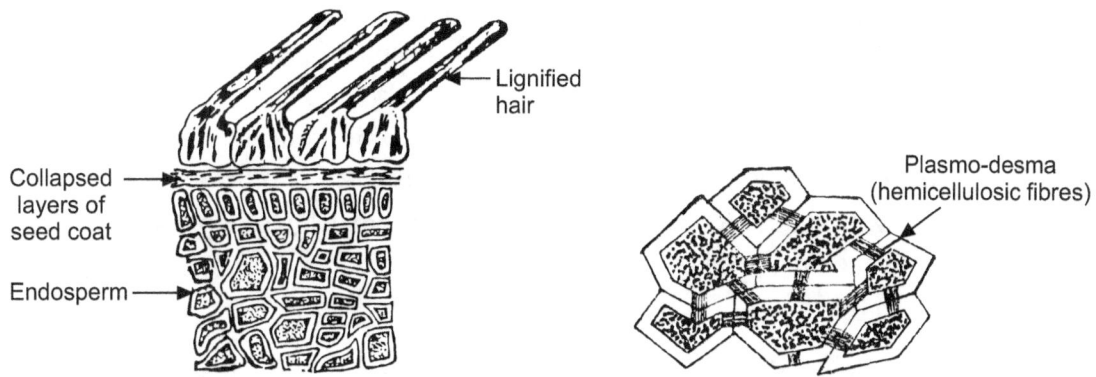

Fig. 1.23: T.S. of Nux vomica Seed   Fig. 1.24: Endospermic cells of
Nux vomica Seed

Chemical Constituents

Nux vomica seeds contain 1.5 - 5 % of bitter indole alkaloids. Chief constituents of nux vomica are strychnine and brucine, while vomicine, α-colubrine, pseudostrychnine and strychnicine are also present. Apart from seeds, other parts of the plant contain alkaloids. Seeds also contain 3.0 % of fat. Bark contains brucine and traces of strychnine. Wood and root of the plant also contain strychnine.

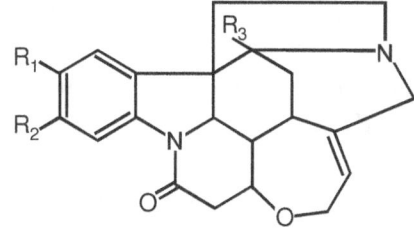

Strychnine	$R_1 = R_2 = R_3 = H$
Brucine	$R_1 = R_2 = OCH_3, R_3 = H$
α - colubrine	$R_1 = H, R_2 = OCH_3, R_3 = H$
β - colubrine	$R_1 = OCH_3, R_2 = R_3 = H$

The other minor, but, chemically related alkaloids are isostrychnine, N-oxystrychnine, protostrychnine, β-colubrine, and novacine.

Nux vomica also contains a glycoside viz. loganin, chlorogenic acid and fixed oil.

The alkaloids can be isolated with the use of dilute sulphuric acid and lime. Strychnine sulphate is meagerly soluble in water and alcohol.

Chemical Tests

The thin sections of nux vomica seed are defatted and the following tests are performed.

1. Stain the transverse section of nux vomica with ammonium vanadate and sulphuric acid Manddin's reagent. The endospermic cells become purple due to the presence of strychnine.

2. Stain the transverse section of nux vomica with concentrated nitric acid. Endospermic cells take yellow colour due to the presence of brucine.

3. Strychnine with sulphuric acid and potassium dichromate gives violet colour which turns to red and finally yellow.

Uses

Due to its bitter taste, nux vomica is used as bitter stomachic and tonic. It is a stimulant to central nervous system. It increases the blood pressure and is recommended in certain forms of cardiac failure. It stimulates respiratory and cardiovascular systems. Brucine possesses very less physiological actions and is about one-sixth in potency as compared to strychnine. But as far as the bitterness is concerned, it is four times bitter than strychnine. Brucine is used for denaturing alcohol and inedible fats, as a standard for bitterness and as a dog poison.

During 1993-94 and 1994-95, India has exported nux vomica alkaloids of Rs. 443.5 lakhs and Rs. 230.8 lakhs.

Adulterants

1. Dried seeds of *Strychnos nuxblanda* Hill, are used as adulterant to nux vomica seeds. These are similar in size, pale in colour with a distinct ridge on the edge of the seeds. Nuxblanda seeds are regular in shape and contain traces of alkaloids.

2. Dried seeds of *Strychnos potatorum* are another adulterant to authentic drug. The seeds are also known as clearing nuts. They are smaller and thicker with yellowish buff colour. Seeds contain diaboline and traces of strychnine and brucine.

Allied Drugs

1. The seeds of *Strychnos wallichiana* are used as substitute to nux vomica, as their alkaloidal content and composition are comparable to the genuine drug.

2. The dried seed of *Strychnos ignatii* is another allied drug. Seeds are about 2.5 cm in diameter, ovoid in shape, dark green in colour with unlignified detached trichomes. It contains 2.5 % to 3 % alkaloids of which 60 % is strychnine. The seeds are used for the manufacture of strychnine.

(F) DRUGS CONTAINING IMIDAZOLE ALKALOIDS

PILOCARPUS

Synonym

Jaborandi.

Biological Source

The drug consists of the leaves of closely related plants of the genus *Pilocarpus*, belonging to family Rutaceae. The genus includes various species known by different names like *Pilocarpus jaborandi* (Pernambuco jaborandi), *P. pennatifolius* (Paraguay jaborandi), *P.microphyllus* (Maranham jaborandi), *P. trachylophus* (Ceara jaborandi), *P. selloanus* (Rio jaborandi), *P. spicatus* (Aracati jaborandi), *P. heterophyllus* (Barqui simento jaborandi) and *P. racemosus* (Guadeloupe).

Now-a-days, *P. microphyllus* i.e. Maranham jaborandi is the main source of this drug.

Geographical Source

It is indigenous to South America and especially grown in Brazil. It is found in Venezuela, Caribbean islands and Central America.

History

Dr. Coutinho in 1874 sent the plant to Europe from Pernambuco, hence the name Pernambuco jaborandi or Pilocarpus jaborandi. Later, Byasson in 1875 showed its alkaloidal nature and further Gerrard and Hardy isolated the main alkaloid pilocarpine.

Organoleptic Characters

The characters of main commercial variety, Maranham jaborandi are discussed here.

Jaborandi leaves are greyish green to greenish, brown in colour and have a slight aromatic odour along with bitter taste of alkaloids. When tested, the leaf causes increase in salivary secretion. It is an, imparipinnate compound leaf with 7 leaflets. The leaflets are asymmetrical, obovate and sessile in shape and 2 - 6 cm long and 1 - 3 cm wide in size. The terminal leaflet is symmetrical and oval in shape. The leaflets are present on the winged and glabrous rachis. The leaflet shows pinnate venation. They contain numerous oil cells.

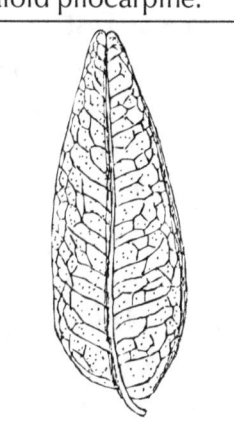

Fig. 1.25: Pilocarpus jaborandi leaf

Chemical Constituents

The leaflets contain imidazole alkaloids among which pilocarpine is most important. Other alkaloids are isopilocarpine, pilocarpidine, pilosine, pseudopilocarpine, and isopilosine.

The range of total alkaloids in different species is between 0.5 to 1 %.

The oil cells observed in the leaf give volatile oil containing different monoterpenes like limonene, α - pinene, sabinene and sesquiterpenes.

Pilocarpine

Isopilocarpine

Pilocarpidine, $R_1 = C_6H_5$, $R_2 = H$
Pilosine, $R_1 = C_6H_5CHOH$,
$R_2 = CH_3$

Jaborandi Alkaloids

The main alkaloid pilocarpine occurs as viscous oil or hygroscopic crystalline solid without any colour and odour. It is soluble in water and organic solvents, but insoluble in petroleum ether. It is the lactonic derivative of pilocarpic acid. The hydrolysis of pilocarpine results into pilocarpic acid, with loss of optical activity. Treatment with alkali produces isopilocarpic acid which is the stable stereoisomer. The alkaloids are totally deteriorated on long storage.

Chemical Test

To the pilocarpine solution, small quantity each of dilute sulphuric acid, hydrogen peroxide solution, benzene and potassium chromate solution is added. On shaking, organic layer gives bluish-violet colour and yellow colour appears in aqueous layer.

Uses

The drug is mainly used in the form of pilocarpine hydrochloride. It is a physiological antagonist of atropine. It acts directly on the autonomic effector cells of those structures innervated by post-ganglionic cholinergic nerves. Hence, it causes contraction of the pupil of the eye, and increase in sweating and salivation.

It is used in ophthalmology for the treatment of glaucoma.

Dose

Its recommended dosage is 0.05 - 0.1 ml of 10 per cent solution, topically.

(G) DRUGS CONTAINING STEROIDAL ALKALOIDS

Some of the important drugs covered under this class are *Solanum* species; kurchi bark, and veratrum. The active chemical principles of such drugs contain mainly steroidal (cyclopenteno phenanthrene) entity, along with basic nitrogen. Either they are used as medicines, as in case of kurchi and veratrum, or as a precursor for synthesis of various other steroids as in *Solanum* species. They belong either to C_{27} or C_{21} group of steroids.

VERATRUM

Two important species of genus *Veratrum* are *Veratrum viride* and *Veratrum album*. Both contain protoveratrine as active principle.

Veratrum contains two groups of alkaloids called jeveratrum and ceveratrum alkaloids. The alkamine part of both these groups is polyhydroxylated $C_{27}N$ fused polycyclic. The alkamines of jeveratrum group contain only 2 or 3 oxygen atoms while in ceveratrum, they have 7 - 9 oxygen atoms. The members containing ceveratrum alkaloids are only therapeutically active, and their examples are cevadine, germerine, veratridine, protoveratrine A and protoveratrine B.

Ceveratrum nucleus

(a) VERATRUM VIRIDE

Synonyms

American or Green hellebore.

Biological Source

It consists of dried rhizome and roots of *Veratrum viride* Aiton, belonging to family Liliaceae.

Geographical Source

The drug is obtained from wild growing plants in many parts of United States like states of New York, North Carolina, Georgia, Tennessee, etc. It is also found in some parts of Canada.

Organoleptic Characters

Colour   :   Brown

Odour   :   Unpleasant

Taste   :   Acrid

Size   :   Rhizomes are 5 - 8 cm in length and 2 - 3.5 cm in diameter

Shape   :   Subcylindrical with numerous stout yellowish brown roots.

It is a perennial about 1 - 2 m in height, large leaves, which are oval and strongly ribbed, star shaped, many flowers in panicle.

Uses

The medicinal action is due to its many alkaloidal constituents. It lowers blood pressure and decreases heart rate. It used as a liquid extract or tincture in pregnancy associated hypertension.

(b) VERATRUM ALBUM

Synonym

White hellebore, European hellebore

Biological Source

It is the dried rhizome of *Veratrum album* Linne, belonging to family Liliaceae.

Geographical Source

It is native to central and southern Europe, China and Japan.

Habitat

It is a decidous hardy perennial herb, flowers in June - July bears white flowers. Stem is hairy and 50 - 125 cm.

Organoleptic Characters

Colour :   Brown

Odour :   Unpleasant characteristic when fresh, dried with no odour

Taste :   Burning, acrid and bitterish

Size   :   5 - 15 cm in length and 2 - 3 cm in diameter

Shape :   Tuberous, fleshy with number of long white fibres at the end of the roots.

Fig. 1.26: *Veratrum album* plant

Chemical Constituents

It contains mainly alkaloids veratrine and also germidine, germitrine, protoveratrine, cevadine, veratrine, pseudojervijne, veratrosine, etc.

Both Protoveratrine A and B are soluble in chloroform, but insoluble in water and light petroleum.

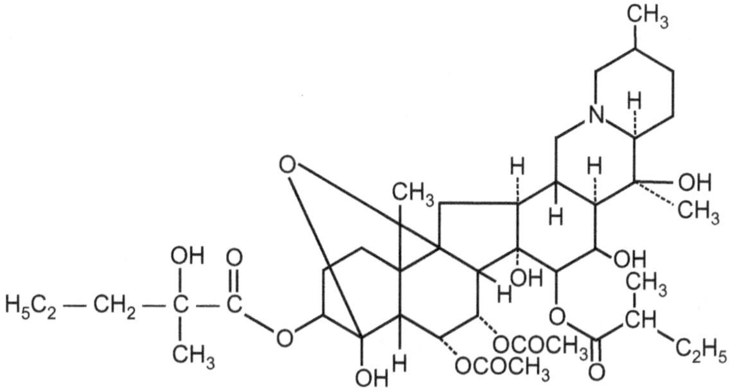

Protoveratrine A

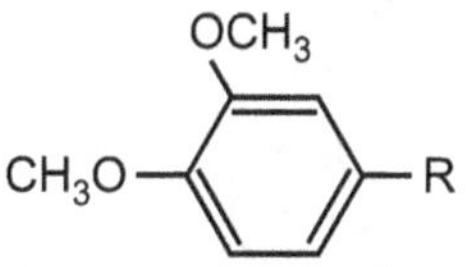

Veratridine 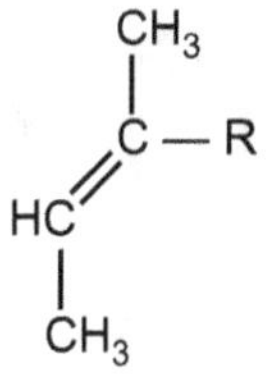   **Cevadine**

Uses

Veratrum album is mainly used as a source of protoveratrine A and B. Among these, protoveratrine A is medicinally more potent. They are used for the management of hypertension in pregnancy, especially in preclampsia and exclampsia conditions.

KURCHI

Synonym

Holarrhena.

Biological Source

It is the dried stem bark of *Holarrhena antidysenterica* (wall) belonging to family Apocynaceae. It is collected from 8 - 10 years old plant and freed from attached wood, and peeled into small pieces. It should contain not less than 2 % of total alkaloids of kurchi.

Geographical Source

Kurchi is indigenous to India and found throughout India in parts ascending upto 1000 metres in Himalayan region. It is also found in Orissa, Assam, Uttar Pradesh and Maharashtra.

Cultivation and Collection

The drug is obtained from wild source only. For the collection of bark, the plants which are 8 - 10 years old, are selected. Longitudinal and transverse incisions are made on the trunk from July to September. After detachment, the bark is separated from the wood and dried. The recurved pieces of the bark are marketed.

Organoleptic Characters

Kurchi bark appears buff to pale brown on outer surface, while slightly brownish on inner surface. The outer surface is longitudinally wrinkled and bears horizontal lenticels. The pieces are recurved with varying size and thickness. The drug shows a short and granular fracture. It has no odour, but bitter and acrid taste.

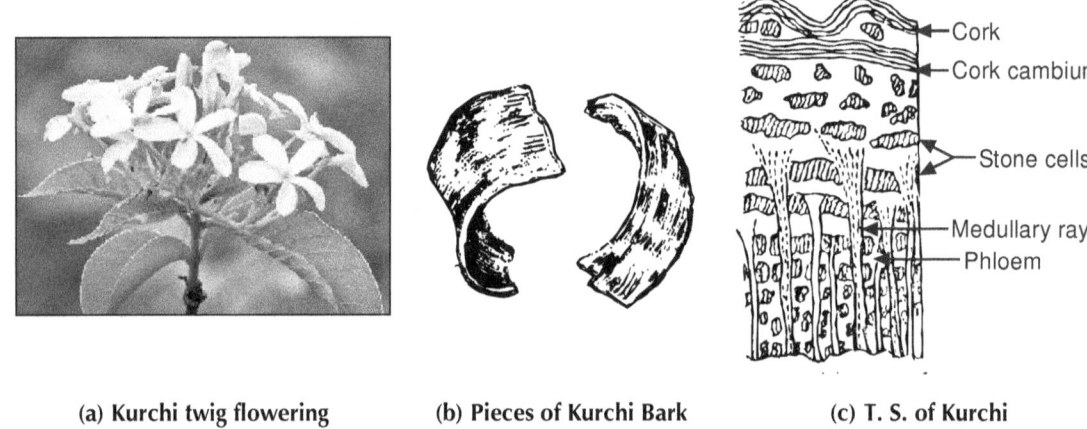

| (a) Kurchi twig flowering | (b) Pieces of Kurchi Bark | (c) T. S. of Kurchi |

Fig. 1.27: Kurchi herb and bark

Microscopic Characters [Fig. 1.27(c)]

In the periderm portion, cork has both tangentially and radially elongated cells. Cork cambium has several layers. Stone cells are present in cortex, either singly or in groups or in horizontal layers. It does not show phloem fibres. Phloem contains sieve tubes, companion cells, phloem parenchyma and stone cells. Medullary rays are multiseriate. In many stone cells, prismatic calcium oxalate crystals are present.

Chemical Nature

Kurchi contains about 25 total alkaloids (1.5 to 3 %). They are C_{21} group steroidal alkaloids. The active alkaloids are conessine (kurchicine), norconessine, isoconessine, dioxyconessine, conessimine, holarrhimine and holarrhidine.

Conessine is also present in root bark alongwith some other steroidal alkaloids.

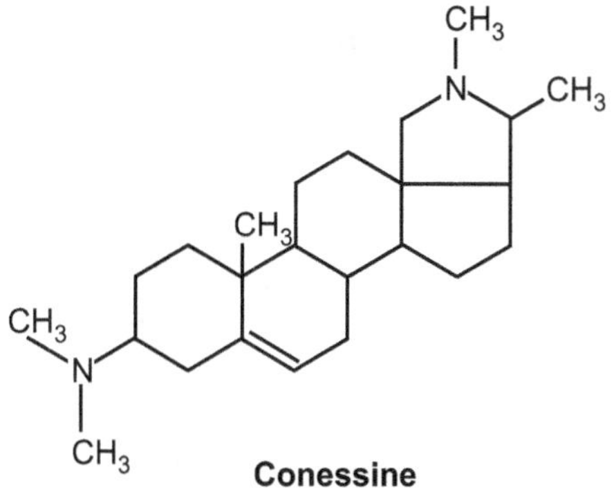

Conessine

Standards

   (1) Acid insoluble ash   - not more than 1 %

   (2) Alcohol (60 %) soluble - 4 - 6 %

   (3) Foreign organic matter - not more than 5 %

Uses

Kurchi is antiprotozoal in activity and used to treat amoebic dysentry. Conessine is highly active against Entamoeba histolytica. A traditional preparation of kurchi bark, viz. "kutajarishta" is commonly used, especially for chronic amoebiasis.

(H) DRUGS CONTAINING ALKALOIDAL AMINES

EPHEDRA

Synonym

Ma-Huang.

Biological Source

It consists of the dried young stems of *Ephedra gerardiana* (wall.) Stapf, and *E. nebrodensis* (Tineo.) Stapf, belonging to family Gnetaceae (Ephedraceae). Ephedra should contain not less than 1 % of total alkaloids, calculated as ephedrine.

Geographical Source

The main source of ephedra is from China, Pakistan, North-West parts of India, Australia, Kenya, Spain and Yugoslavia.

History

The drug originally belongs to Chinese System of Medicine. It has been used in China since last 5000 years. In Chinese language, it is called as Ma-Huang where 'Ma' denotes astringent taste and 'Huang' is for yellow colour of drug. The references about this drug are found in the herbal of the emperor Shen Nung (2700 B.C.) and in 'Chinese medicinal plants' (1596 A.D.) by Pen T'sao Kang Mu. In those times, it was used for treatment of respiratory problems, fever and also for improving circulation. The drug was for the first time explored chemically by Yamanishi in Japan and he isolated ephedrine in crude form in 1885, which was further obtained in pure form by Nagai and Hari. Merck of Darmstadt, a German firm, carried out detailed search on *Ephedra helvetica* and isolated ephedrine in 1888. K. K. Chen and C. F. Schmidt are mainly credited for introduction of ephedra and ephedrine in modern therapeutics.

Cultivation, Collection and Preparation

Ephedra can be cultivated at an altitude of 2500 to 3000 m. Annual rainfall should not exceed 50 cm. It can be propagated by seeds or by layers or divisions of the root stock. Seeds are sown early in the spring at a distance of 5 cm, keeping the distance of one meter between 2 rows. The plants are collected after attaining the age of 4 years for the extraction of alkaloid. During this period, proper irrigation and weeding are necessary. The alkaloidal content of the drug varies from season to season. It is found to be maximum in autumn; when plants and twigs are dark in colour. Twigs are generally dried in sun or even by artificial ways. After drying, they are stored in dry and well closed containers, away from light.

Organoleptic Characters (Fig. 1.28)

Ephedra is a gymnospermous plant bearing thin stems which are woody, cylindrical and grey to greenish in colour (about 5 mm in diameter).

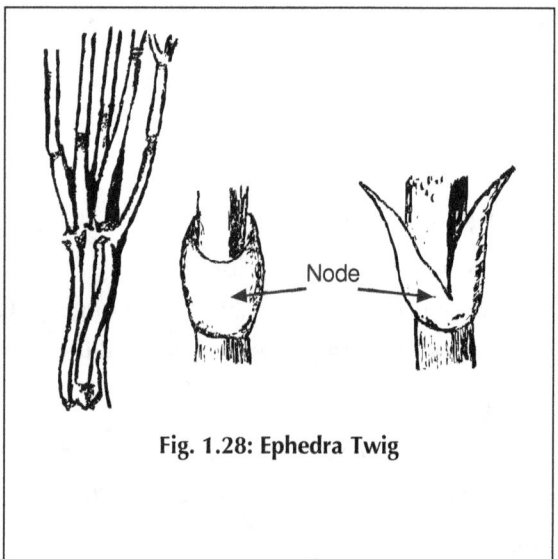

Fig. 1.28: Ephedra Twig

It shows the internodes at a distance of about 3 to 3.5 cm. Ephedra bears the scaly leaves from the nodes in a whorl of 2. The bases of the leaves are dark brown and they are joined on all sides of the node-forming a sheath. It bears a terminal bud, which is short and usually constricted at base. The male spikes are solitary, ovate, sessile and crowded.

Microscopic Characters (Fig. 1.29)

The T.S. of ephedra shows the following characteristics.

(i)   Unicellular epidermis made up of quadrangular cells along with thick-walled cuticle.

(ii) Vertical rows of sunken stomata and papillae on the ridges.

(iii)   Chlorenchymatous cortex.

(iv)   Non-lignified, hypodermal fibres.

(v)   Lignified pericyclic fibres.

(vi)   Crystals of calcium oxalate in the cortex.

(vii)   Parenchymatous dark brown coloured pith.

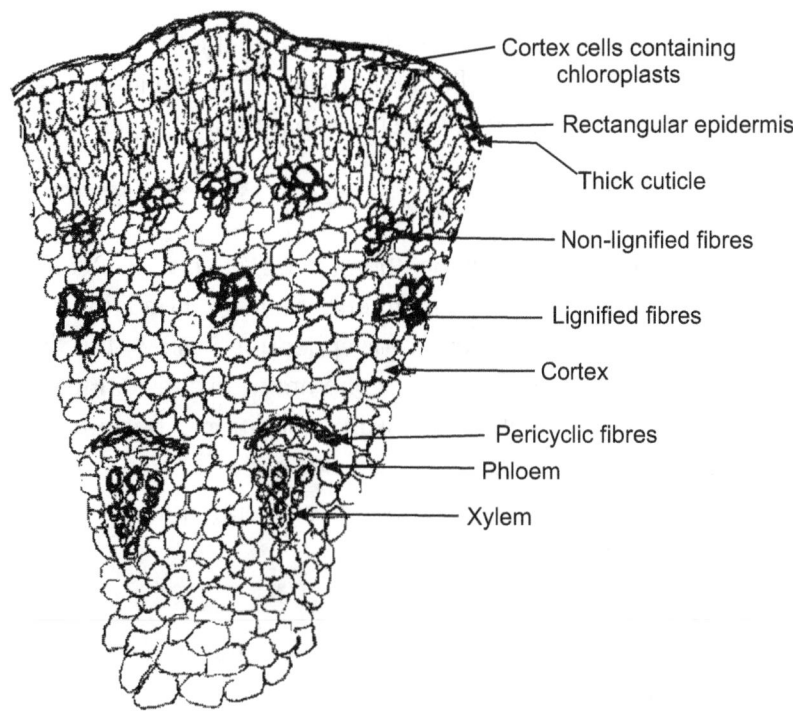

Fig. 1.29: T.S. of Ephedra Stem

Chemical Constituents

Ephedra contains the amino alkaloids. They are ephedrine, nor-ephedrine, n-methyl ephedrine, pseudo-ephedrine, etc.

(–) Ephedrine $R_1 = H$, $R_2 = CH_3$

(–) Nor-ephedrine $R_1 = H$, $R_2 = H$

(–) n-methyl ephedrine $R_1 = CH_3$, $R_2 = CH_3$

Chemically, ephedrine ($C_{10}H_{15}NO$) is 1-phenyl-1-hydroxy-2-methylaminopropane and is soluble in water, alcohol, organic solvents and oils. It is odourless and colourless, deliquescent and decomposes when exposed to air.

Along with the amino alkaloids, macrocyclic alkaloids called ephedradines are present in roots. The drug also contains oxazolidone.

Chemical Test

Ephedrine is dissolved in water and dilute hydrochloric acid and then treated separately with copper sulphate and sodium hydroxide. The solution gives violet colour. If shaken with solvent ether, the organic layer shows purple and aqueous layer shows blue colour.

Uses

Ephedra and its alkaloids show sympathomimetic effects. Hence, it is used as a bronchodilator in asthma and also in the treatment of allergic conditions like hay fever. As compared to adrenaline, the onset of action for ephedrine is slow, but the effect is much prolonged, as it is not quickly hydrolysed by mono amino oxidase in the body. Ephedrine is also used to correct the low blood pressure conditions, because of its peripheral contraction of arterioles. Ephedrines have hypotensive effects.

In 1995-96 and 1996-97, India has exported total ephedrine salts of worth ₹ 820.8 lakhs and ₹ 1555 lakhs respectively.

Dose

Ephedrine hydrochloride or sulphate 25-50 mg, 6-8 times a day, orally or parenterally and 0.1 ml 1-3 % solution, 2-3 times a day intravenously.

Other Species and Allied Drugs

The genus Ephedra has about 45 species, amongst which nearly 25 species contain ephedrine. The prominent species containing ephedrine are *E. equisetina and E. sinica* (both Chinese), *E. intermedia, E. major, E. helryetica and E. alata*. They contain from 35 - 87 % of ephedrine in total alkaloids. The other plants containing ephedrine are *Aconitum napelles* (Ranunculaceae); *Sida cordifolia*; and *S. rhombifolia* (Malvaceae); *Roemeria refracta* (Papaveraceae); and *Taxas baccata* (Taxaceae).

Allied Drugs

The plants having chemical contents similar to colchicine type of alkaloids belong to different genera, such as *Dipidax, Gloriosa, Androcybium, Camptorrhiza*, etc.

The other genera in which colchicine is present are from the same family Liliaceae, like *Androcymbium, Bulbocodium, Dipidax, Littonia, Fritillaria, Ornithoglossum*, etc. and *Narcissus* and *Crocus* from families Amaryllidaceae and Iridaceae respectively.

COLCHICUM

Synonyms

Meadow saffron seeds, autumn crocus

Biological Source

It consists of the dried ripe seeds of *Colchicum luteum* Baker and *Colchicum autumnale* Linn, belonging to family Liliaceae. Colchicum corm is also used medicinally.

Geographical Source

It is found and cultivated in various parts of Europe, like England, Czechoslovakia, Holland, Poland and Yugoslavia. It is also cultivated in India (in Western Himalaya and Kashmir regions).

History

Though, it was known from the time of Dioscorides, it was not much used, owing to its toxic nature. In the medieval times, Arabian people were using it for treatment of gout. It was reintroduced in European countries towards beginning of seventeenth century and first appeared in the London Pharmacopoeia in 1616. Pelletier and Caventou isolated colchicine in 1820.

Cultivation, Collection and Preparation

In nature, colchicum propagates by repeating the life cycle with the corm which is present as a swollen underground stem with sheathing leaves. Towards the end of summer, the fully grown corm develops daughter corms in the axil of scaly leaf near the base. These daughter corms develop parasitically on parent corm and subsequently, the parent corm withers away. After this, the daughter corms develop into new plants.

In Jammu and Kashmir and different parts of Europe and Africa, the drug is obtained by propagation with seeds. The propagation is done by sowing the seeds in boxes at an altitude of 1000 - 3000 m. The seedlings are transplanted in open fields at a distance of 1 m. The plants bear the capsular fruits after one year of vegetative growth. The fruits are collected before dehiscence and dark seeds are separated, processed and graded. The corms are isolated and the adhering scales and coats are removed. The corms are sliced transversely and dried below 65°C.

Organoleptic Characters (Fig. 1.30)

(a) Colchicum Seeds

Colchicum seeds are very hard in nature and show a reddish-brown testa. The seeds have a projection at the hilum and from there develops strophiole, which is an outgrowth of testa. The seeds are 2 - 3 mm in diameter, having bitter and acrid taste and no odour.

The corms are 2-3 cm in diameter and used in the sliced form which are reniform and ovate in shape, with 2-5 mm, thickness. They have a short fracture, bitter taste and no odour.

| (a) Colchicum autumnale herb | (b) Colchicum seeds |

Fig. 1.30

(b) Colchicum Corms

Colour   : Yellowish-brown

Odour   : None

Taste   : Bitter and acrid

Size   : Slices are about 2-5 mm in thickness

Shape   : Sub-reniform or ovate in outline

Extra features : Fracture is short and cut surfaces are white and starchy, showing greyish points.

Fig. 1.31 : Colchicum Corms

Microscopic Characters

The section of seed shows parenchyma and endosperm. The parenchymatous cells are reddish- brown with thick walls. The endospermic cells show pitted walls and contain aleurone grains and fixed oil. The strophiole portion of seed contains starch.

The corm has epidermis, parenchyma and vascular tissue. The parenchymatous cells have abundant starch grains. The epidermis has circular stomata. In vascular part, the xylem vessels are spiral or annular.

Chemical Constituents

Colchicum seed contains 0.2 - 1 % of amino alkaloids of which colchicine is the main constituent. The seeds contain upto 0.8 % of colchicine and in corms, it is upto 0.6 %.

Colchicum also contains demecolcine. Both the alkaloids contain tropolone or cycloheptatrien-ol-one ring structure.

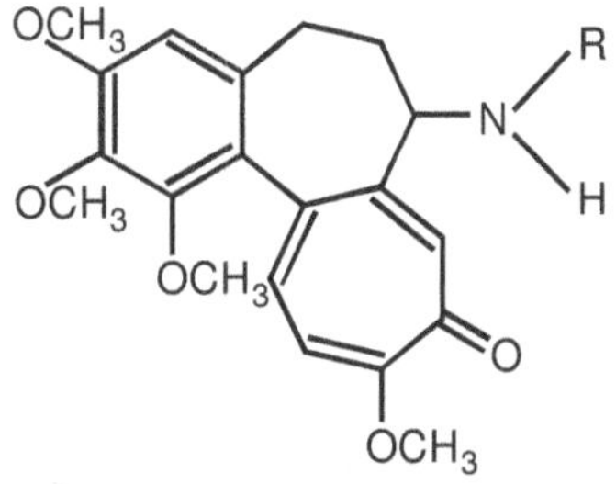

Colchicine, R = COCH$_3$, Demecolcine, R = CH$_3$

Colchicine ($C_{22}H_{25}O_6N$) is obtained as pale yellow crystals, amorphous or in powder form. It has a bitter taste and is odourless. It darkens on exposure to air. Colchicine is freely soluble in alcohol and chloroform, soluble in 25 parts of water and in 220 parts of solvent ether.

Chemical Tests

(1) Colchicine gives yellow colour with 70 % sulphuric acid.

(2) Alcoholic solution of colchicine, when treated with ferric chloride gives red colour.

Uses

Colchicum is a specific drug for treatment of gout and rheumatism. Colchicine also possesses antitumour activity.

Apart from medicinal use, colchicine is widely accepted and practised as a chemical agent for bringing the polyploidy (increase in number of chromosomes) and hence used in horticulture and cultivation of medicinal plants.

Dose

Colchicine: 500 – 650 μg, 1 - 3 times a day, orally

500 μg to 1 mg,1 - 2 times a day, intravenously

(I) DRUGS CONTAINING GLYCOALKALOIDS

SOLANUM KHASIANUM

Biological Source

It consists of dried berries of *Solanum khasianum* C.B. Clarke, belonging to family Solanaceae.

Geographical Source

The plant is found widely growing at various altitudes in India right from coastal region upto 2000 metres. It is found in hilly regions of Assam, Manipur, NEFA, Sikkim, Nilgiris,

Central India and also in Myanmar and China. Now-a-days, it is cultivated on commercial scales in Maharashtra.

Habitat

A stout highly-branched shrub upto 1 - 1.5 metre tall with straight pricles, Leaves: ovate, lobed, lobes are triangular, prickly on both surfaces. Flowers: white coloured, in lateral 1 - 4 flowered racemes.

Cultivation and Collection

In view of its solasodine content, it has commercial significance. Solasodine, a steroidal glycoalkaloid, has similar applications as that of diosgenin.

Fig. 1.32 : *Solanum khasianum* plant with fruits

The cultivation of this plant is scientifically studied and the observations of those trials are given here in brief. The seeds are used for propagation, either through nursery beds or by direct broadcasting. In February, the seeds are sown in nursery beds. The seed beds are covered with sand or farmyard manures and weeding is done periodically. When the seedlings show sufficient growth, they are transplanted into open fields. The raising in nurseries is preferred to direct broadcasting. The plant grows in various climatic and agricultural conditions. The well drained soil and sunny atmosphere are preferred. The seedlings are transplanted in moist soil at 50 × 50 cm distance. Urea, potash and superphosphate are given as fertilizers. In the initial period, irrigation is done once in a week and then in later stages as per requirement. After six months, the plants are harvested for collection of berries. They are immediately dried in shade or artificially at low temperature to reduce the large content of moisture.

Organoleptic Characters

It bears yellowish to greenish berries which are globose and 2.5 cm in diameter with compressed smooth brown seeds.

Chemical Constituents

The berries contain about 3 % of steroidal glycoalkaloid called solasodine. A new glycoalkaloid solakhasianin having rhamnose and galactose as sugar components have been isolated. Mucilage surrounding part of the seeds contain highest amount of alkaloid. Immatured and over-ripe fruits contain neglegible content of alkaloid, while it is maximum when fruits change colour from green to yellow. Colour change of fruits takes place about two months after setting the fruits to the plants.

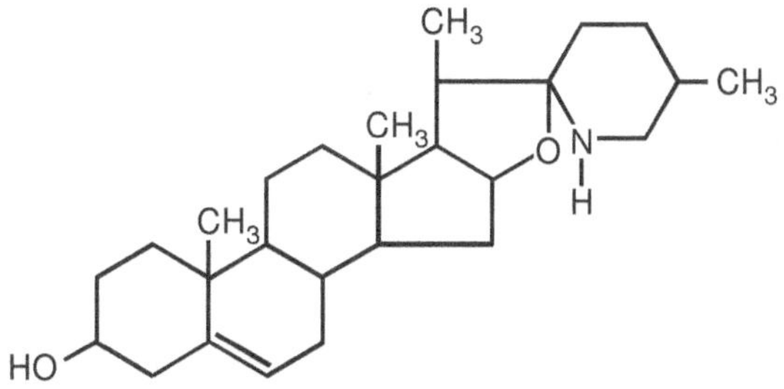

Solasodine

The berries also contain 8 - 10 % of greenish-yellow fixed oil.

Uses

Solasodine is used as a precursor for steroidal synthesis. Like diosgenin, it is first converted to 16-dehydro-pregnenelone acetate. The later is a precursor for steroids, like corticosteroids, pregnane, androstanes and 19 - NOR steroids. All of these are useful as sex hormones, oral contraceptives.

Isolation

For the isolation of solasodine, the berries are powdered and the oil is removed by defatting. The defatted material is extracted with ethanol. The extract is concentrated, treated with conc. Hydrochloric acid and refluxed for 6 hours. After this, ammonia is added to basify the extract and again refluxed for 1 hour. It is filtered and the residue is washed, dried and dissolved in chloroform. This mixture is filtered and solasodine in the form of residue is obtained by evaporating the solvent.

Allied Species

Many other species of Solanum containing small quantities of solasodine are *S. eleatnifolium, S. inacanum, S. indicum, S. surratense, S. seaforthianum, S. mammosum, S. trilobatum,* etc.

(J) DRUGS CONTAINING PURINE ALKALOIDS
COFFEE SEED

Synonyms

Coffee bean.

Biological Source

It is the dried ripe seed of *Coffea arabica* Linne or *C. liberica* Hiern, and deprived of most of the seed coat. It belongs to family Rubiaceae.

Geographical Source

It is found in Ethiopia, Brazil, India, Vietnam, Mexico, Guatemala, Indonesia and Sri Lanka.

Coffee beverage is popular in different parts of world. The amount of caffeine present is also more than in tea. In middle east countries, it is known by name 'qahuah'. It is a strong decoction of coffee seed powder. The word has its origin in Turkish and Arabic languages. The major suppliers of coffee, now-a-days, are Brazil and India. Karnataka, Kerala and Tamil Nadu grow large plantation of coffee. (*Fig. 1.33*). At present it is cultivated in Maharashtra also.

Habitat

Coffee plant is an evergreen shrub which bears drupe type of fruit with an ellipsoidal or spheroidal shape. Each fruit has 2 locules, with one seed in each chamber. Each plant gives about 2 - 3 kg of coffee seeds. The fruits are dried to separate the seeds. The seeds are separated by wetting them and mechanically separating, followed by drying in heaps, which causes fermentation.

The separated seeds or beans are green in colour. They are roasted by which the colour and odour is effected. The seeds acquire dark brown colour and possess an agreeable odour and bitter taste.

India produced 1.65 and 2.35 lakh tones of coffee during 1998 - 99 and 99 - 2000 respectively.

Fig. 1.33: Coffee Plant with fruits

Chemical Constituents

The main constituents of coffee bean are caffeine, tannin, fixed oil and proteins. It contains 2 - 3 % caffeine, 3 - 5 % tannins, 13 % proteins, 10 - 15 % fixed oils, chlorogenic or caffeotannic acid and sugars in the form of dextrin, glucose, etc. In the seeds, caffeine is present as a salt of chlorogenic acid. During roasting process, the agreeable smell of coffee is developed which is due to an oil called caffeol composed of mainly furfural alongwith minor quantities of phenol, pyridine and valerianic acid.

Extraction of Caffeine

Caffeine is prepared either by synthesis (from urea or uric acid) or extracted from natural sources. Coffee bean is one of the major sources for it. For the extraction, coffee roasters are used in which caffeine sublimed during roasting is recovered. It is the commercial method for extraction of caffeine.

Uses

It is used as a source of caffeine. The main effects of coffee i.e. stimulant and diuretic actions are due to caffeine. It is, sometimes, used to combat the toxic effects due to CNS depressant drugs. During 1997 - 98 and 1998 – 99, India exported coffee worth of ₹ 17.07 crores and 17.51 crores respectively.

Other Preparations

Decaffeinated coffee: This product has been introduced in developed countries. It has been specially designed, because of addiction effects of coffee. It has all the agreeable odour of coffee beans, but contains a meagre amount (about 0.08 per cent) of caffeine.

TEA LEAVES

Synonym

Camellia thea.

Biological Source

It contains the prepared leaves and leaf buds of *Thea sinensis* (Linne) O. kuntze, belonging to family Theaceae (Ternstroemiaceae).

Geographical Source

Large areas of land are put under cultivation of tea in India, Sri Lanka, China, Indonesia and Japan. It is available as **black tea** from India and Sri Lanka and **green tea** from China and Japan.

Black tea is obtained by fermenting the heap of fresh tea leaves and further drying with artificial heat. **Green tea** is obtained by putting tea leaves in copper pans and then drying by artificial heat.

Organoleptic Characters

It is a small evergreen shrub. When cultivated, reaches to the height of 1.0 - 1.5 metres, while wild growing plants reach upto 6.0 metres. Plant is much branched and bears grey bark.

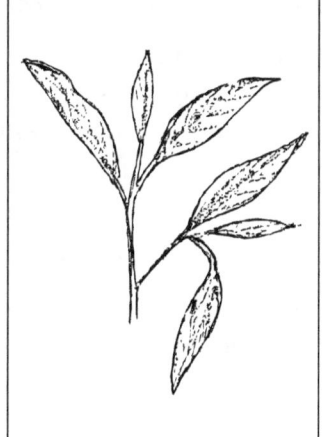

Fig. 1.34: Twig of tea-herb

Leaves   : Dark green, lanceolate or elliptical, blunt at apex, base is tapering margin shortly serrate. Young leaves are hairy, while matured leaves are glabrous.

Flowers : Flowers are solitary or in groups of 2 or 3 in the leaf axils, and drooping.

Odour   : Characteristics

Taste   : Bitter

Preparation of Green Tea

It is prepared by exposing the freshly collected leaves to the air until most of the moisture is removed. Then they are roasted and stirred continuously until leaves become moist and flaccid. Then they are passed to rolling table and rolled into balls and subjected to a pressure which removes the moisture. Then the leaves are shaken out on the copper pans and roasted again till the leaves assume dull green colour. Then the leaves are winnowed, screened and graded into various varieties.

Chemical Constituents

Tea leaves are considered as a rich source of caffeine (1 - 3 %). It is extracted from tea dust and tea leaf waste or sweepings. It also contains theobromine and theophylline in minor quantities. The colour of tea leaves is due to gallotannic acid (15 %). The agreeable odour is due to presence of a yellow volatile oil. Tea leaves also contain an enzymatic mixture called thease.

Caffeine   **Theobromine**   **Theophylline**

Use

Tea is useful as a CNS stimulant in the form of beverage besides, it is a diuretic as well.

Caffeine

Caffeine [$C_8H_{10}O_2N_4$] occurs as a white powder without any odour, but possesses bitter taste. It is a weak base and feebly soluble in water, alcohol, chloroform and solvent ether. But, its solubility in water is sharply increased in the presence of benzoates, bromides, citric acid and salicylates.

Chemical Tests

1. Caffeine (also the other purine alkaloids) gives **murexide colour reaction.** Caffeine is taken in a petridish to which hydrochloric acid and potassium chlorate are added and heated to dryness. A purple colour is obtained by exposing the residue to vapours of dilute ammonia. The purple colour is lost on addition of fixed alkali.
2. Caffeine also produces white precipitate with tannic acid solution.

Uses

Caffeine is widely accepted and used as a central nervous system stimulant, due to its cerebral vasoconstrictor effect. It is also given along with ergotamine tartarate to potentiate the action of latter as a specific analgesic in migraine.

Chapter 2

TERPENOIDS AND RESINS

Introduction

Terpenes are hydrocarbons and are components of resins and also volatile oil. Word terpene is derived from turpentine. When terpenes are modified chemically such as by oxidation or rearrangement of carbon skeleton, the resulting compounds are known as **terpenoids** or **Isoprenoids**.

Carterpillars also emit terpenes in their osmeteria. (Osmeterium is a fleshy organ found in the prothoracic segment of larve of butterflies.)

Terpenoids are regarded as derivatives of polymers of **isoprene**, $H_2C = C - CH = CH_2$
$$\overset{|}{CH_3}$$

(i.e. C_5H_8) usually joined head to tail and widely distributed in the plant kingdom.

Terpene hydrocarbons are classified as under:

Isoprene*/Hemiterpene	C_5H_8
Monoterpenes	$C_{10}H_{16}$
Sesquiterpene**	$C_{15}H_{24}$
Diterpene	$C_{20}H_{32}$
Triterpenes	$C_{30}H_{48}$
Tetraterpenes	$C_{40}H_{64}$
Polyterpenes	$(C_5H_8)n$

Terpenoids are abundantly available in volatile oils. They consist of a complex mixture of terpenes or sesquiterpene, alcohols, aldehydes, ketones, acids, and esters. The separation of individual components is accomplished by vacuum fractionation and by chromatographic methods. The unsaturated hydrocarbons are conveniently separated as their crystalline addition products with hydrochloric acid or hydrobromic acid, or nitrosyl chloride.

* This does not occur free in nature. Isoprene itself is considered as only hemiterpene, while prenol (3 methyl-2 buten-1-ol) and isovalaric acid (3 methyl butanoic acid) are the hemiterpenoids.

** Prefix sequin means one and half.

MONOTERPENES

These are subdivided into three groups: acyclic, monocyclic and bicyclic.

1. Acyclic monoterpenes

Important hydrocarbons are ocimene and myrcene.

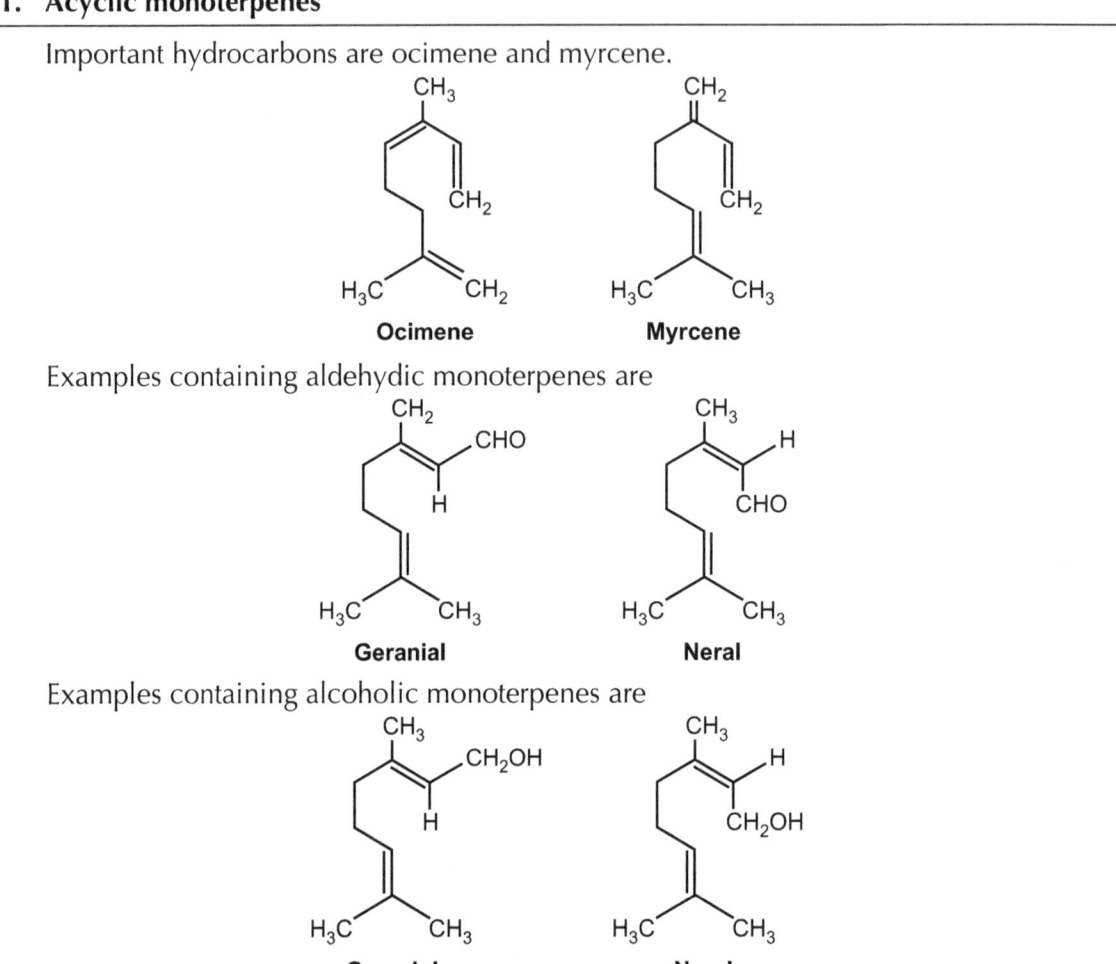

Ocimene   Myrcene

Examples containing aldehydic monoterpenes are

Geranial   Neral

Examples containing alcoholic monoterpenes are

Geraniol   Nerol

2. Monocyclic monoterpenes

Examples containing only hydrocarbons are:

d-Limonene   α-Terpinene   β-Terpinene

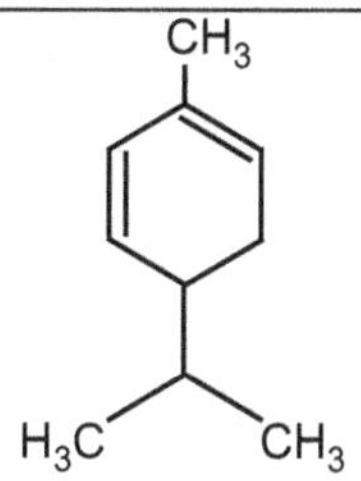

α-Phellandrene 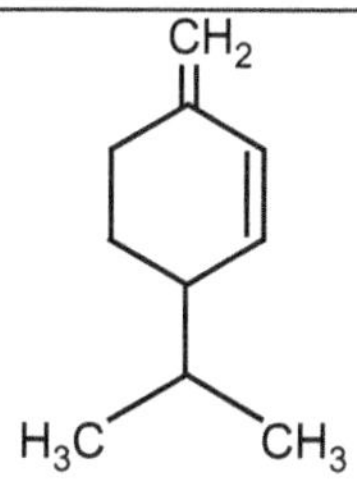   **β-Phellandrene**

Monocyclic monoterpenes containing alcohol are

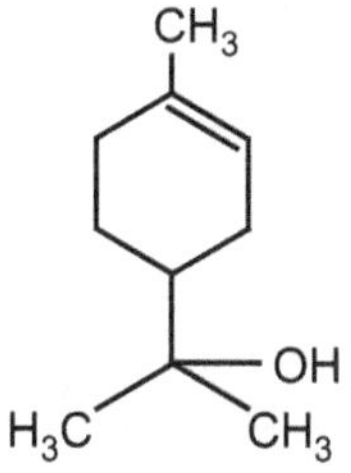

α-Terpineol 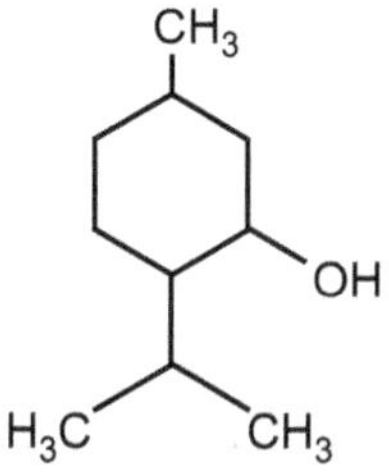   **Menthol**

Monocyclic monoterpenes containing aldehydes are

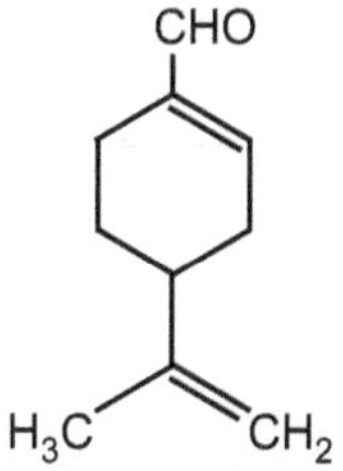

Perillaldehyde 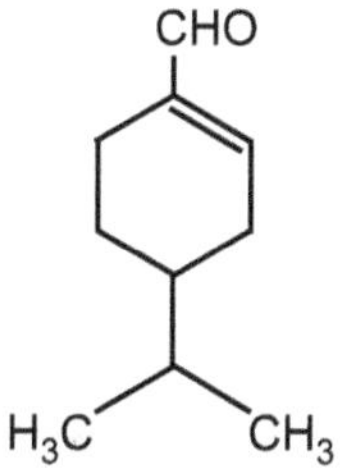   **Phellandral**

SESQUITERPENES

1. Monocyclic sesquiterpenes

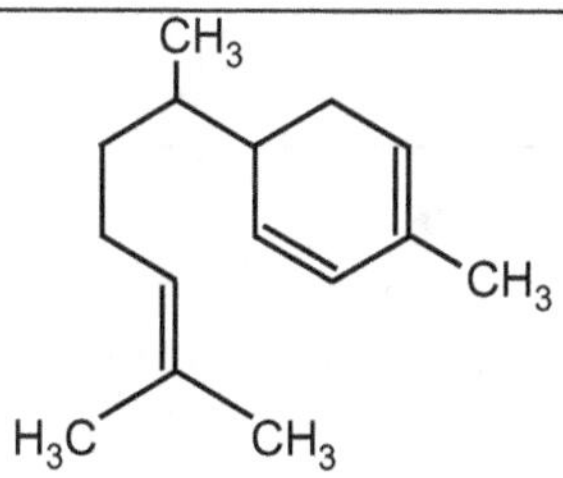

Zingiberene

2. Bicyclic sesquiterpenes

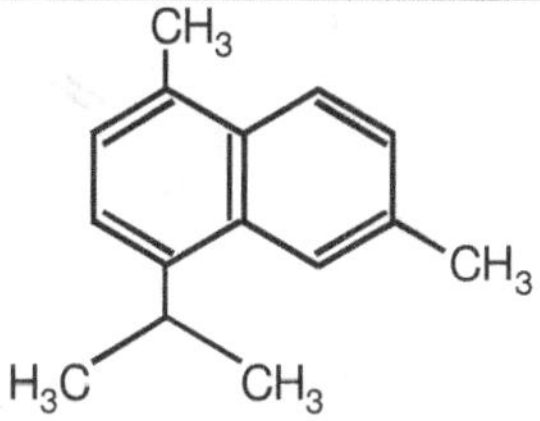

Cadalene 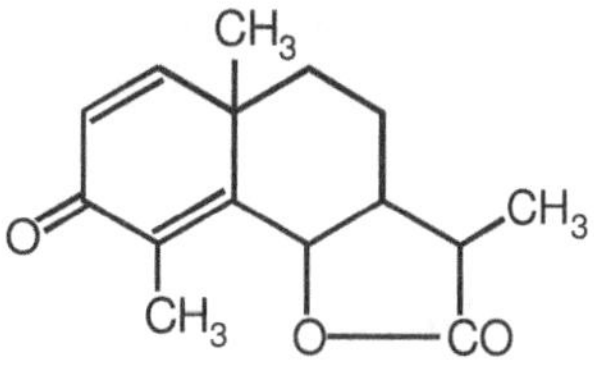   **Santonin**

DITERPENES

These are formed by the union of four isoprene units and are found mainly in the plant resins.

1. Acyclic diterpene

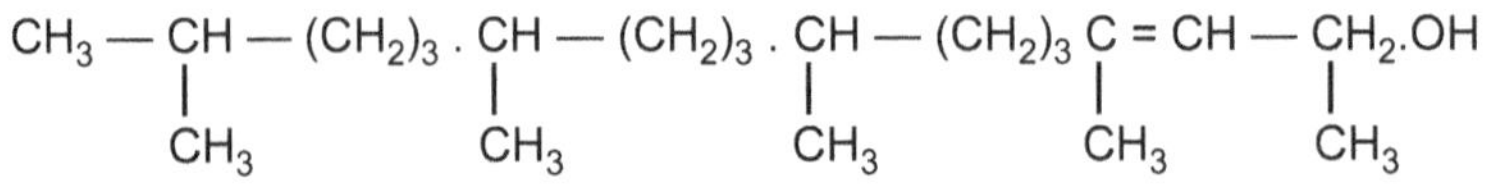

Phytol

2. Monocyclic diterpene

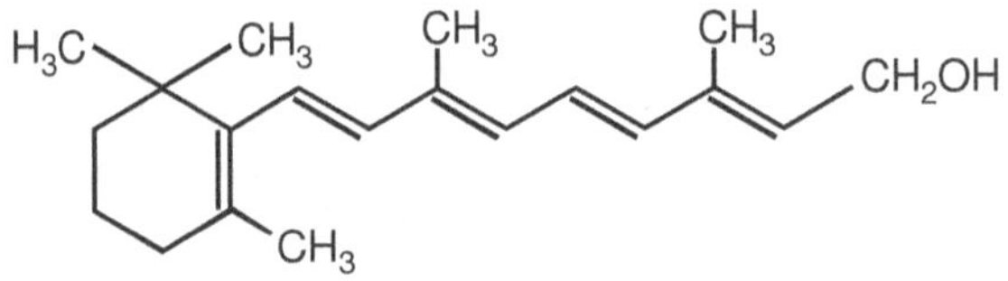

Vitamin A₁

3. Bicyclic diterpene

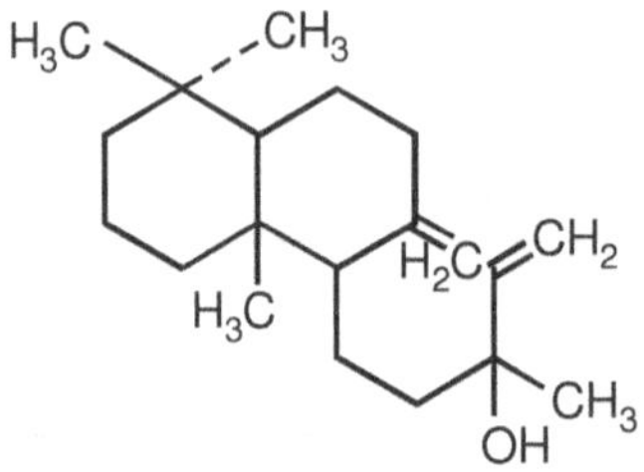

Manool

4. Tricyclic diterpenes

The resin acids form the major nonvolatile part of many natural resins, such as

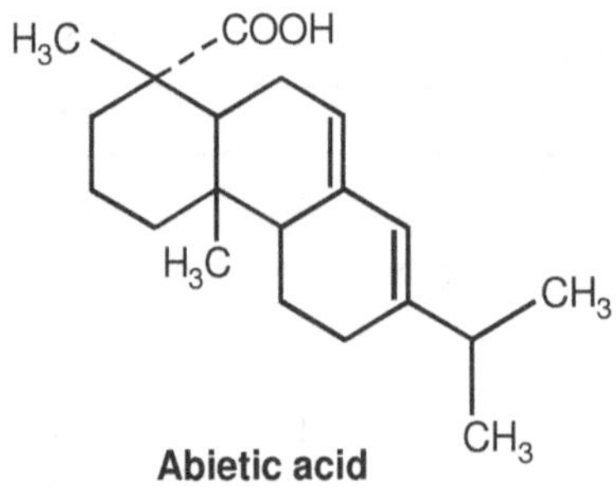

Abietic acid

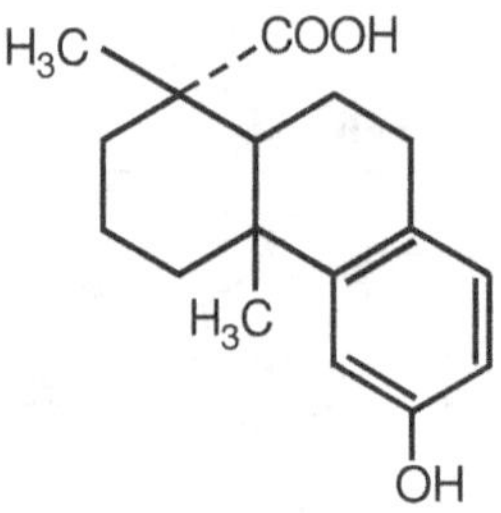

Podocarpic acid

TRITERPENES

The triterpenes are also widely distributed in the plants and animals kingdom. They are classified into three groups:

1. Acyclic triterpene; 2. Tetracyclic triterpene; 3. Pentacyclic triterpene.

1. Acyclic triterpene

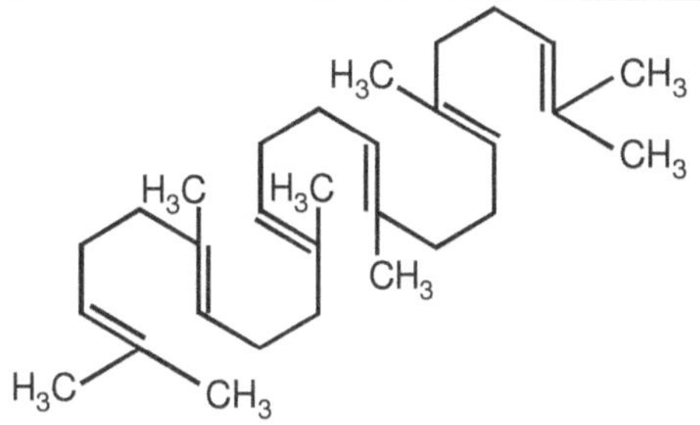

Squalene

2. Tetracyclic triterpenes

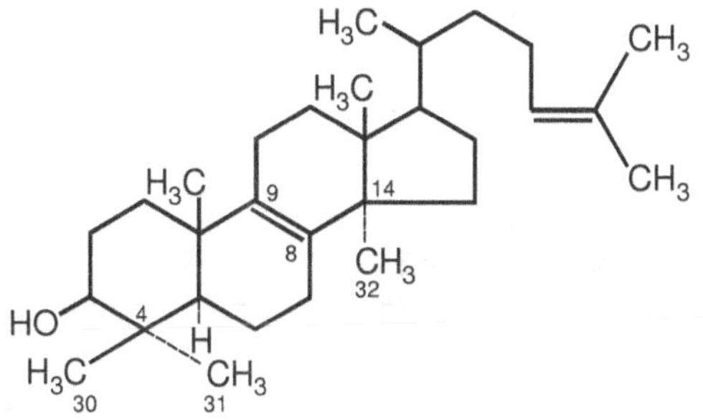

Lanosterol 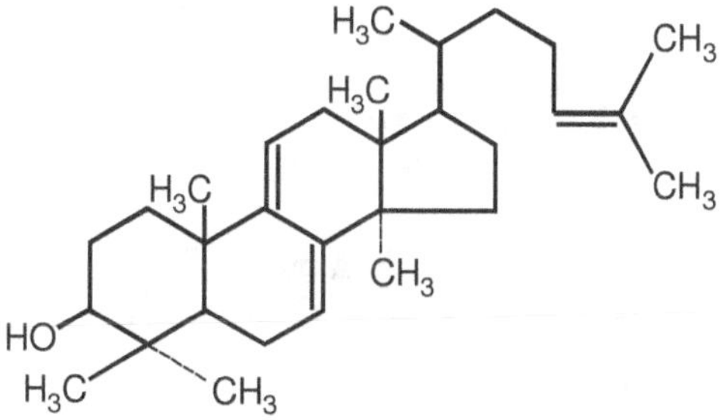   **Agnosterol**

3. Pentacyclic triterpenes

These compounds are subdivided into three subclasses.

α-Amyrin class

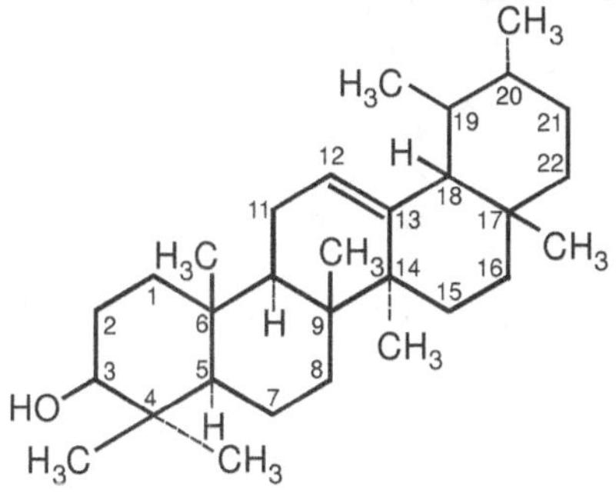

α-**Amyrin** 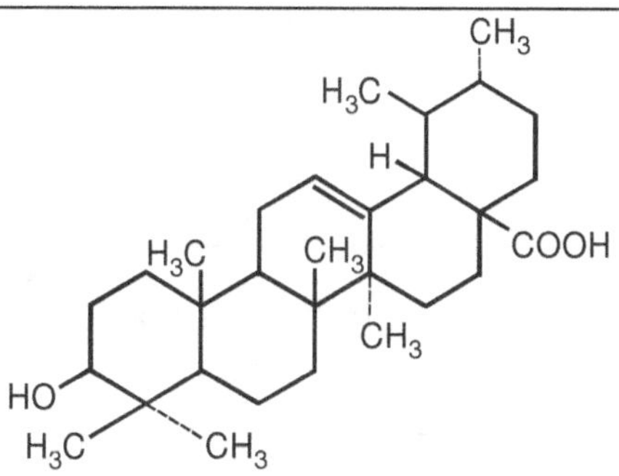   **Ursolic acid**

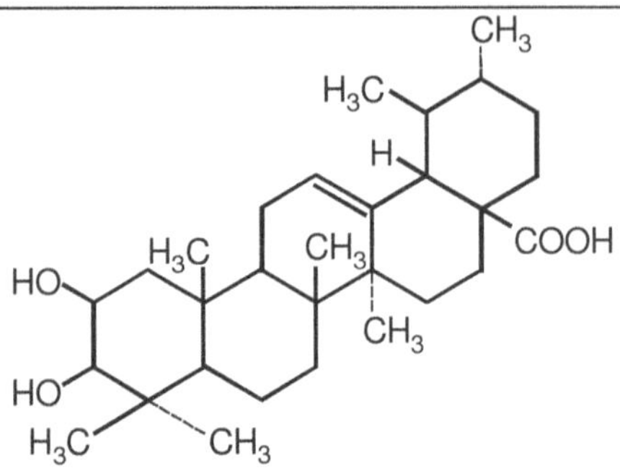

Asiatic acid

β-Amyrin class

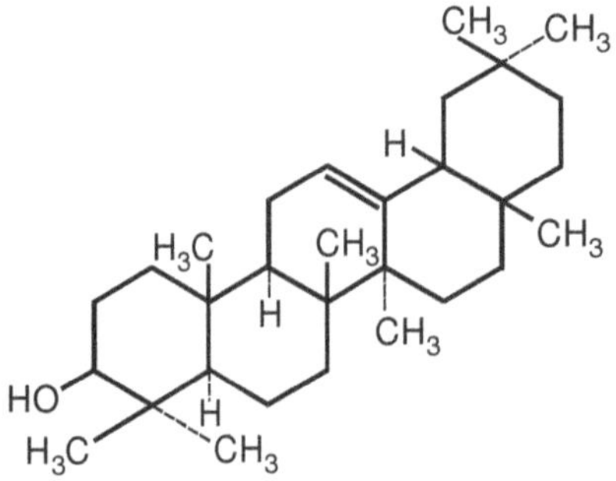

β-Amyrin

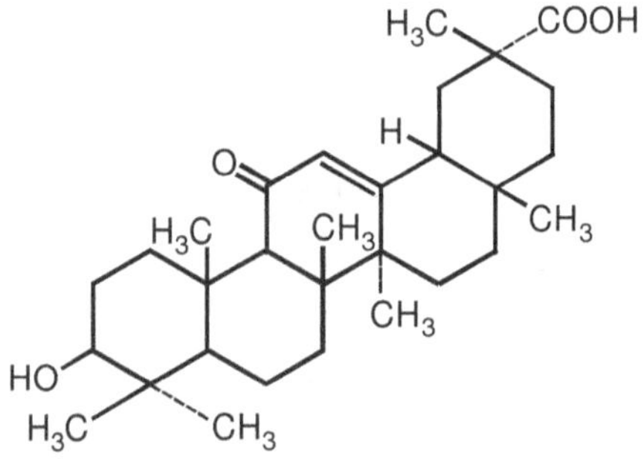

Glycyrrhetic acid

Lupeol group

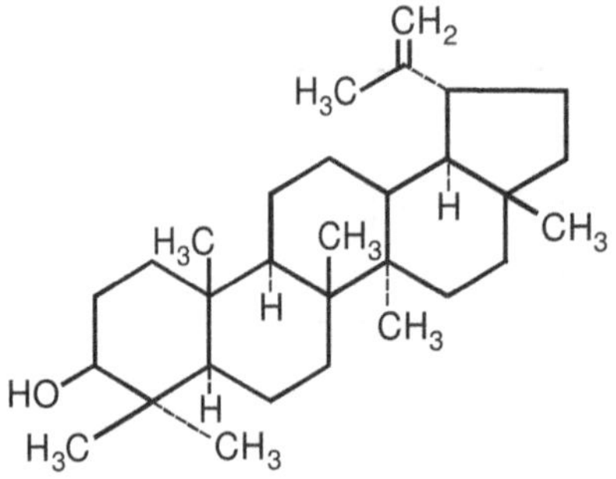

Lupeol

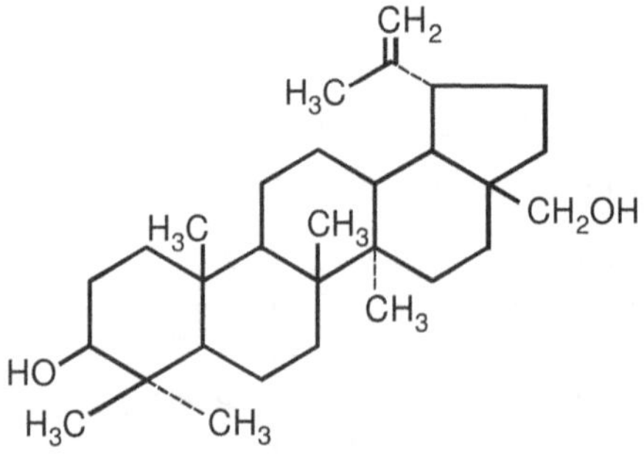

Betulin

Actually, the term *terpene* represents the hydrocarbons while *terpenoids* include the hydrocarbons, as well as their oxygenated derivatives.

Terpenes and terpenoids are found in all volatile oils, resins and resin combinations of plant or animal origin. Drug containing terpenoids are known as Terpenoidal drugs.

Structure and Classification

Terpenoids can also be classified according to the number of cyclic structures they contain. The *Salkowski test* can be used to identify the presence of terpenoids.

Meroterpenes are any compound, including many natural products, having a partial terpenoidal structure.

Since the terpenes are components of volatile oil, it is very essential to know first, about volatile oils in detail.

Their occurance, distribution in natural drugs, classification, chemistry, methods of extraction, their biogenesis (biosynthesis) qualitative and quantitative methods of analysis are described below :

VOLATILE OILS

Volatile oils are odourous principles, that evaporate when exposed to air at room temperature. They are also called as "etheral oil" or "essential oil". The term *essential oils* is applied to volatile oils, as they represent odoriferous principles or "essences".

Volatile oils may act as repellents to insects, thus preventing destruction of flowers and leaves or they also serve as insect attractants helping in cross fertilization.

Volatile oils are colourless when fresh, but on long standing they may darken in colour. To prevent such darkening, volatile oils should be stored in well closed, preferably amber colour glass containers in cool and dry place. Volatile oils are soluble in alcohol, ether and other non-polar solvents and practically insoluble in water. They are usually lighter than water. (The density of volatile oils is less than water except clove oil). They have high refractive indices and most of them are optically active.

Occurrence and Distribution

Volatile oils are secreted by different specialized cells in different families, are listed below in Table 2.1.

Table 2.1 : Occurrence of volatile oils

Name of specialized cells that secrete volatile oil	Name of family
1. Glandular hairs	Labiatae
2. Modified parenchymal cells	Piperaceae
3. Oil tubules called vittae	Umbeliferae
4. Lysigenous or schizogenous passage	Pinaceae and Rutaceae

Volatile oils may occur in all tissues like

Rose	:	Only in petals.
Cinnamon	:	In bark and leaves.
Umbeliferous fruits	:	In pericarp.
Mint	:	In the glandular hairs of stem and leaves.
Orange	:	In rind and in flower.

Based on biosynthetic origin, the constituent of volatile oils may be divided into two classes :

1) Terpene derivatives formed via acetate mevalonic acid pathway.

2) Aromatic compounds formed via shikimic – phenyl propanoid route.

Chemistry of Volatile Oils

Volatile oils are mixtures containing diverse types of compounds, very rarely they consist of single chemical compound. Volatile oils consist largely of terpenes.

Terpenes are defined as natural products where, structures may be divided into isoprene units. These units arise from acetate via mevalonic acid. These 5 carbon units are branched-chain compounds containing two unsaturated bonds.

$$CH_2 {=} \overset{\overset{\displaystyle CH_3}{|}}{C} - CH = CH_2$$

Isoprene (C_5H_8)

During formation of terpenes, the isoprene units are linked in head to tail fashion. Thus classification of these compounds depend upon number of units incorporated into a terpene.

$$C - \overset{\overset{\displaystyle C}{|}}{C} - C - C + C - \overset{\overset{\displaystyle C}{|}}{C} - C - C$$

Head　　　　　　Tail ¦ Head　　　　　　Tail

Isoprene unit　　　Isoprene unit

Monoterpene	:	$C_{10}H_{16}$ - composed of two isoprene units
Sesquiterpene	:	$C_{15}H_{24}$ - contains 3 isoprene units
Diterpene	:	$C_{20}H_{32}$ - contains 4 isoprene units
Triterpene	:	$C_{30}H_{48}$ - contains 6 isoprene units

Most often, monoterpenes are found in volatile oils. They occur in acyclic, monocyclic, and bicyclic form as hydrocarbons and as oxygenated derivatives such as alcohols, aldehydes, ketones, phenols, oxides and esters.

Volatile oil also composed one another major class of constituents known as "phenylpropanoids". These compounds contain C_6-phenyl ring attached with C_3-propane side chain. The phenyl propanoids found in volatile oils are phenols or phenol ethers.

Volatile oils are composed of numerous and diverse types of constituents, they can be classified as follows :

(1) Hydrocarbons, (2) Alcohol, (3) Aldehydes, (4) Ketones, (5) Phenols, (6) Phenol-ethers, (7) Peroxides and oxides, (8) Esters or non-terpenoids.

The stereochemistry of different constituents determines quality of odour. Different geometric isomers like ortho/meta/para or cis/trans responsible for strength of odour. In nature, many terpenes exist in both enantiomeric forms (optically active). Among the monoterpenes that occur as (+) form in certain species and (–) enantiomeric form in others or may occur as racemic mixture. For example, limonene, α-terpinol, α-fenchol occur as racemic mixture in certain plants or as (+) and (–) form in other species. The physiologic response elicited by each isomer may differ. For example, (+) – carvone is odourous principle in caraway whereas (–) carvone produces spearmint odour.

Table 2.2 : Classification of volatile oils and volatile oil containing drugs based on their composition

Sr. No.	Name of drugs and class	Botanical name	Important constituents and their percentage
A.	**Terpenes or sesquiterpenes**		
1.	Turpentine	*Pinus* spp.	Pinenes, Camphene
2.	Tea-tree	*Melaleuca alternifolia*	Cyclic monoterpenes.
B.	**Alcohols**		
1.	Coriander	*Coriandrum sativum*	Linalol (65 – 80%)
2.	Sandalwood	*Santalum album*	Santalols (sesquiter alcohols) penes
C.	**Esters and alcohols**		
1.	Lavender	*Lavendula officinalis*	Linalol, linalyl acetate
2.	Peppermint	*Mentha piperita*	Menthol (45%), Menthyl acetate (4-9%).

Contd...

D.	**Aldehydes**		
1.	Cinnamon bark	*Cinnamomum zylenicum*	Cinnamic aldehyde (60 – 75%), eugenol, terpenes.
2.	Cassia bark	*Cinnamomum cassia*	Cinnamic aldehyde (upto 80%)
3.	Lemon	*Citrus limon*	Citral and citronellal (75 – 80%)
E.	**Ketones**		
1.	Caraway	*Carum carvi*	Carvone (60%)
2.	Dill	*Anethum graveolens*	Carvone (50%), limonene, Dill-apeol
F.	**Phenols**		
1.	Cinnamon leaf	*Cinnamomum zeylanicum*	Eugenol (80%)
2.	Clove	*Syzygium aromatium*	Eugenol (90%) acetyl eugenol.
G.	**Ethers**		
1.	Anise	*Pimpinella anisum*	Anethol (80-90%)
2.	Eucalyptus	*Eucalyptus globlus*	Cineol
H.	**Peroxides/oxides Chenopodium**	***Chenopodium spp.***	**Unsaturated terpene peroxide**
I.	**Non-terpenoid**		
1.	Mustard	*Brassica spp.*	Glucosinolates
2.	Winter green	*Gaultheria procumbens*	Methyl salicylate

Extraction of Volatile Oils

Volatile oils are usually obtained by distillation method. Method of distillation depends upon the plant part containing the oil. On commercial scale three different distillation methods are used :

1) Water or hydro distillation,
2) Water and steam distillation,
3) Direct steam distillation.

Water or hydrodistillation is applied mostly to dried plant material and that are not subject to injury by boiling. e.g. turpentine oil is composed entirely of terpenes, which is not affected by boiling.

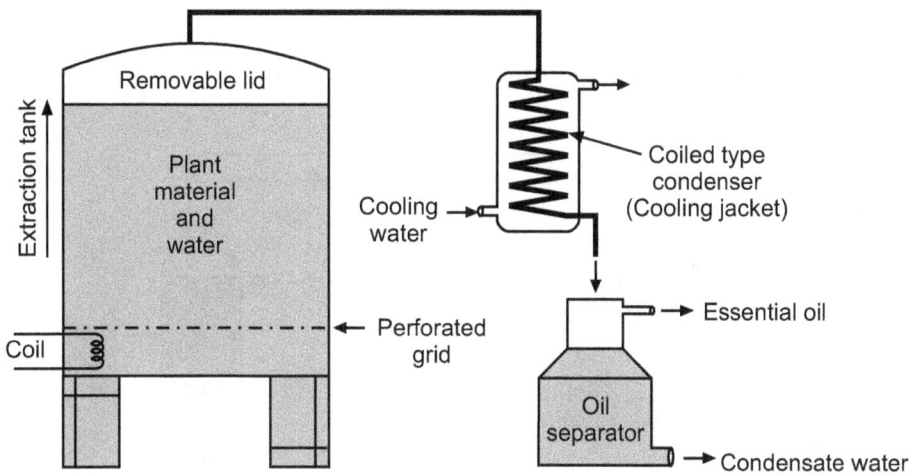

Fig. 2.1 : Hydrodistillation

Water and steam distillation is mainly used for the material where components get damaged or decomposed by boiling. Dried or fresh plant parts can be used for such distillation method.

Examples are cinnamon and clove oil; the steam is passed through macerated drug bed and oil globules are carried by steam and then condensed. The oily layer of condensed distillate is separated from aqueous layer.

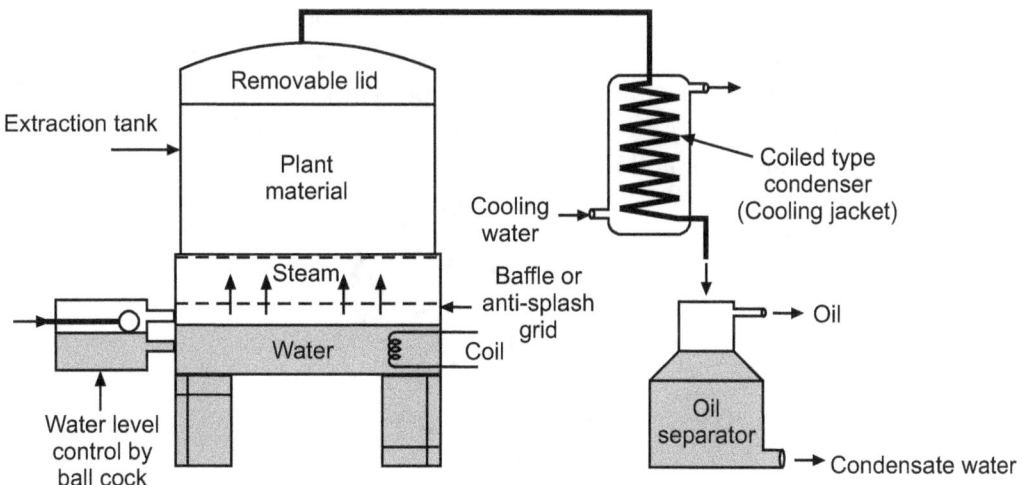

Fig. 2.2 : Water and Steam distillation

Direct steam distillation is employed for fresh plant drug, like spearmint and peppermint. The steam is generated at bottom tank and it is passed to perforated container when drug is placed. Steam is forced through fresh plant material and carries oil droplets through vapour pipe attached at top of tank to condensing chamber. During steam distillation some components may hydrolyse and some may decompose due to high temperature.

Glycosidic volatile oils like mustard oil are obtained by enzymatic hydroysis of glycosides.

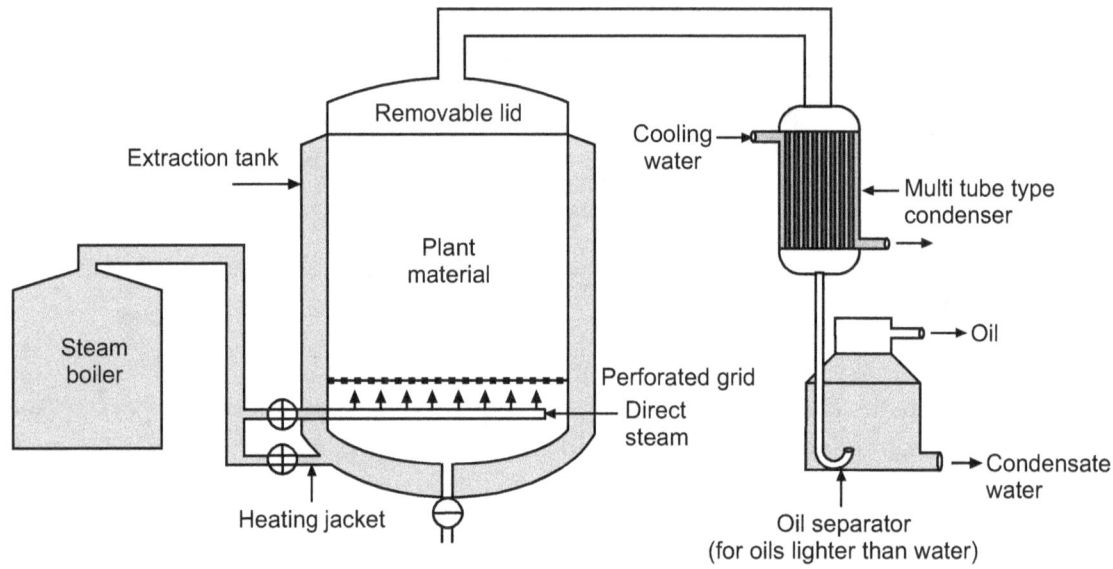

Fig. 2.3 : Direct steam distillation

Some volatile oils are obtained by mechanical means or by expression. The general method for citrus oil involves puncturing of oil glands by rolling the fruit over sharp projections. The projections penetrate oil glands located in outer portion of peel. This is known as Ecuelle method. After pressing a fine spray of water, washes mashed peels. This oil-water emulsion is then separated by centrifugation.

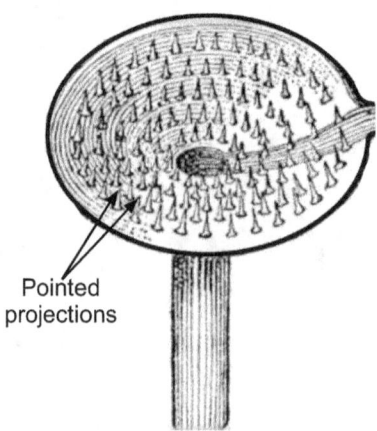

Fig. 2.4 : Ecuelle apparatus for isolation of volatile oil

The volatile oils obtained from flower petals employees enfleurage technique. In this method, odourless fixed oil or fat is spread in a thin layer on glass plates. The petals are spread on fat for few hours, then repeatedly old petals are replaced by fresh petals. After this, oil may be removed by extraction with alcohol.

There are two types of processes:

In **cold enfleurage**, a large framed plate of glass, called a chassis, is smeared with a layer of animal fat, usually lard or tallow (from pork or beef, respectively), and allowed to set. The petals or whole flowers, are then placed on the fat and their scent is allowed to diffuse into the fat over the course of 1-3 days. The process is then repeated by replacing old petals with fresh ones until the fat has reached a desired degree of fragrance saturation. This procedure was developed in southern France in the 18th century for the production of high-grade concentrates.

In **hot enfleurage**, solid fats are heated and petals are stirred into the fat and are replaced with fresh material until the fat is saturated with fragrance. This method is considered the oldest known procedure for preserving plant fragrance substances.

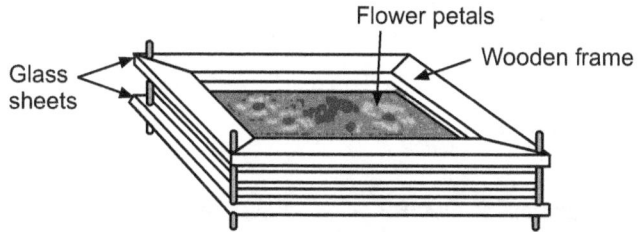

Flowers are spread on glass plate in wooden frame known as chassis

Fig. 2.5

In both instances, once the fat is saturated with fragrance, it is then called the "enfleurage pomade". The enfleurage pomade was either sold or it could be further washed or soaked in ethyl alcohol to draw the fragrant molecules into the alcohol. The alcohol is then separated from the fat and allowed to evaporate. The used fat is usually used to make soaps since it is still relatively fragrant.

In perfume industry, volatile oils are extracted by solvent extraction using petroleum ether or benzene. The extraction is generally carried out at temperature about 50°C so that natural odour is maintained. This is most important feature required in perfume industry, hence it is preferred method to obtain oil than distillation method.

Medicinal and commercial uses of volatile oil :

1) The volatile oil containing crude drugs are mostly used as spices and condiments like clove, cinnamon, caraway, coriander etc.

2) The volatile oil and crude drugs are also used for flavouring purpose e.g. cinnamon, clove, lemon.

3) Volatile oils possess carminative action (e.g. Dill), but few possess additional therapeutic significance, such as – they are administered as inhalations (e.g. eucalyptus oil, orally (e.g. peppermint oil), as gargles and mouth washes (e.g. thymol). Many essential oils are used in aromatherapy.

4) Volatile oils are used not only for perfumes and cosmetics, but also are essential for manufacture of soaps, toiletries and for masking odour to household cleaners, etc.

BIOGENESIS OF VOLATILE OIL CONSTITUENTS

The biogenetic pathway involves formation of terpenoid from mevalonic acid which is formed from acetyl Co-A. Geranyl pyrophosphate acts as key intermediate in biogenesis of most of terpenoids.

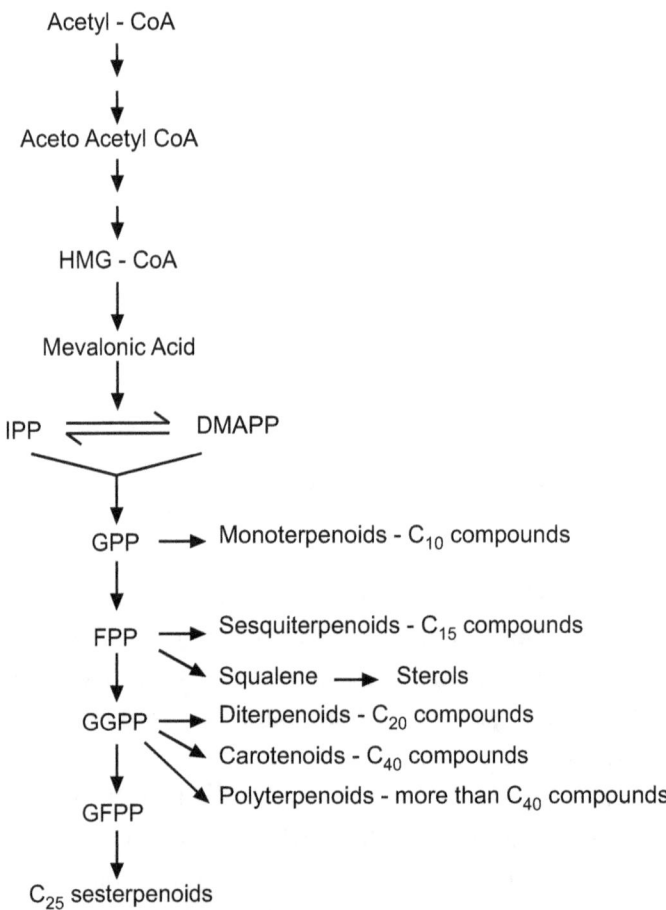

Fig. 2.6 : General biogenetic pathway for terpenoid compounds

Here, IPP   :   Isopentyl pyrophosphate

DMAPP :   Dimethyl allyl pyrophosphate

GPP   :   Geranyl pyrophosphate

FPP   :   Farnesyl pyrophosphate

GGPP :   Geranyl geranyl pyrophosphate

GFPP :   Geranyl farnesyl pyrophosphate

In certain volatile oils, the principal constituent is phenyl propanoid which is formed from aromatic amino acids like phenyl alanine and tyrosine via shikimic acid pathway.

BIOGENESIS OF PHENYLPROPANOID COMPOUNDS

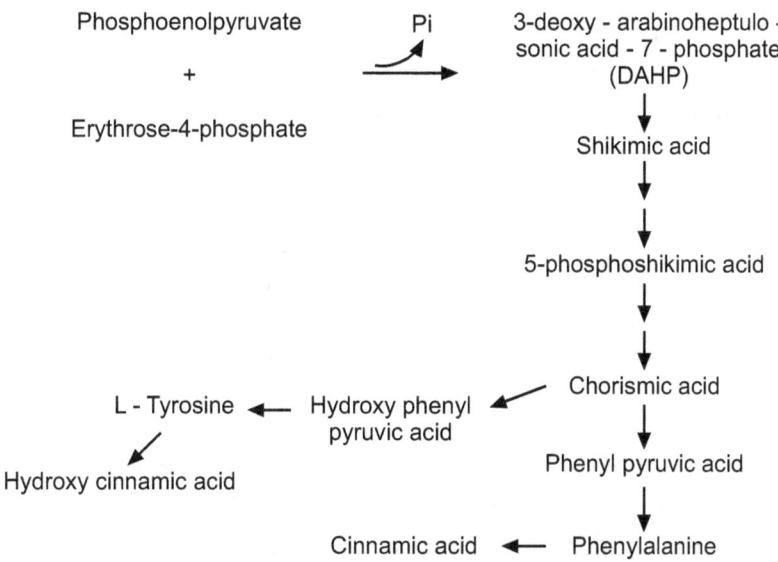

Fig. 2.7 : General bigenetic pathway for phenyl isopropanoid compounds

Determination of volatile oils as per WHO guidelines (Quality Control methods for herbal material)

To determine volume of oil present in plants, the plant material is distilled with water and the distillate is collected in graduated tube. The Clavenger's apparatus is used for distillation.

1) The determination is carried out by steam distillation.

2) The distillate is collected in a graduated tube, using xylène R or the solvent specified for the herbal material concerned, and then the aqueous phase is allowed to recirculate into the distillation flask.

Equipment

A suitable apparatus is made from resistant glass and has the following parts:

-    a round-bottomed, short-necked flask, capacity 500 or 1000 ml, the internal diameter of the ground-glass neck being 29 mm at the widest end;

-    a burner allowing fine control and fitted with a flue, or an electric heating device;

-    a vertical support with a horizontal ring covered with insulating material;

- the following sections fused into one piece (Fig. 2.8):
  - a vertical tube (AC), 210-260 mm long, with an external diameter of 13-15 mm;
  - a bent tube (CDE), CD and DE each being 145-155 mm long, and having an external diameter of 10 mm;
  - a bulb-condenser (FG), 145-155 mm long;
  - a tube (GH) 30-40 mm long, with a side-arm tube (HK), at an angle of 30-40°;
  - a vented ground-glass stopper (K') and a tube (K) with an internal diameter of 10 mm, the wide end being of ground glass;
  - a pear-shaped bulb (J) with a volume of 3 ml;
  - a tube with a volume of 1 ml (JL), graduated over 100-110 mm in divisions of 0.01 ml;

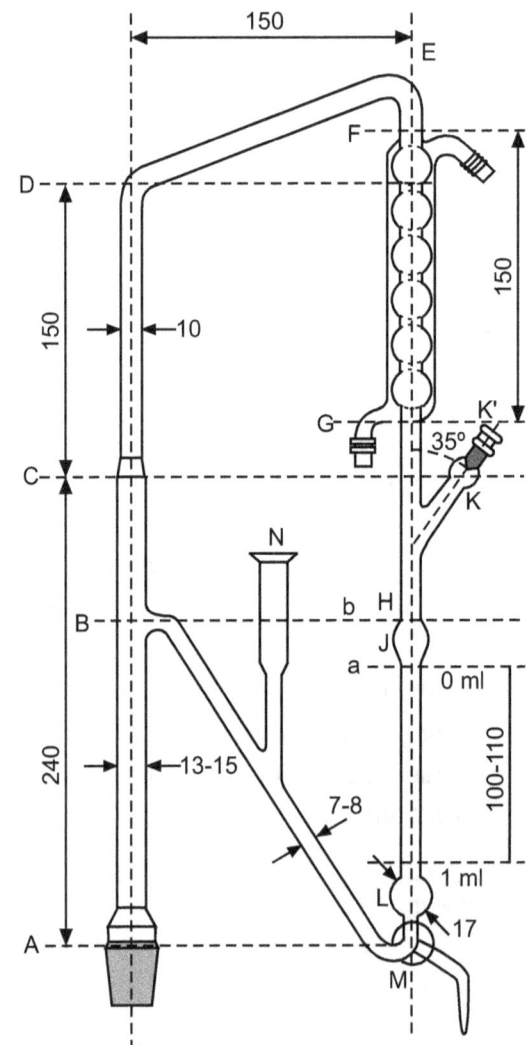

Fig. 2.8 : Apparatus used to determine volatile oils (dimensions in mm)

- a bulb-like swelling (L), with a volume of about 2 ml;
- a three-way tap (M);
- a connecting tube (BM), with an external diameter of 7-8 mm, which is fitted in the middle with a security tube (N); the junction (B) should be 20-25 mm higher than the uppermost graduation.

Before use, clean the apparatus thoroughly by successive washings, for example with acetone R or a suitable detergent, then rinse with water, drain and assemble in a suitable place.

Preparation of Sample

The preparation of the sample depends on the texture of the material and the location of the volatile oils.

Hard and compact herbal material (e.g. bark, roots or rhizomes), should be coarsely powdered; thick leaves should be finely cut; materials such as citrus peel are crushed under water.

Material consisting of thin floral parts or thin laminae or containing volatile oils in the epidermal glands should be distilled whole.

Method

Place the volume of distillation liquid specified in the test procedure for the herbal material concerned in the flask, add a few pieces of porous porcelain and join the condenser to the apparatus. Introduce water by tube N until it reaches level B. Remove stopper (K') and introduce the appropriate volume of xylene R or the solvent specified for the given herbal material, using a graduated pipette and placing its tip at the bottom of tube K. Replace stopper, heat the liquid in the flask until it begins to boil and adjust the distillation rate to 2-3 ml per minute, unless otherwise specified in the test procedure.

Introduce the specified quantity of the herbal material being examined into the flask and continue the distillation as described above for the time and at the rate given in the test procedure. After a further 10 minutes record the volume of oil collected in the graduated tube and subtract the volume of solvent (xylene) previously noted. The difference represents the volume of volatile oils in the sample of herbal material taken. Calculate the oil content in ml per 100 g of herbal material.

(A) LOWER TERPENOIDS (MONOTERPENOIDS)

CLOVE

Synonyms

Caryophyllum; Clove flower; Clove bud; Laung.

Biological Source

Cloves consist of dried flower buds of *Eugenia caryophyllus*, (Family : Myrtaceae). It should contain not less than 15 % (v/w) of clove oil.

Geographical Distribution

It is indigenous to Amboyna and Penang Molucca islands. It is now cultivated chiefly in Zanzibar, Pemba, Madagascar, West Indies, Sri Lanka and India. In India, cloves are grown in Nilgiri, Tenkasi-hills and in Kanyakumari district of Tamil Nadu state. It is also cultivated in Kottayam and Quilon districts of Kerala.

Cultivation and Collection

Deep rich loamy soil with high humus content is suitable for clove cultivation. It is also found growing favourably in open sandy loam and laterite soil of South Kerala region. Water logging of soil must be avoided. It needs warm humid climate and grows well in the vicinity of sea. The annual rainfall in the range of 150 to 250 cm is another requirement for cultivation of clove. Clove thrives best in the location ranging from sea level upto 900 m. It is propagated by seed germination. The seeds are sown from August to October. The seeds are placed in nursery beds at a distance of 10 cm. It takes from four to five weeks for seed germination. The seedlings of clove are slender and delicate, with poor growing rate. After nine months, they are transplanted to the pots where they are allowed to grow for a year. Thereafter, they are again transferred to the field and are provided with shade in initial stages of growth. Clove can also be grown with arecanut, coconut or nutmeg plants. The plants are provided with suitable fertilizers like ammonium sulphate, super phosphate and potash. Generally, fertilizers are given in two doses; first in May/June and second in October. The plant starts bearing after 7 to 8 years and satisfactory yield per hectare of drug is achieved only after 15 to 20 years of growth. Under normal conditions of soil, clove tree produces on an average, 3 kg of the drug. Cloves are handpicked or collected by beating with bamboos. This operation commences when cloves start changing their colour from green to slightly pink. When the tree is tall and cloves are beyond reach, platform ladders are used for collection. The cloves are dried in sun and freed from foreign material and graded. The cloves on drying become perfectly crimson or brownish-black in colour.

Organoleptic Characters (Fig. 2.9)

Colour : Crimson to dark brown.

Odour : Slightly aromatic.

Taste : Pungent and aromatic followed by numbness.

Size : About 10 to 17.5 mm in length, 4 mm in width, and 2 mm thick.

Shape : Hypanthium is surmounted with 4 thick acute divergent sepels surrounded by dome shaped corolla. The corolla consists of unexpanded membranous petals with several stamens and single stiff prominent style. Cloves are heavier than water.

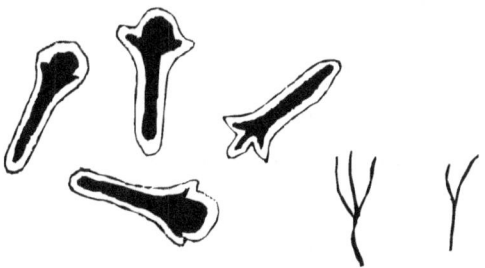

Fig. 2.9 : Cloves and Clove Stalks

Microscopic Characters (Fig. 2.10)

In the transverse section, clove hows the following characters. The epidermis of clove is covered with thick cuticle. The epidermis itself consists of straight walled cells and large

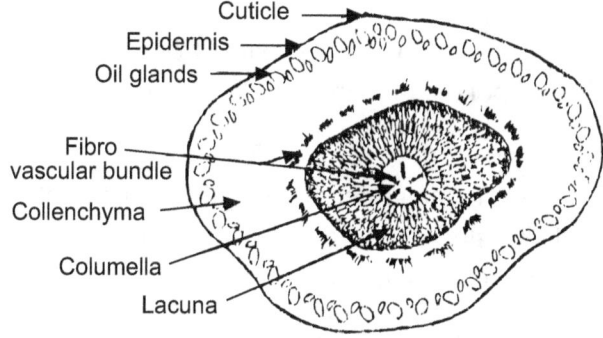

Fig. 2.10 : T.S. of Clove (Hypanthium)

anomocytic stomata. The oil glands, which are ovoid and schizolysigenous are found in all parts of the drug. Phloem fibres, which are isolated, are occasionally found in the spongy tissue. Cluster crystals of calcium oxalate and small number of stone cells are found in the drug. Clove does not contain starch.

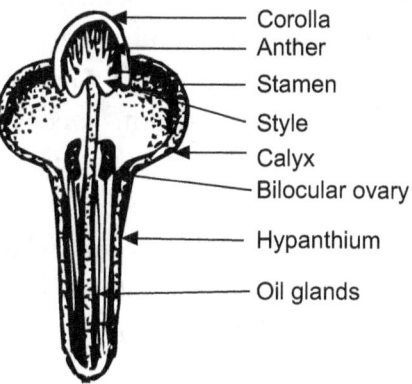

Fig. 2.11 : Vertical Section of Clove

Chemical Constituents

The drug contains about 15 to 20 % of volatile oil; 10 to 13 % of tannin (gallotannic acid), resin, chromone and eugenin. The volatile oil contains eugenol (about 70 to 90 %), eugenol acetate, methylamylketone, caryophyllenes and small quantities of esters and alcohols .

Eugenol

Chemical Test

If the transverse section of clove is treated with strong potassium hydroxide solution, the needle-shaped crystals of potassium eugenate are observed.

Uses

Clove is used as a dental analgesic, carminative, stimulant, flavouring agent, an aromatic and antiseptic. Exhausted cloves are used in preparation of cigarettes. The oil is used in perfumery and also in manufacture of vanillin.

Adulterants

1. **Mother cloves :** These are dark brown, ovate ripened fruits of clove tree. They are slightly aromatic and contain starch. They are very inferior in volatile oil content.

2. **Blown cloves :** These are expanded flowers of clove tree, wherein the stamens generally get detached. They also contain volatile oil and are similar in colour to cloves. The volatile oil content is less as compared to authentic drug.

3. **Clove stalks :** These are generally used to adulterate powdered clove and detected by presence of isodiametric sclereids and prisms of calcium oxalate. Their ash value and crude fibre content are also high. Genuine cloves should not contain more than 5 % of stalk to pass the pharmacopoeias limit. Due to similarity in colour, odour and taste, clove stalks are mixed with cloves. Clove stalks contain only 5 % of oil.

4. **Exhausted cloves :** These are the cloves from which oil has been removed by distillation. They are dark in colour, more shrunken and when pressed with finger nails, do not show presence of oil. Exhausted cloves float on water.

Storage

Clove and its powder should be stored in air-tight containers in cool and dry places.

CINNAMON

Synonyms

Cinnamon bark; Kalmi-Dalchini, Ceylon cinnamon.

Biological Source

Cinnamon consists of dried inner bark of shoots of coppiced trees of *Cinnamomum zeylanicum* Nees, belonging to family Lauraceae. It should not contain less than 1.0 % of volatile oil.

Geographical Distribution

Cinnamon, the evergreen tree of tropical area is considered to be native of Sri Lanka and Malabar coast of India. It is also found in Jamaica and Brazil. However, most of the world requirements are met by Sri Lanka and hence true cinnamon is known as Ceylon cinnamon.

Cultivation, Collection and Preparation for Market

Eventhough cinnamon can be propagated by planting the cuttings and layers; commercially, it is generally propagated by seed, as it is the easiest method to adopt. Cinnamon is a crop of tropical countries. It needs sandy or siliconous soil with an admixture of humus. The altitude at which it grows favourably is 800 to 1000 metres. Sheltered situation with an annual rainfall of 200 - 250 cm is ideal for cultivation of cinnamon. The seeds are sown in well prepared nursery bed located at suitable places in June and July. The seeds are sown at a distance of 10 cm and covered with small layer of soil and watered properly. It takes approximately 20 days to germinate the seeds. Seedlings are provided with the shades and are allowed to grow for about 10 - 12 months. Transplantation is done in October/November or in rainy season by keeping the distance of 2 metres in between two plants. Shades are provided with the pendals of coconut leaves. The field is weeded 2/4 times in a year. For healthy growth, each plant should be manured with 100 g each of ammonium sulphate and superphosphate in the first year. Subsequently, it is increased, depending upon the age of the plant. Fertilizers are applied in two equal doses, first in monsoon and second in October/November to encourage the growth of side shoots.

Trees are coppiced to induce formation of shoots. The trees are allowed to grow further unless they turn to uniform brown colour by formation of cork. Harvesting is done in rainy season when it is easy to peel off the bark from shoots. Longitudinal incisions are made on shoots and transverse markings are given so as to form rings at the nodes, which also connect longitudinal incisions producing the strips, which are then peeled off. Strips, thus formed, are made into bundles, wrapped in coir matting and allowed to ferment for

24 hours. Fermentation results in loosening of the outer cork and cortex, which is then removed by scrapping with curved brass knives. During drying, the bark contracts and gets converted into quill. The smaller quills are inserted into larger quills to form compound quills. Quills are arranged end to end, upto the length of 90 cm, when soft and fresh quills are rolled by hand and slightly pressed so as to avoid swelling and splitting into pieces. The drug is dried in shade over the mats. The quills are collected, packed into bundles of different grades and sold. Small pieces and debris produced during the handling of the quills are known as quislings and featherings. These are also used for manufacture of cinnamon oil.

One hectare plantation of cinnamon, on an average, produces 200 – 300 kg bark and 2 - 3 kg of cinnamon leaf oil per year.

Organoleptic Characters (Fig. 2.12)

Colour : The outer surface is dull yellowish-brown, while the inner surface is dark yellowish-brown.

Odour : Aromatic, sweet followed by warm sensation.

Taste : Found in the form of compound quills.

Size : About 1 m in length and 1 cm in diameter. The thickness of the bark is approximately 0.5 mm.

Fracture : Splintery.

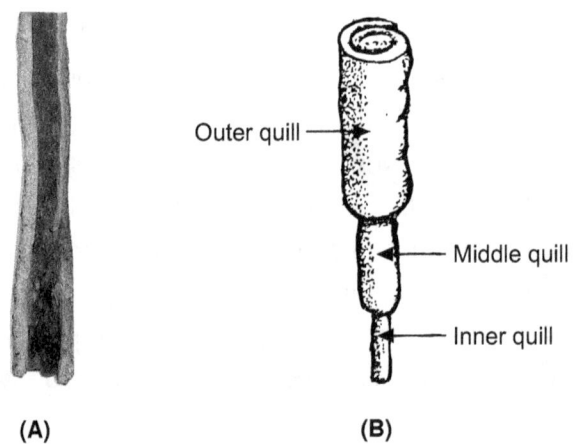

Outer quill

Middle quill

Inner quill

(A)   (B)

Fig. 2.12 : Cinnamon Bark A : Single quill, B : Compound *Quill*

Extra Features

The outer surface of the bark is marked with wavy longitudinal striations with small holes of scars left by the branches. The inner surface also shows the longitudinal striations. Bark is free of cork.

Microscopic Characters (Fig. 2.13)

Transverse section of cinnamon shows the following characteristics. Being an inner bark, the cork and primary cortex are absent. Rarely, patches of primary cortex may be present. Sclerenchymatous pericycle is prominent. The stelar part shows phloem, phloem fibres, biseriate medullary rays and secretory cavities containing volatile oil and mucilage. Starch grains in cortical parenchyma and medullary rays and calcium oxalate crystals in parenchymatous cells are also present.

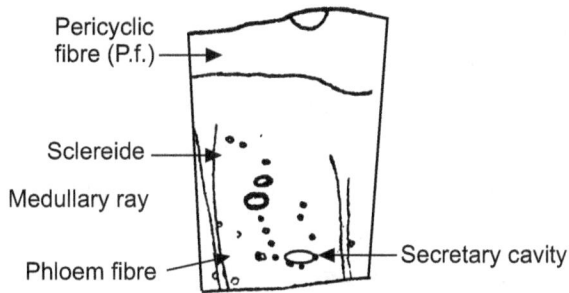

Fig. 2.13 : T. S. of Cinnamon Bark

Chemical Constituents

Cinnamon bark contains about 0.5 to 1.0% of volatile oil, 1.2% of tannins (phlobatannins), mucilage, calcium oxalate, starch and a sweet substance known as mannitol.

Bark yields 14 -16% of 90% alcohol-soluble extractives.

The volatile oil is the active constituent of the drug. It is light yellow (when freshly distilled) in colour and changes to red on storage.

Cinnamon oil contains 60 - 70% cinnamaldehyde, 5 - 10% eugenol, benzaldehyde, cuminaldehyde and other terpenes like phellandrene, pinene, cymene, caryophyllane etc.

Cinnamic aldehyde   Eugenol

Chemical Test

On addition of a drop of ferric chloride solution to a drop of volatile oil, a pale green colour is produced. With ferric chloride, cinnamic aldehyde gives brown colour and eugenol gives blue colour, resulting in formation of pale green colour.

In cassia oil, brown colour is obtained, as it contains only cinnamic aldehyde .

Uses

Bark is used as a carminative, stomachic and mild astringent. It is also used as a flavouring agent, stimulant, an aromatic and antiseptic. Commercially, it is used as a spice and condiment, and also in the preparation of candy, dentifrices and perfumes.

Substitutes and Adulterants

Jungle cinnamon : It is the bark obtained from wild growing trees, which is dark in colour, less aromatic than the cultivated trees, and slightly bitter.

Cinnamon chips : These are pieces of untrimmed bark. They can be distinguished from genuine drug by presence of abundant cork cells and by poor yield to 90 % alcohol.

Saigon cinnamon : It consists of bark of the trees of *Cinnamomum loureirii* (Family : Lauraceae). It is exported from the port of Saigon. It is also grown in China and Japan. The bark is greyish-brown in colour with light patches and sweet taste. Quills are 30 x 0.7 cm, unpeeled and contain 2.5 % of volatile oil.

Java cinnamon : It is derived from *Cinnamomum burmanii* (Family : Lauraceae). Bark is less aromatic, peeled and found in the form of double quills. Histologically, medullary rays contain small tubular crystals of calcium oxalate, not found in *C. zeylanicum*. It contains about 75 % of cinnamaldehyde in the oil. It also gives poor yield to 90 % alcohol as compared to Ceylon cinnamon.

CORIANDER

Synonym

Coriander fruits

Biological Source

These are fully dried ripe fruits of the plant known as *Coriandrum sativum* Linn. (Family : Umbelliferae). The fruits should contain not less than 0.3 % of the volatile oil.

Geographical Distribution

The plants are cultivated throughout European countries, principally in Russia, Hungary and Holland. The drug is also cultivated in India, Egypt and Morocco. In India, it is widely grown in Andhra Pradesh (Guntur, Anantpur), Maharashtra (Jalgaon and Satara), West Bengal (Howrah and 24 - Pargana), Uttar Pradesh and Jammu and Kashmir.

Cultivation and Collection

Coriander is grown as kharif, as well as, rabi crop. It needs light to heavy black soil. About 15 to 20 kg of fruits per hectare are required for cultivation. It is sown by drilling method. It is rotated with wheat, grain, jowar and onion and also grown with cotton, sugarcane and brinjal as mixed crop. The crop is ready for harvesting after 100 days of growth. J - 16, J - 214, K - 45 and New Pusa are few of the improved varieties of coriander. About 2 lakh hectares of land in India is under cultivation of coriander.

Oganoleptic Characters [Fig. 2.14 (a)]

Colour   :   Yellowish-brown to brown.

Odour   :   Aromatic.

Taste   :   Spicy and characteristic.

Size   :   Fruits are 2 to 4 mm in diameter and 4 - 8 mm in length.

Shape   :   Coriander is a sub-globular cremocarpous fruit with about 10 primary ridges and 8 secondary ridges.

Primary ridges are wavy and inconspicuous, while secondary ridges are straight. It is further described as an endospermic and coelospermic. The weight of 100 fruits is approximately 1 g.

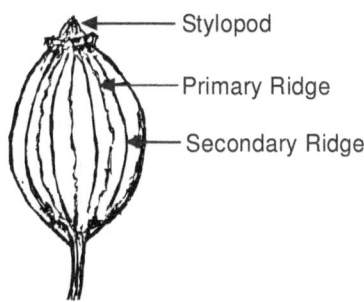

Fig. 2.14 (a) : Coriander Fruit

Microscopic Characters [Fig. 2.14 (b)]

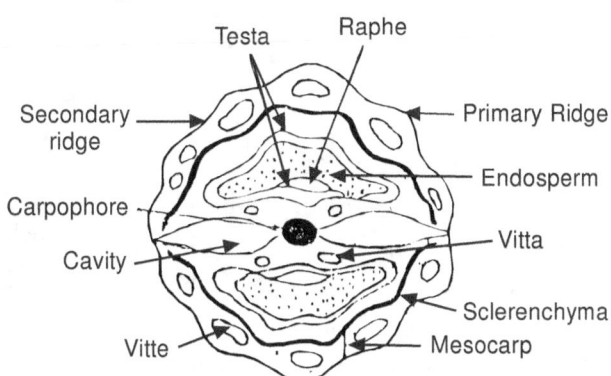

Fig. 2.14 (b) : T.S. of Coriander Fruit (Cremocarp)

The epidermis of the pericarp is made up polygonal tabular cells with stomata, several epidermal cells contain prism of calcium oxalate. Mesocarp consists of inner and outer layer of parenchyma with a layer of sclerenchyma in between them. Inner epidermis of pericarp consists of parquetry cells. The seed is characteristic to umbelliferous fruits. Trichomes and lignified reticulate parenchyma absent. No starch grains are present. Fixed oil globules in the endosperm. Volatile oil in the vittae. Aleurone grains are present in polygonal thick walled cellulose parenchyma of endosperm.

Chemical Constituents

Coriander yields from 0.3 to 1 % of volatile oil. The fixed oil (13 %) and proteins (20 %) are other contents of the drug. Volatile oil contains 90 % of D-linalool (coriandrol), and small quantities of L-borneol, geraniol and pinene. Coriander leaves are rich in vitamin A content.

Coriandrol

Uses

The fruits, as well as, volatile oil are used as an aromatic, carminative, stimulant and flavouring agent. Coriander oil is used alongwith purgative to prevent gripping. It is an ingredient of compound spirit of orange and cascara elixir.

Substitutes

It is substituted by Bombay coriander fruits, which contain less volatile oil and are ellipsoidal in shape.

LAVENDER OIL

Synonym

Comman Lavendor.

Biological Source

It is the volatile oil obtained by steam distillation of fresh flowering tops of *Lavandula officinalis* Chaix (L. Vera D.C.), family Labiatae.

This plant is also known as true lavender or common lavender. It is indigenous to mountainous or hilly regions of Europe and is supposed to be the most superior in all varieties of lavender. The other variety known as *Lavandula stoechas* is also used for the isolation of oil. In commerce, it is known as French lavender.

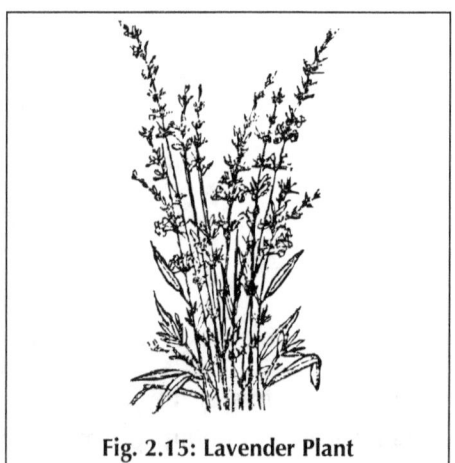

Fig. 2.15: Lavender Plant
(*Lavandula officinalis* Chaix)

Geographical Source

It is found in Portugal and eastwards throughout the Mediterranean region. Lavender is cultivated to some extent in India.

Description

Colour   :   Colourless or yellow liquid.

Odour   :   Characteristic pleasant aroma.

Solubility   :   Slightly soluble in water, soluble in 4 volumes of 70 per cent alcohol, carbon disulphide.

Chemical Constituents

The oil contains about 30 - 40 per cent esters, calculated as linalyl acetate and also linalool, pinene, geraniol and cineol.

Uses

It is used as aromatic, carminative and as flavouring agent in perfumery and cosmetics.

SANDAL WOOD

Synonyms

Yellow sandal wood, *Lignum santali.*

Biological Source

It is the dried heartwood of *Santalum album* Linn., belonging to family Santalaceae.

Geographical Distribution

The plants (Fig. 2.16) are found in India and Malaysia. Sandalwood tree is an evergreen plant of 10 - 12 m height found widely distributed in India.

Fig. 2.16 : Sandal Wood Plant

The systematic cultivation of these parasitic plants is undertaken mainly in South Indian states of Karnataka and Tamil Nadu. The leaves and other parts of the tree are free of volatile oil. The plant bears very beautiful flowers and fruits. Trees more than 30 years of age are normally selected for the collection of the oil. All parts of the wood contain volatile oil.

The fully grown plants are uprooted and the bark from roots and stems is removed alongwith little sap wood. The wood is yellowish or pale red in colour. It is very much dense, hard, heavy and splits easily. The wood surface shows darker and lighter zones. It is cut in small pieces and subjected to steam distillation. It contains about 2.5 % oil.

Organoleptic Characters

Colour : Yellowish or pale reddish.

Odour : Strong and fragrant.

Taste   : Slightly bitter.

Chemical Constituents

The main product of sandal wood is the volatile oil (2.5 %) called sandal wood oil. All the wood elements of this drug contain oil. Sandal wood oil contains about 95 % of two isomeric sesquiterpene alcohols, α–santalol (b.p. 300 - 301°C) and β - santalol (b.p. 170 - 171°C). The oil also contains an aldehyde santalal $C_{15}H_{22}O$, santene, santenone, teresantol.

Uses

It is used as a source of sandal wood oil. The oil is used for symptomatic treatment of dysurea and in diminishing the frequency of micturition marked in the tuberculosis of the bladder. The oil is mainly used as a perfume in cosmetics and incense sticks. The wood is utilised for other purposes like carvings and manufacture of boxes.

Sandal wood oil

It is pale yellow colourless viscid liquid unpleasant in taste and with characteristic persistant flavour. It is soluble in alcohol and chloroform, while insoluble in water. Sandal wood oil has following standards.

Specific gravity   :   0.973 to 0.985

Optical rotation   :   – 15 to – 20°

Refractive index   :   1.500 to 1.510

Esters   :   Not less than 2.0% as santolyl acetate.

Alcohols   :   Not less than 90% as santalol.

Constituents

Oil mainly contains 95% of two isomeric alcohols α and β santalol and in addition it also contains santalol, sentene, santanone, teresantol, santalone and santalene.

Uses

As perfume in cosmetics and in incense sticks.

ARTEMISIA

Synonyms

Santonica; Worm seeds.

Biological Source

These are the unexpanded flower-heads of *Artemisia cina Berg*, *Artemisia brevifolia Wall*, *Artemisia maritima* Linn. and other species of Artemisia, belonging to family Asteraceae. It is collected late in spring or early in summer when the flower-heads are young. It should contain not more than 2 per cent of stems, and not less than 0.75 per cent of santonin.

Geographical Source

It is found growing wild in the Kurran valley in Pakistan, Turkey and from Kashmir to Kumaon in Himalayas, as well as, in West Tibet, upto an altitude of 4000 metres. It is also found in Punjab, Uttar Pradesh and Haryana.

Organoleptic Characters

Colour : Flowers are yellow in colour, while other parts are whitish-grey.

Odour : Aromatic and sweet.

Taste : Bitter and camphoraceous.

The drug consists of yellowish or brownish flower-heads, which are oval in shape. Flowers are fertile with tubular corolla and short cylindrical tube and narrow limb. Calyx is absent.

Fig. 2.17 : Artemisia cina herb

Chemical Constituents

Santonica contains essential oil and two crystalline substances i.e. santonin and artemisin. The volatile oil content varies from 1.0 - 2 per cent, while the percentage of santonin is about 2.0 per cent. The volatile oil contains cineole, pinene and resin. The chief active constituent of the drug is santonin. Santonin is a sesquiterpene lactone which is anhydride of santonic acid. The amount of santonin present varies considerably depending upon the type of species and time and nature of collection. If the flower-heads are unexpanded and quickly dried, they yield over 3.0 per cent of santonin.

Artemisin   **Santonin**

Identification

Boil 1g finely powdered drug with 10 ml alcohol and filter. To the filtrate, add sodium hydroxide and heat again. The liquid develops red colour.

Uses

Santonica is used as a strong anthelmintic, especially for round worms. It has less or no effect on hook worms and tape worms. The crude drug, at present, is rarely used in therapeutic and has been totally replaced by santonin. Santonin is found to create remarkable disturbances of vision. Santonin is cumulative in action. The B.P. variety of the drug is obtained from *Artemisia cina*.

Substitutes

Artemisia is substituted by a tall aromatic shrub, known as *Artemisia vulgaris* Linn. (Compositae) found in all mountaneous districts of India. It is found at Mount Abu in Rajasthan, in Konkan, Uttar Pradesh, Tamil Nadu and Jammu and Kashmir in Himalayas, up to an altitude of 4000 metres. It occurs in Sikkim and Sri Lanka too.

(B) DITERPENOIDS

Diterpenes or diterpenoid are C_{20} compounds, derived from four isoprene units, and in contrast to mono or sesquiterpenes, are non-volatile in nature. These C_{20} natural compounds are biosynthetically prepared from geranyl pyrophosphate. They are present both in plants and animals of terrestrial or marine origin. The plant families rich in diterpenoids are Pinaceae, Podosocarpaceae and Taxodiaceae (all conifer resins); Leguminosae, Cistaceae and Burseraceae (all angiosperm resins). The other families containing appreciable quantities of diterpenes are Labiatae, Ranunculaceae and Euphorbiaceae. They have also been found in marine animals (Coelentrates) like soft corals and sea fans. Different parts of the same plant may contain different diterpenes; and percentage of diterpenes varies alongwith seasons.

Most of the diterpenes appear to be stress compounds, produced as a response to environmental stress. They are also considered as defence chemicals prepared against parasites and mechanical injury. Apart from these activities, certain diterpenes have specific roles. Gibberellins are plant growth regulators, phytol is an important part of chlorophyll with crucial role in photosynthetic process while retinol having essential role in mammalian visual function. Besides their active biological role in plants and animals, many diterpenes have important pharmacological activities.

COLEUS

Synonym

Forskohlii

Biological Source

It consists of roots of *Coleus forskohlii*, Syn. *Plectranthus barbalus* belonging to family *Labiatae* (Lamiaceae), and should contain not less than 0.4 per cent of forskolin on dried basis.

Geographical Source

The plant grows perennially over the tropical and subtropical regions including India, Pakistan, Sri Lanka, Brazil and Tropical East Asia. In India, it occurs at high altitudes upto the height of 2500 metres in Himalayas, in the regions from Garhwal, Kumaon to Nepal. It also occurs in Deccan Peninsula and Parasnath hills in Bihar. It is common on dry and barren hills.

Cultivation and Collection

About 2500 tonnes of leaves and roots are harvested every year from commercial cultivation in Gujarat and Kanchipuram district of Tamil Nadu.

It is propagated by using stem cuttings in spring. All types of soils are suitable for cultivation. Coleus is harvested in autumn. Irrigation once in ten days is enough. It is highly disease resistant crop. It is a crop of 6-7 months duration. It fetches the value of ₹ 1.5 lakh per tonne. Yield per hectare is about 1 to 1.5 tonnes.

Traditionally, it has been used in India for pickles and for this purpose it is cultivated to some extent.

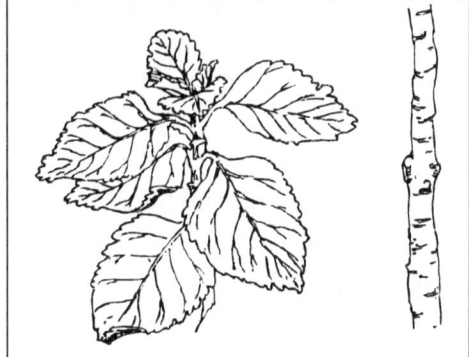

Fig. 2.18 : Coleus forskohlii twig and root

Organoleptic Characters

It is a branched, aromatic perennial herb 1 - 2 feet in height, leaves have camphor-like flavour with several, fasciculated, succulent, radially spread roots.

Chemical Constituents

It contains the diterpene Forskolin about 0.6 % (coleonol) was discovered at the Hoechst Research Centre, Mumbai, India and Central Drug Research Institute (CDRI), Lucknow, India. It also contains various diterpenoid derivatives. The leaves give coleon E (methylenequinone), barbatusin and coleon F. The roots contain coleonol B, coleonol C, deoxycoleonol and labdane diterpenoids (I, II and III).

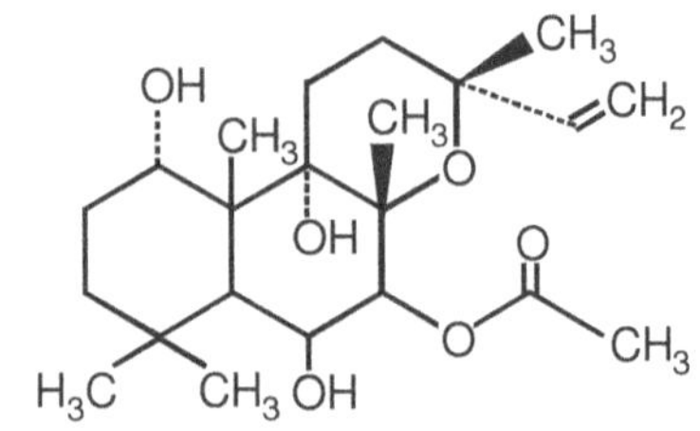

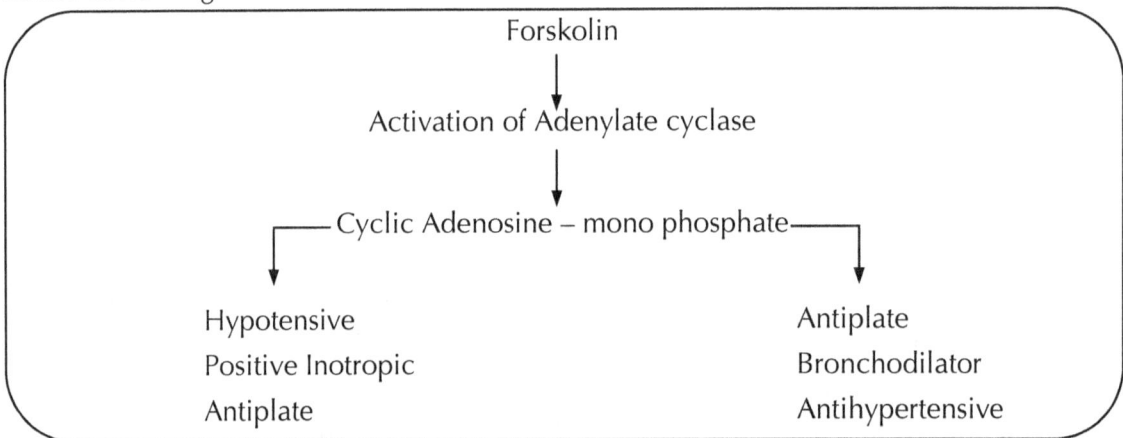

Forskolin

Uses

Forskolin has vasodilator and cardio stimulant effects. Major biological effects of forskolin include activation of adenylate cyclase, positive inotropic action, blood pressure lowering, and decreasing intra-occular pressure. Forskolin inhibits human platelet aggregation induced by epinephrine or collagen. It reduces intra occular pressure and hence useful in glaucoma.

Forskolin
↓
Activation of Adenylate cyclase
↓
Cyclic Adenosine – mono phosphate

Hypotensive
Positive Inotropic
Antiplate

Antiplate
Bronchodilator
Antihypertensive

TAXUS

Synonyms

Yew, Talispatra, Himalayan yew, Birmi.

Biological Source

This consists of dried leaves, bark and roots of various species of *Taxus*, belonging to family Taxaceae. The four important species with parts used are as under.

1. *Taxus baccata* (English or European yew) mainly leaves.
2. *Taxus brevifolia* (Pacific yew) mainly stem bark.
3. *Taxus Canadensis* (Canadian or American yew) Leaves and roots.
4. *Taxus cuspidate* (Japanese yew) leaves.

5. *Taxux wallichiana* :

It contains not less than 0.04 percent of Paclitaxel (Taxol) culculated on dried basis.

Fig. 2.19 (a) : Yew tree and bark   Fig. 2.19 (b) : Twig of Yew tree

Geographical Source

It is very slow growing evergreen gymnospermous tree. Found in India, Canada and America. It is reported in temperate Himalayan region of India upto an altitude of 2000 – 3500 meters.

Organoleptic Characters

Leaves

Colour	: Dark green
Taste	: Bitter
Size	: 1 - 3 cm × 1 - 2 cm
Shape	: Lanceolate, flat

Leaves are arranged spirally on the stem, leaf bases are twisted to align the leaves in two flat raws on either side of stem except on erect leading shoots.

Bark   : Thin and scaly brown

Seed cones : Each contains one seed which is 4 - 7 mm surrounded by aril, Arils get matured after 6 - 9 months.

Standards

Alcohol soluble extractives	:	not less than 11.0%
Water soluble extractive	:	not less than 17.0%
Total ash	:	not more than 4.0%
Acid insoluble ash	:	not more than 0.7%
Loss on drying	:	not more than 7.0 % at 105°C

Chemical Constituents

The main constituent paclitaxel or taxol is present in all parts of the plant especially in leaves, roots and bark.

Taxanes are the most important group of chemical constituents and uptil now 40 different Taxane compounds have been found, all of which are diterpenoid structures. Among them three most important members are Taxol, cephalomannine and 10 - deacetyl baccatin. In all species, with little variations, taxol occurs from 0.007 % to 0.01 %. Presently, it is mainly obtained from stem bark of *T. brevifolia*. But the method of isolation is tedious and like vinca, yields are also less. It needs at least 60 years old 3 - 4 trees to get 1 gm of taxol. Yields 50-150 mg of taxol are obtained from 1 kg dried yew bark. About 10 kg bark is available from an average tree. Considering the slow growing nature of yew tree, it has been already predicted that this will lead to severe ecological problem. Obviously alternative sources, like total synthesis or biotechnological route through tissue culture are also presently under development. It has been reported that leaves contain 10-deacetyl baccatin III, which can be comparatively easily converted to Taxol. The leaves can be quickly regenerated after harvesting. Among the various yew species, most of the compounds are anticancer. The most potent compounds include Taxol (containing a rare oxetane ring and amide side chain), cephalo mannine (0.031 per cent), baccatin – III (0.084 per cent), and 10 - deacetyl baccatin III.

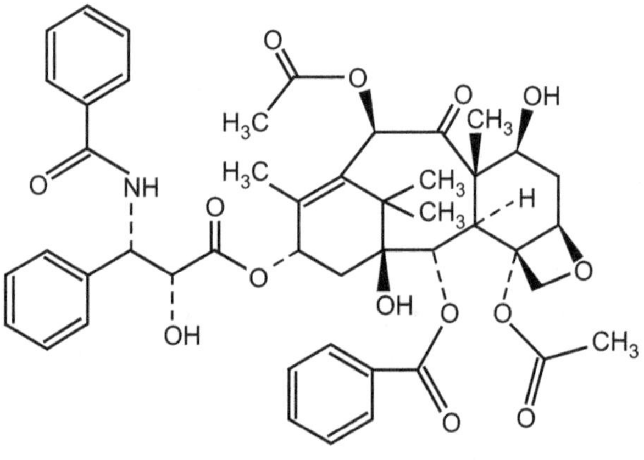

Paclitaxel (Taxol)

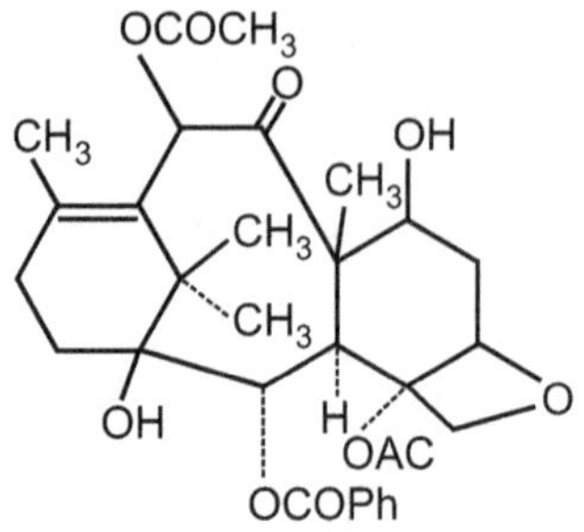

10-Deacetyl baccatin III

A derivative of Taxol, called taxotere has been reported to have better bio-availability and pharmacological properties and has been claimed as a promising anticancer agent.

Uses

Used as anticancer, analgesic, anti inflammatory, antipyretic and anti convulgant. The biological target of Taxol is microtubules produced from α and β-tubulin. The microtubules are responsible for the formation of mitotic spindle necessary for cell division. α and β-tubulin polymerise to give microtubules and for this process microtubule associated proteins (MAP) and guanosine triphosphate (GTP) are necessary. Taxol brings out the polymerisation to microtubules in absence of MAP and GTP. Due to this, microtubule formation is much enhanced which causes detrimental effects on dividing cells which leads to blockade of cell cycle. Eventually, multiple abnormal esters are formed from microtubules and get distributed in cytoplasm. These structures are non-functional. Taxol also inhibits cell migration thus, preventing spread of metastatic cancer cells. Taxol has been approved by USFDA for treatment of refractory ovarian cancer. It has also a promising role against non-small cell lung carcinoma, gastric and cervical cancers and also carcinomas of head, neck, prostate and colon.

(C) TRITERPENOIDS

Among various terpenoid groups, this is the largest one. Triterpenoids are widely distributed in plant kingdom but few in animals. They are present in either free state or as esters or glycosides. Biosynthetically, triterpenoids are C_{30} compounds prepared from six isoprene units. They are further classified as: (i) Tetracyclic triterpenoids and (ii) Pentacyclic triterpenoids.

Steroids are degraded triterpenes.

Triterpenes are very commonly present in most of the dicotyledonous plants. The plant families producing appreciable quantity of triterpenoids are cucurbitaceae, Caryophyllaceae, Leguminosae, Apocynaceae etc. Azadirachtin from *Azadirachta indica* is a prominent triterpenoid from plant kingdom. They are also present in marine sources like squalene, ambrein and lanosterol from shark, ambergris and wool fat respectively.

They are mostly stress compounds (phytoalexins) produced by the plants as a response to environmental stress and ecological interaction.

GINSENG

Synonyms

Ninjin, Pannag, Panax.

Biological Source

Ginseng is the dried root of various species of *Panax*, like *P. ginseng* (Korean ginseng), *P. japonica* (Japanese ginseng), *P. notoginseng* (Chinese ginseng) and *P. quinquefolium*

(American ginseng), belonging to family Araliaceae. It contains not less than 0.4% of Ginesenosides calculated on dried baris.

Geographical Source

It grows widely in Korea, China and Russia. Presently, ginseng is commercially cultivated in Korea, China, Japan, Russia, Canada and United States of America. In India at present it is cultivated in Kohima, Tunsang district of Nagaland. It is also available in Arunachal area.

Like some of the well known ayurvedic medicines, ginseng has generated large interest because of its novel pharmacological actions. An international symposium was arranged at Lugano in 1975 to discuss the analytical, pharmacological and clinical aspects of ginseng, which was sponsored by World Health Organisation.

The term *Panax* indicates curve all (*Pan and axos*), while *ginseng* is derived from Chinese words *shen sang*, which stands for manroot, because the shape of the root resembles the human body. The references about ginseng are found in ancient Chinese literature, stating its medicinal properties. Now-a-days, ginseng is considered as adaptogen. It increases non-specific resistance and defence mechanism of the body.

Cultivation and Collection

The cultivation technology adopted in Korea is briefly described.

Ginseng is propagated by means of seeds in nursery beds and then transplanted into open fields i.e. permanent beds. The ripe seeds are collected from four year old plants. They are sown in November in nursery beds. There are 3 types of nursery beds viz. Yang-Jik, To-Jik and Ban-Yang-Jik. The first type gives high quality seedlings. After attaining sufficient growth, the seedlings are dug up in the following May and transplanted to permanent beds for next 3 - 5 years. Ginseng requires clay loam or sandy loam soil. It grows at altitudes from 100 - 800 metres. The soil with high amount of potassium gives better results. About 10 - 15 seedlings are planted in one square metre. About 7 -10 days after transplantation, shades are provided to plants to protect them from excessive sunlight. Generally, use of fertilizers is avoided, but before transplantation, the soil is mixed with large amount of green grass. Periodically, weeding is done. The plants are harvested 3 - 5 years after transplantation. Generally, they are harvested between July to October. White ginseng is obtained by removing the outer layers of the roots. Red ginseng is obtained by first steaming the roots and after that they are dried. But, removal of outer layers may lead to loss of active constituents.

Organoleptic Characters (Fig. 2.20)

Ginseng roots are tuberous corpulent roots. They are yellowish brown, white or red in colour depending on type. They are translucent and possess the stem scars.

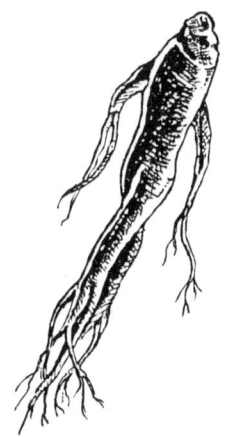

Fig. 2.20 : Ginseng root

Chemical Constituents

Ginseng contains a mixture of several saponin glycosides, belonging to triterpenoid group. They are grouped as follows:

(1) Ginsenosides;

(2) Panaxosides; and

(3) Chikusetsusaponin

Ginsenosides contain aglycone dammarol, while panaxosides have oleanolic acid as aglycone. About 13 ginsenosides have been identified. Panaxosides give oleanolic acid, panaxadiol and panaxatriol on decomposition.

Oleanolic acid	*Panaxadiol*	**Panaxatriol**

Glycosides of Ginseng

Standards

Foreign organic matter	not more than 2.0 %
Total ash	not more than 7.0 %
Acid insoluble ash	not more than 1.0 %

Sulfated ash	not more than 12.0 %
Alcohol soluble extractive	not less than 22.0 %
Water soluble extractive	not less than 27.0 %
Loss of drying	not less than 10.0 % at 105°C with 1.0 gm drug

Uses

Ginseng is an important immunomodulatory drug. It shows a wide range of activities. It increases the natural resistance (non-specific resistance) and enhances the power to overcome the illness or exhaustion. It has both stimulant and sedative properties. It is used as aphrodisiac. It is believed to be useful in adrenal and thyroid dysfunctioning. In old days, ginseng was used for a number of ailments, like curing the giddiness and prolonging life of elderly and diabetic persons. It is given as demulcent and in gastritis and anaemia.

Although, ginseng shows a low toxicity, long term use leads to poisoning, similar to that of corticosteroids.

Ginseng extracts are also used externally in cosmetics.

(D) TETRATERPENOIDS

They are C_{40} compounds of terpenoids groups and biosynthetically prepared by tail-to-tail condensation of geranyl geraniol. They contain long sequence of conjugated double bonds.

ANNATTO

Synonyms

Arnotta, Annotta, Lipstic pods.

Biological Source

This consists of dried seeds of the plant *Bixa orellana* L. family Bixaceae.

Geographical Source

The plant is cultivated in Peru, Jamaica, Mexico, Kenya, India, Brazil. About 40% of the world requirement is met by Peru while India contributes only 10%.

Organoleptic Characters

Colour	:	Seeds are brick-red
Odour	:	Slightly sweet and peppery
Taste	:	Hotness scale 1 to 2
Size	:	3 to 5 mm
Shape	:	Triangular

Cultivation and Collection

It is sown from the seeds or from cuttings. It needs tropical setting in a loamy soil at an altitude of 1000 meters. Plant stands alone as profusely fruiting shrub. It is about 2 to 6 meters in height and servives for 50 years. Plant bears pointed leaves and pinkish white flowers. It bears prickly heart shaped pods. Each pod bears about 50 seeds.

Preparation for the Market

Bixa is commercially grown for dye and also for the seeds which are used as spice.

Fully matured prickly pods are collected and dried. The fruits are then macerated in water for a while. The dye settles, is collected and dried, made into cakes.

The seeds from pulp are separated and washed thoroughly for further processing and use.

Chemical Constituents

Annatto seeds are covered with aril and contain bixin dye. Annatto seeds are found to contain about 12 % of annatto oleo resin of which 50 % is water soluble. Volalile oil covers only 0.3 - 0.8 %, while pigment covers 4 - 5 %.

The main constituent of the pigment is known as Bixin which constitutes about 70 - 80 % of pigment. Bixin is a carotenoid carboxylic acid and is responsible for yellow colour. Isobixin, trans-bixin, nor-bixin are the other isomers of it. Bixin is naturally present in *cis form and gets* converted to *trans-bixin* during extraction. Bixin, in pure form, is insoluble in water but, soluble in organic solvents and alkaline aqueous solutions. Oil soluble annatto is available in the market for commercial use.

Bixin

Bixin is a monomethyl ester of nor-bixin (a dicarboxylic acid) and gets readily hydrolysed to dicarboxylic acid by alkali during extraction. Annatto extracts are the potassium salts of nor-bixin.

When compared to β-carotene in the tinctorial strength, bixin is quite stable. However, it looses its tinctorial strength on storage. Light and heat has adverse effect on its tinctorial power. Annatto is most stable at pH 8.

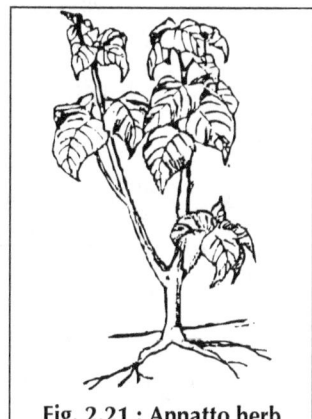

Fig. 2.21 : Annatto herb

Uses

Bixin is antioxidant and protects against ultra violet light. It also has liver protective properties.

Annatto is used as colouring agent for foods, cosmetics, alcoholic and non-alcoholic beverages, dairy desserts, fats and oils and in margarine.

SAFFRON

Synonyms

Hay saffron, Kesar, Crocus.

Biological Source

Crocus consists of dried stigmas and upper parts of styles of plant known as *Crocus sativus* Linn, family Iridaceae.

Geographical Source

It is cultivated in India (Kashmir), Spain, France and Greece.

Cultivation and Collection

The plants are raised from corms planted during July/August. The flowering takes about one year. Flowers are collected in early morning in November and December, stigmas and upper style portions are detached manually, and the drug is dried by artificial heat. It is stored in dry place.

India's share in global supply is 50 tones and is about 10 % of world requirement. Approximately, 5000 hectares of land is under cultivation in Kashmir and Himachal Pradesh.

Organoleptic Characters (Fig. 2.22)

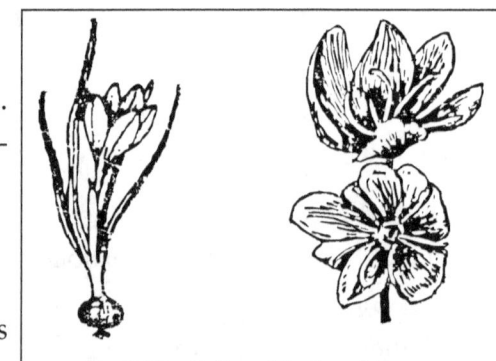

Fig. 2.22 : Saffron Plant and Flower

Colour : Stigma dark red to reddish-brown. Style, yellowish-brown to yellowish-orange.

Odour : Strong, characteristic and aromatic.

Taste : Characteristic and bitter.

Size : Stigmas are 25 mm long, and styles about 10 mm long.

Shape : Stigma trifid and styles cylindrical.

Stigmas may be attached to the apex of styles or may be separated. About 12000 flowers weigh 100 g.

Chemical Constituents

Saffron contains red colouring matter known as Crocin and crocetin, bitter principle picrocrocin and traces of volatile oil. Protocrocin, a carotenoid glycoside splits during drying into two molecules of picrocrocin and one molecule of crocin. Crocin further hydrolyses to crocetin and gentiobiose while picrocrocin yields glucose and safranal. It yields about 50 to 60 % of extractives to cold water. It also contains non-reducing substances and crystalline hydrocarbon. The crocins are responsible for the blue colour when treated with concentrated sulphuric acid.

Chemical Tests

1. Add a drop of sulphuric acid to dry stigma. It turns blue, gradually changing to purple and finally purplish-red.

2. Saffron imparts yellowish orange brown colour to water.

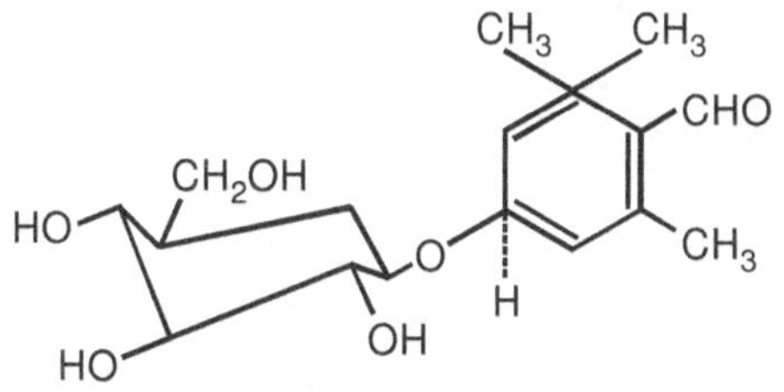

Picrocrocin

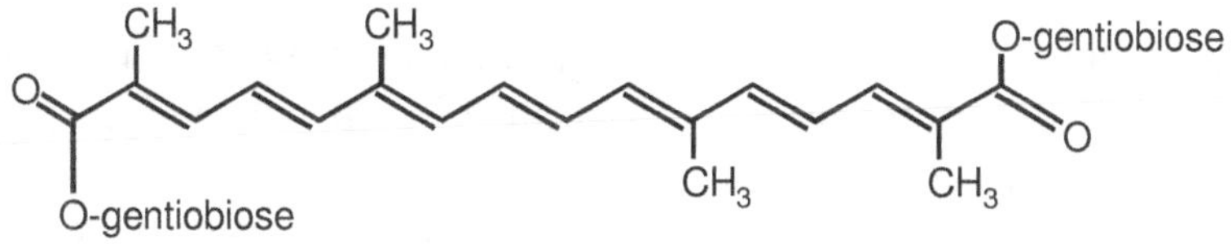

Crocin

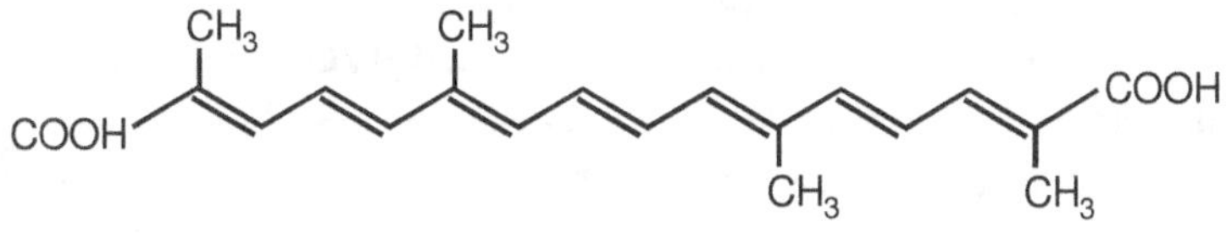

Crocetin

Uses

Saffron is used as a colouring (food dye) and flavouring agent. It is also used as antispasmodic, emmenagogue and a stimulant.

Substitutes and Adulterants

Due to high price of drug in the market, saffron is adulterated. In India, it is commonly adulterated with florets of safflower, botanically known as *Carthamus tinctorius* Linn, family Compositae, which are orange in colour. Safflower florets impart orange colour to alcohol, whereas no colour is observed with authentic drug. The weight of the drug is sometimes, increased by the addition of glycerine and ammonium nitrate. Such type of adulteration can be detected by determining water-soluble extractive.

(E) RESINS AND RESIN COMBINATIONS

Resins are amorphous products of complex chemical nature. These are mixtures of essential oils, oxygenated products of terpene and carboxylic acids found as exudations from the trunk of various trees. They are transparent or translucent solids, semi-solids or liquid substances containing large number of carbon atoms. Most of the resins are heavier than water. They are insoluble in water, but soluble in alcohol, volatile oils, fixed oils, chloral hydrate and non-polar organic solvents like benzene or ether. They are hard, electrically non-conductive and combustible masses. When heated, they soften and ultimately melt. They are usually formed in schizogenous or schizolysigenous cavities or ducts as end products of metabolism. Chemically, they contain organic acids, alcohols, esters, and neutral resins. Depending upon the type of the constituents of the resin, they are further classified as: (a) Acid resin, (b) Ester resin, and (c) Resin alcohols.

1. Acid resins

Following are few examples of this type of resins alongwith their acids; colophony (abietic acid), safetid (sandracolic acid), copaiba (copaivic and oxycopaivic acids), myrrh (commiphoric acid) and shellac (alleuritic acid).

2. Ester resins

This group contains esters as the chief constituents of the resins, e.g. benzoin and storax. Benzoin contains coniferyl benzoate and storax contains cinnamyl cinnamate.

Resin alcohols

The contents are the complex alcohols of high molecular weight. They are either found in free state or as esters. The examples are balsam of peru with peruresinotannol, gurjan balsam with gurjuresinol and guaiacum resin with guaic-resinol.

Resins and oils in homogenous mixtures are called as **oleoresins**, e.g. copaiba, Canada balsam, capsicum, etc. **Oleo-gum** resins are the homogenous mixtures of volatile oil, gum and resin, e.g. myrrh, guggul and safetida. **Glycoresins** are made up of resins and sugars and are present in jalap and ipomoea. If the resin contains benzoic acid and / or cinnamic acid, it is called as a **balsam**, e.g. balsam of tolu, storax, balsam of peru, etc.

Resenes: These are the complex natural substances without any specific chemical properties. They are inert chemically. They neither form any salt nor they get hydrolysed. Examples of the drug containing resenes are the gum copal, gutta purcha, asofoetida, colophony and dammar.

PODOPHYLLUM

Synonyms

Indian Podophyllum, Podophyllum Radix, Himalayan May-apple.

Biological Source

Podophyllum consists of dried rhizomes and roots of *Podophyllum hexandrum* Royal or *Podophyllum emodi* Well, belonging to family Berberidaceae. American podophyllum consists of dried rhizomes and roots of *P. peltatum*.

Geographical Source

It grows in the forests of the Himalayas from Kashmir to Sikkim in Himachal Pradesh and parts of Uttar Pradesh.

Cultivation and Collection

The rhizomes and roots are obtained from wild grown plants growing at an altitude of 3000 to 4000 m. Underground rhizomes remain dormant in winter and produce aerial shoots in April to May. Shoots flower during summer and die in November. Rhizomes and roots are dug up in spring or autumn, washed, cleaned and dried in the sun. The drug collected in the month of May has higher resin content than that collected in November. Actually, the roots contain more resin than the rhizomes and hence, the roots are preferred.

Organoleptic Characters (Fig. 2.23)

Colour   : The rhizomes are yellowish-brown to earthy brown.

Odour   : Slight and characteristic

Taste   : Bitter and acrid.

Size   : Rhizomes are 2.5 cm in length and 1 - 2 cm in thickness. Roots are about 7 cm in length and 2.5 mm in thickness.

Fracture : Both roots and rhizomes are brittle and even.

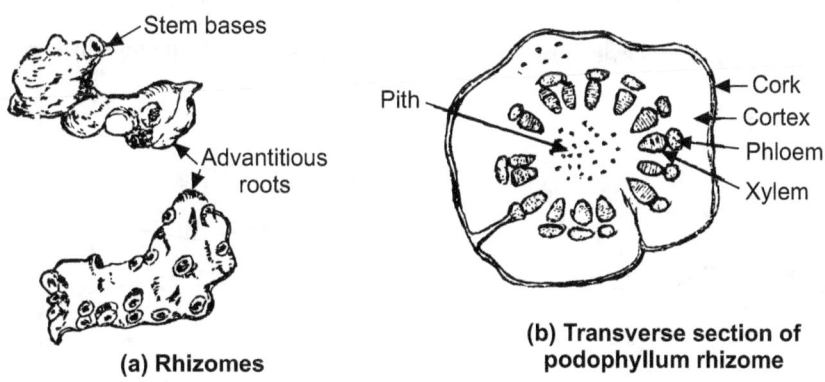

(a) Rhizomes

(b) Transverse section of podophyllum rhizome

Fig. 2.23 : Indian Podophyllum Rhizome (Natural Size)

Extra Features

Rhizomes are irregular and knotty, somewhat flat and dorsiventral, upper surface of the root has presence of 3 to 4 cup shaped scars.

Microscopic Characters

Rhizome: Outermost layer of rhizome consists of six layers of thin walled polygonal, tabular cork cells, while the cortex is made up of cellulosic parenchyma containing compound starch grains, calcium oxalate crystals (cluster type) are also present in the parenchyma. On the inner side of the vascular bundles short sclerides are present, xylem vessels are short and irregular. Pith shows the presence of pitted-sclerides.

Roots: T. S. of root exhibits the presence of epiblema which are strongly thickened, cortex is similar to rhizome but without calcium oxalate crystals. Exodermis and endodermis contain suberin. Stele consists of four to nine-arch arrangements.

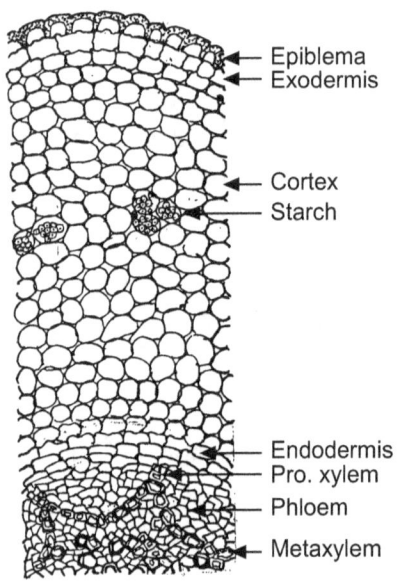

Fig. 2.24 : T. S. of Podophyllum root

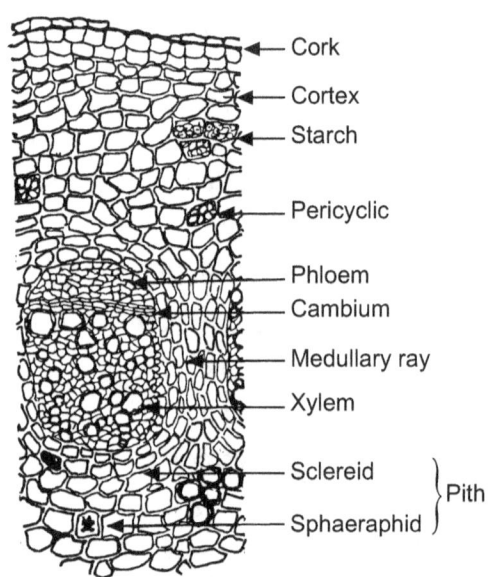

Fig. 2.25 : T. S. of Podophyllum rhizome

Chemical Constituents

Podophyllin

Etoposide

Indian Podophyllum contains from 7 - 15 % of resin known as podophyllin. Resin content varies in roots and rhizomes with the area and the season of collection. Roots contain more resin than the rhizomes. The active principle in podophyllin resin is known as podophyllotoxin which constitutes at least 40 % in Indian variety. α - and β-peltatins are present only in the American *Podophyllum*, but absent in *Podophyllum hexandrum*. The flavonoid astragalin and several other glucoside of podophyllotoxin are the other constituents of Indian podophyllum. Quercetin, about 8 per cent kaempferol, asiragalin, essential oil (responsible for odour of the drug) are the other contents of it. Chemically, Podophyllin is a lignan compound i.e. substance whose, chemical structure is based on 2 - 3 di-benzyl butane. Etoposide (4-demethylepipodophyllotoxin ethylidene-glucoside) is semi-synthetically processed and used in testicular and lung cancer.

Table 2.3 : Chemical nature of podophyllin

	R_1	R_2	R_3
Podophyllotoxin	CH_3	OH	H
α-peltatin	H	H	OH
β–peltatin	CH_3	H	OH
Demethylpodophyllotoxin	H	OH	H
Desoxypodophyllotoxin	CH_3	H	H
Podophyllotoxone	CH_3	O	H

Chemical Tests

Macerate 0.5 g of the drug with 10 ml. of alcohol and filter. To the filtrate, add strong copper acetate solution (0.5 ml.), brown precipitate is produced.

Standards

FOM	:	not more than 2.0%
Total ash	:	not more than 6.0%
Acid insoluble ash	:	not more than 2.0%
Alcohol soluble extractives	:	not less than 17.0%
Water soluble extractives	:	not less than 1.0%

Uses

Because of cytotoxic action, podophyllum is used in the treatment of veneral and other warts. It is also purgative, cholagague and bitter tonic. The active constituents of the drug, viz. podophyllin is a resin and has recently been successfully used in controlling some forms of cancer. Its cytotoxic effect i.e. mitotic arrest is similar to colchicine. It is used in semi-synthetic production of etoposide.

GUGGUL

Synonyms

Scented Bdellium, Gum guggul, Commiphora

Biological Source

Guggul is the oleo-gum-resin obtained by making deep incisions at the basal part of stem bark of *Commiphora weightii* belonging to family Burseraceae, and should contain not less than 1.0 % and not more than 1.5 % Guggulsterones (Z & E).

Guggul is one of the noted drugs from Ayurveda and Unani system. In recent times, its demand in therapeutics has been substantially increased.

Geographical Source

Guggul plant is native to Africa especially in its arid zones like Ethiopia, Somalia, Kenya, Zaire and Zimbabwe. It grows widely in various subtropical regions. In India, guggul plant is mainly found in Rajasthan and Gujarat States. Ajmer and Jaisalmer districts of Rajasthan are the prominent habitats.

Cultivation and Collection of Guggul Plant

It grows upto 2 - 3 metres as a woody tree and shows spinescent branches on pale yellow to brownish stem. It has characteristic silvery and paper like bark peelings. It bears compound leaves with ovale subsessile leaflets and they are serrated with smooth upper surface. The guggul tree grows well in sandy loam soil with more gypsum content, with a pH 7.5 - 9. In general, it requires low land use soils.

Guggul plant can be propagated both by seeds and stem cuttings. Seeds are a natural mode of propagation. In the arid or semi-arid zones, slopy well drained highly degraded lands are preferred for this purpose.

The seeds are collected from matured red berries in July-September when the viability is more. The plants are raised through nursery beds and transplanted after six months. For vegetative propagation, 25 - 30 cm long stem cuttings are planted in June or October-November.

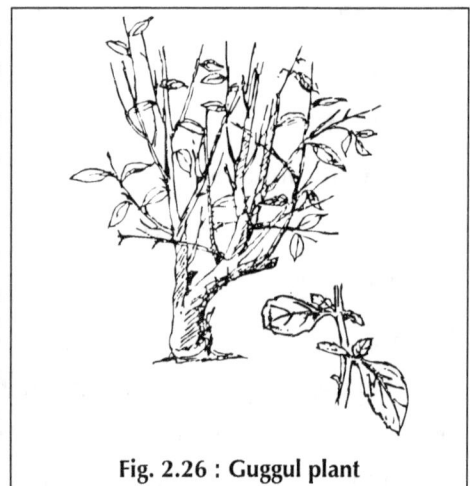

Fig. 2.26 : Guggul plant

CIMAP has identified a clone of guggul plant called *'Maru - Sudha'* which contains higher percentage of E and Z Guggulosterones.

Oleo-gum-resin is collected from at least 5 years old plants. It is tapped from main stem with 7.5 cm diameter on which deep circular incisions are made. It should be noted that the resin ducts occur only in bark portion near cambial layer. Guggul oozes out as yellowish white aromatic latex like matter. It has been reported that dose of 400 ml ethaphon (2 - chloro-ethyl phosphoric acid) three times a year enhances upto 22 times the secretion of guggul. Thick branches of tree give best grade of guggul. Each plant gives from 0.5 - 1 kg of guggul per year.

Description

Colour	:	Brown to pale yellow or dull green.
Odour	:	Agreeable, aromatic and balsamic.
Taste	:	Characteristic bitter.
Size	:	0.5 to 1.00 to 2.5 cm in diameter.
Shape	:	Rounded or irregular masses or agglomerated tears. Tears are somewhat transparent, with waxy surface and brittle in nature. Guggul is gummy to touch and tears are normally with fractured surface.
Solubility	:	When triturated with water, it forms white emulsion. It is partly soluble in alcohol.

Chemical Constituents

The gum-resin portion of guggul contains steroids, diterpenoids, carbohydrates and aliphatic esters. They are present in a complex mixture form, but the resin does not contain cinnamic acid, benzoic acid or their esters which are normally found in many oleo-gum-resin of pharmaceutical significance. The purified gum gives pentosan, pentose and furfural. Steam distillation of guggul gives pale yellow volatile oil, containing the terpenes like myrcene and caryophylline. Guggul contains z - guggulosterone, E - guggulosterone and three new sterols viz. guggulosterol I, II and III.

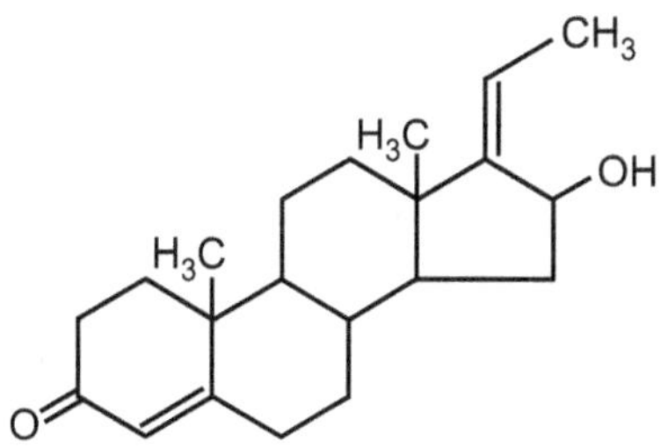

Guggulosterone - z 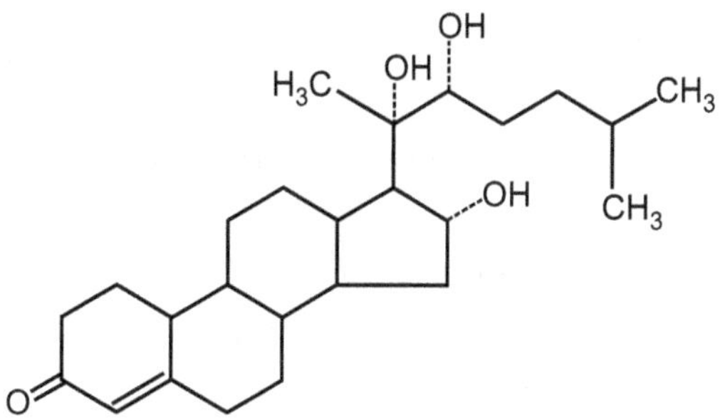   **Guggulosterol - I**

Guggul contains therepeutically active steroids shown as under:

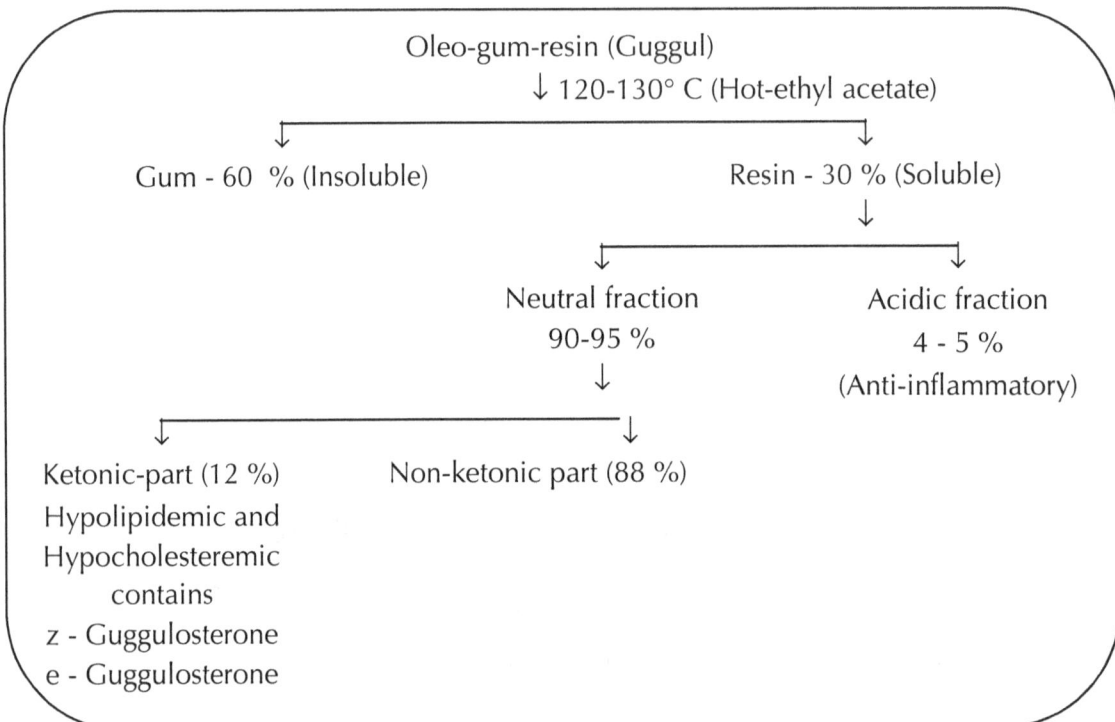

Chemical Test

To the ethyl acetate extract of guggal add acetic anhydride boil, cool and add two ml of sulphuric acid, green colour develops at the junction due to sterols.

Standards

Water soluble extractives	- not more than 48 %.
Alcohol soluble extractives	- not more than 40 %.
Ash value	- not more than 5.5 %.
Acid insoluble ash	- not more than 3.5 %.
Loss on drying	- not more than 11.8 %.

Uses

It is used as anti-inflammatory, anti-rheumatic hypolipidemic and hypo-cholesteremic drug.

It lowers low density lipoproteins and supports weight contact.

'Guggulip' developed from *Commiphora mukul* is an antihyperlipidaemic product.

Adulterants

Guggul is found as adulterated with resins of various *Commiphora* species like *C. abyssinica, C. roxburghii, C. molmol* and also with *Boswellia serrata*.

BOSWELLIA

Synonyms

Kunduru, Sallaki guggul, Indian Olibanum tree, Sallaki

Biological Source

The oleo-gum-resin obtained from plant known as *Boswellia serrata* belonging to family Burseraceae. It contains not less than 1.0 % of total 11-keto-β-boswellic acid and acetyl-11-keto-β-boswellic acid.

Geographical Source

About 10 species of genus *Boswellia* occur in tropical parts of Asia and Africa. *B. serrata,* the species found in dry hilly areas of Bihar, Madhya Pradesh, Gujarat. It is a medium sized but highly branching tree. It grows upto 12-15 feet in height. The type of leaves distinguishes Indian olibanum into two varieties called *var serrata,* having pubescent and serrate leaves and *var. glabra* having glabrous and entire leaves.

Method of Preparation

Oleo-gum-resin is obtained by tapping process, between November and June. The average yield per tree per annum is maximum upto 1 kg. The trees with more girth and stunted growth have low yields. For exudation, shaving is done, at 2.5 feet height, after 4-5 days.

Description

The oleo-gum-resin of Indian olibanum has following characters and compositions.

Colour : golden to dark brown

Odour : turpentine like, agreeable on burning

Taste : Aromatic-bitter

Size : Agglomerates of various size and shapes tears are 2 × 5 cm. Translucent, brittle, club or pear shaped.

Fig. 2.27 : *Boswellia serrata* twig

Standards

Moisture	-	not more than 12 %
FOM	-	not more than 2.0 %
Alcohol soluble extractives	-	not more than 35 %
Ash	-	not more than 10 %

Acid insoluble ash　　　-　not more than 2.0 %

Melting point　　　　　-　73 - 78°C

Heavy metals　　　　　-　not more than 20 ppm

Chemical Constituents

Oleo-gum resin approximately consists of:

Volatile oil　: 8 - 9 %

Gum　　　　: 20 - 23 %

Resin　　　　: 55 %

Volatile oil is composed of sesquiterpene alcohols, anisaldehyde, d-α-thujone, α-pinene, d-α-phellandrene and phenolic compounds. Similar to turpentine oil, this oil is soluble in colophony and dammer, but more volatile in nature. Acidic components of volatile oil are known as compholenic acid and compholytic acid.

Gum is mainly composed of arabinose with small amounts of xylose and galactose. Gum also contains oxidizing and diastatic enzymes. The highly brittle resin is soluble in various organic solvents.

Boswellia resin: Boswellia mainly contains boswellic acids. Boswellic acids belong to pentacyclic triterpenoids which are the active therapeutic contents. Important of them are β-boswellic acid, acetyl-β-boswellic acid, acetyl-11-keto-β-boswellic acid and 11-keto-β-boswellic acid of which acetyl-11-keto-β-boswellic acid is the main anti-inflammatory compound on which drug is standardized. Additionally it also contains diterpenic alcohol serratol and α and β amyrin.

Tetracyclic triterpenic acids present in resin are known as elemolic acid and elemonic acid.

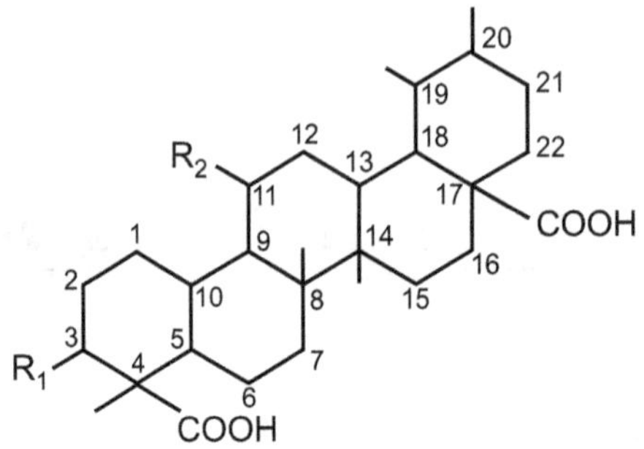

β-Boswellic acid 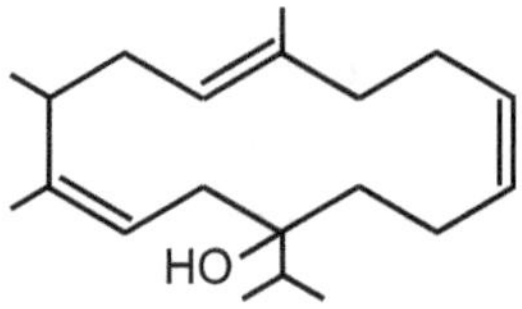　　　　　　　　　　　　　　Serratol

Table 2.4 : Chemical nature of Boswellic acids

Sr. No.	Type	R_1	R_2
1.	β-boswellic acid	— OH	— H
2.	Acetyl-β-boswellic acid	$O — CO — CH_3$	— H
3.	Acetyl-11-keto-β-boswellic acid	$O — CO — CH_3$	= O
4.	11-keto-β-boswellic acid	— OH	= O

Uses

It is anti-imflammatory and antiarthritic. Indian olibanum is mainly used in treatment of rheumatoid arthritis. It is known to regain integrity of vessels in joints from damage or spasm. It is also used in preparation of incence sticks and as a fixative in perfumes.

CANNABIS

Synonyms

Cannabis Indica or Indian Hemp; Ganja; Marihuana.

Biological Source

Cannabis consists of dried flowering tops of the cultivated female plants of *Cannabis sativa* Linn., (Family : Cannabinaceae (Moraceae)).

Geographical Distribution

It is indigenous to India. Cannabis is produced commercially in Mexico and Africa. In India, it is cultivated in Maharashtra, Bengal and Madhya Pradesh.

Cultivation and Collection

Commercially, it is cultivated for various purposes e.g. for fibres, oil and for narcotic substances like charas, bhang, ganja etc. For the production of fibres, it is cultivated in Almora, Garhwal, Nainital, and also in Kashmir, Nepal and Kerala.

The cultivation of cannabis (Fig. 2.28) is undertaken only under licence from the government. Since it is a ' *Narcotic Drug* ', its cultivation is regulated by government. It needs light loamy or sandy soil and humid tropical climate. It is cultivated as a kharif crop and sowing of the seeds is done in the month of June or July. The distance between two rows is about 1 metre and it needs about 6 to 9 kg of seeds per hectare. The plant is kept free of weeds and, if necessary, thinning is done. It flowers in the month of November or December and harvesting is done in the month of December or January. The average yield of ganja per hectare is 275 kg, but may vary depending upon suitability of climatic conditions. The average crop of seeds per hectare is 1100 to 1700 kg.

Fig. 2.28 : *Cannabis* **Sativa Plant**

Narcotic Substances from Cannabis

The narcotic substances obtained from the hemp plant are bhang or hashis, ganja and charas. The method of preparation and types of plants used for extracting the drug vary and only the female plants are used for preparation. Male plants are not selected, because the resinous material is formed only in female unfertilized plants.

Bhang or Siddhi

Bhang and siddhi are two different names of the same product. Bhang is prepared by cutting leaves and flowering tops of the plant, exposing them to sun and dew, drying and pressing the drug. The product is stored in earthenware vessels.

Ganja :

Ganja consists of dried flowering or fruiting tops of female plants from which no resin has been removed. It is collected only from cultivated plants. For preparation of ganja, plants are collected when lower leaves fall on ground and flower stalks begin to turn yellow. The floral shoots are cut off and are spread out in ridges and furrows. The ridges are levelled down and crushed to press the floral shoots into compact sheaves. The turning of material is done at regular intervals. After that, the material is collected and arranged in flat heaps. It is then subjected to pressure under the press. The heaps are turned over and broken up, so as to form thick layers. After 3 to 4 days, ganja is ready for storage. Two types of ganjas are available in market. The first variety is flat or Bombay ganja, while the other is known as round or Bengal ganja. In case of flat ganja, the individual pieces of plants are pressed by treading, wherein resinous material of the flowering tops sticks together to form flat mass. The flat ganja coming from Ahmednagar district of Maharashtra State is well known in commerce. Round ganja is regarded as better quality, where the resin-free parts of plants are removed and every piece (flowering top) is rolled individually, so as to form cylindrical mass. It is prepared in Bengal.

Charas :

Charas is the resinous exudation collected from leaves of the hemp plants, the resinous secretion, appearing just before flowering of the plant, is collected by rubbing fresh tops between hands or by beating them on cloth or carpet. The adhering material is scrapped off to yield charas of the market. It is collected even by walking through cultivated plants after wearing leather aprons. The resinous secretion, which sticks to leather aprons is scrapped off and collected.

Organoleptic Characters

Colour : Dull-green.

Odour : Strong, characteristic and narcotic.

Taste : Somewhat acrid and pungent.

Shape : Flattened or cylindrical masses consisting of branches upper part of the stems with bracts, bractioles, distillate flowers, fruits and seeds.

Stems which are not more than 3 mm in diameter also constitute the drug. Stems are thin, straight cylindrical and longitudinally furrowed. Bracts are 1.5 to 2 cm long, simple or lobed with subulate stipules. Bractioles are in pairs, present in the axial of bract. Flowers are formed in axial of each bractiole with 2 long brownish-red hairy stigmas. Achene type of fruits, about 5 to 6 mm in length and 4 mm in width, ovate glossy green or yellowish-green in colour with single seed.

Tetrahydrocannabinol

Chemical Constituents

Indian hemp comprises 15 to 20 % of resin which contains major active euphoric principle 1-3-4 trans tetrahydrocannabinol (commonly known as Δ^1 THC). It contains volatile oil, trigonelline and choline. The resin also contains cannabinol, cannabidiol, cannabidiolic acid, cannabichromene and cannabigerol. Indian hemp seeds contain about 20 % of fixed oil.

Identification

Shake about 0.1 g of the drug with 5 ml of light petroleum (60 - 80°) and filter. To 1 ml of the filtrate, add 2 ml of 15 % solution of hydrogen chloride in ethyl alcohol. At the junction of the two liquids, a red colouration appears. After shaking, the upper layer becomes colourless and lower layer acquires pink colour which disappears on addition of water.

Uses

It is a narcotic, sedative and analgesic. It has psychotropic properties due to tetrahydrocannabinol. At present, it is very little used as a drug. It causes intoxication, euphoria and later mental disturbances.

Storage

It should be stored in well closed containers after thorough drying.

BIBLIOGRAPHY

- Pharmacognosy, Trease GE and Evans W. C. 16th Edition 2002, W.B. Saunders Elsevier Publication, U.S.A.

- Pharmacognosy, Tyler V. E. Brady Lynn R and Robbers J. E. 9th Edition, 2011, Philadelphia, U.S.A.

- Text book of Pharmacognosy, Wallis T.E., 5th Edition 1967, J & A Churchill Ltd. London (U.K.)

- Pharmacognosy, C. K. Kokate, A. P. Purohit, S. B. Gokhale, 51st Edition, 2015, Nirali Prakashan, Pune 5.

- Pharmaceutical Chemistry of Natural products, V. Alagarsamy, 1st Edition, 2012, Elsevier India.

- Pharmacognosy and Pharmacobiotechnology, Ashutosh Kar, 2nd Edition, 2008, New age International Publishers, New Delhi.

- Quality Control of Herbal Drugs: An Approach to Evaluation of Botanicals, Pulok K. Mukherjee, 2002, Reprint 2012 Edition, Business Horizons Publication, New Delhi.

- World Health Organization, Quality Control Methods for Medicinal Plant Materials, 1998, Geneva.

- CRC Hand book of Ayurvedic Medicinal plants, L. D. Kapoor, Taylor and Francis, CRC Press USA.